Jack
and
The War Babies

A NOVEL

J. DAVID ERICKSON

Kaniksu
N.F.

Clearwater River

Lochsa

LoLo
PASS

Selway

Snake River

The Idaho
"Panhandle"

Also by J. David Erickson

the Muddy River Boys
Beyond Muddy River

ISBN 978-0-9846459-4-7 0-9846459-4-2

Jack and The War Babies is fiction. Characters, incidents, and dialogue are drawn from the author's imagination and are not to be construed as real. The author's depictions of actual towns, communities, and places are - in part - creative embellishments, not necessarily reflecting accurate tenor of actual settings, nor the people therein.

Illustrations by Shena Bingham
Book layout by Red Couch Creative, inc.

Printed and bound in the United States of America
Published by Swede Hill Publishing, LLC.

JACK
AND
THE WAR BABIES

A NOVEL

J. DAVID ERICKSON

CONTENTS

PRE-AMBLE

USED CARS AND NEW BOOKS

My friend, Ole, likes to say "I'm Norwegian; but I take a pill for it."
Owning this style of humor, you may be certain that Ole won't mind
my talking about him.
Ole sold his used car business 20 years ago and moved to southern Idaho to retire, play golf, and discover about 200 new friends. He also discovered that he could not bear to retire cold turkey, abandoning his love
of deal-making.

Thus, in retirement Ole continues practicing his homespun "art of
the deal." He buys cars, sells cars, buys again... vintage autos: Corvettes,
Mustangs, and Rancheros, usually convertibles. Every few weeks Ole
arrives at our golf club driving his latest pride and joy. We gather 'round
his newfound treasure as Ole enthuses, usually adding colorful monologue about his deal. His exhilaration is a joy to behold.

Ole's incorrigible passion and singular focus bear strong resem-
blance to passions of aspiring writers. How else to explain the prolif-
eration of writer's leagues, writing seminars, and book signings? We're
dealing with untreatable writers' fever given a shot of energy by the
emergence of digital technology. No more cut, paste, and white-out.
At our fingertips lies literary wealth equal to that of metropolitan libraries. Writing fever has infected even off-stream places like my town
of 3000, where our little community library hosts "newbies" and hope-
fuls, who gather to share methodologies, tribulations, and successes. A
half-dozen of us have actually sold our works, ordinary people sharing
ourselves with the world. A little hyperbole? Sure—but an infectious
element of freedom arms us against critics and naysayers.

My first book, *The Muddy River Boys*, a four year project, was a joyful and mind-expanding adventure. Simply put, the *Muddy River* stories chronicled boyhood escapades during an era when adults turned youngsters loose to roam town and countryside.

The real life "Muddy Boys" congealed into a tribe... couldn't call us a gang back in the day when "gangs" were considered despicable.

Our leaders were as old as 12, gatekeepers for membership and watchdogs for younger kids. One boy, Little Ergie, made the grade at five.

Wimps would not apply. They knew better. Once our leaders decided on a plan, you had to keep up and never give up... running the hills, biking 15 or 20 miles, rafting the river, and sometimes fishing dawn to dusk.

The boys of Muddy River included impulsive risk-takers like brother Jim, and Buck—cautious, but rock-solid willing, and Jack, with unfailing comic demeanor. Fringe members rotated in and out, including a pair of rascals. I can name a dozen "tribesmen," adventurers all, living in an extraordinary place and time. Their treasured stories had to be told.

Remarkably, 65 years later I'm still learning and benefitting from the Muddy River days and their surviving characters. Here's just one serendipitous example...

Naturally, post-boyhood interests and careers took us in different directions. But, to do justice to *Muddy River* the writer needed memory help from scattered Muddy friends. Consequently, I began a search for addresses and phone numbers. With notebook at the ready, I began to call, always with apprehension. Would I learn of illness or worse?

The "worse" turned out to be learning that one of the rascals had passed. But the rest were upright, upbeat, surprised and pleased by my call and mission. I'll be forever grateful that we reconnected, a bonus spilling from the *Muddy River* project.

Typically, long distance conversations with a friends of long ago lasted an hour or more. And four of my guys I met in person... with gratifying results. Following a few minutes of appropriate civilities, we'd seamlessly turn back the clock, replaying ancient memories, laughing, celebrating. Then it hit me, as a bucket of ice water full in the face. Each man was the same—same laugh, same spirit, same joy of life—and the same species unto himself that he was 65 years ago. Back then, we'd arrived on the shores of the Little Muddy River already engineered for life.

Decades passed. Hearts had beaten 3 trillion times; but souls and characters had grown from original root-stalks. Someday, I thought, I'd write about the growth of those special hearts and souls which produced exceptional adults. First, though, our Muddy River days warranted a boyhood chronicle. Four struggling years later I had a manuscript.

Book publishers and reviewers need a category. When pushed, I offered "memoir," knowing not what else to say about genre. Yet memoir often becomes stodgy recounting of dusted off accomplishments, suspiciously self-serving, sometimes amended by white-washed politics. "Memoir" isn't a proper fit for *Muddy River*. I prefer "boy stories"... from their memories, in their own words: daring, adventuring, running "balls out," rafting, fishin', swimmin', muddied, skunk-sprayed, sometimes bloodied, but consistently joyful.

After soft cover *Muddy River Boys* rolled out in 2011, I was invited to present a book talk for a conference in Kalispell, Montana hosted by the Authors of the Flathead. With beginner's trepidation, I accepted. It was a wise decision. Without exaggeration, the kind members of the Authors of the Flathead cemented my decision to hone my skills and launch new writing projects. Who says a man in his 70's cannot add a new layer of life?

A minor reunion of the Muddy River boys just happened to convene at the 'Authors' conference, an opportunity for a delightful surprise. Here's how it played out—

I began by reading excerpts of dialogue between Jack when he was a precocious 8 year old, and me—a lad of 6. The content was from Chapter 7, "Cats, Rats, and Sex Education," wherein Jack explains that the white balloon I'd found floating in the river was really something called a "rubber," and I really shouldn't try to blow it up because it likely had an incredibly weird history. For the 'Authors' I read the exchange of kid to kid sex education, all about "dinkies eventually growing into dinks" and "men and women wrestling plumb naked." At that point the conference went—you might say—adrift. It went further adrift when the writer and original recipient of sex education, introduced 74 year old Jack, the teacher. Jack stood, accepting applause.

Next, a reading from "Chapter 11, Kowabunga! What Happened?" wherein Jack and Buck, unbelievably and unexpectedly, took *girls* to our favorite fishin' hole on the Little Muddy. My brother and I arrived to find Buck and Jack sitting paired with girls by the water's edge, the pony-tailed girls "dibbling painted toe-nails in the water." Our sacred place would be spoilt. "No more swimmin' buck naked or peein' in the sand." Worse, though young and naïve, we feared our leaders would be irreversibly distracted.

Appealing to my audience, some 40 literary folks, I said, "Doggone Buck, it was his crappy idea to bring girls to the Little Muddy River." Gesturing toward Jack and the handsome, wavy-haired gentleman sitting alongside in the back row, I said, "Buck, after 60 years, you are fully forgiven." Buck Bundhund and his world-class smile stood to warm applause.

At this point my audience stirred, looking about for other potential ringers.

Next, a reading to identify more distractions that would separate the Muddy River Boys: growing up activities like team sports, part time jobs, girlfriends. For Jack it was Beverly, his 8th grade sweetheart. I said, "Beverly, will you please stand." From across the room Beverly stood and waved at Jack. Jack stared in disbelief. He threw his hands into the air... "My, oh my, *Beverly!*" Jack and Beverly hadn't seen each other in 40 years. Now they came together, laughing and hugging, to the delight of every person in the room.

Bottom line tip for newbie writers: If and when you are invited to read from your book, bring your own cast of characters.

Obviously, fiction writers haven't the option of using living characters to promote their works. On the positive side, perhaps fiction could reveal a new force, a personal agency as strong as the device I call the "boy story?"

Following a second non-fiction, *Beyond Muddy River*, I began writing short story fiction, finding fascination in studying an endless inventory of human quirks and qualities—admirable, loathsome, farcical... an inventory of adjectives—human clay to mold characters. Talking with Jardine, my long-time fishin' buddy, I said, "I'm writing fiction now. I think I'm pretty good at it."

"Why am I not surprised?" he said, with his all-knowing smile. Confession: Jardine is a superior fish catcher, but no match for my skill in stretching trout to fictional dimensions.

So I opened doors to imagination, and two years later *Jack... and the War Babies* walked out.

I've explained my take on what drives the writer. Well, how about my readers? Some of you—at least—I already "know."

For 30 years I practiced fisheries biology for a well-managed Idaho company that farms, processes, and markets rainbow trout. Though the company is small by American standards, it is a recognized leader in product development and marketing. The company attracted an unconventional roster of "do-ers".

Chris, our marketing director, was comfortable in the fast lane of urban commerce. He hosted a memorable teamwork seminar, wherein he explained his approach to analysis of customer dynamics, how to align marketing strategies with demographics. He carried on at length about demographic determiners, groupings of urbanite, suburban, professional, rural, credentialed or informally educated consumers. When he came to a particularly challenging group, he slowed his presentation, struggling to characterize a group called the "Western Rustics." Like strange citizens of a remote Euro-Asian country, the Rustics' common traits and predictable behaviors proved difficult to explain. Looking at Chris's puzzled face, some of us began to laugh, not at him, but ourselves. "Chris," our weathered production manager volunteered, "That's us, Western Rustics."

Countrified Rustics—Western, Mid-western, Southern, Appalachian; and beyond the stereotypes—you'll see yourself in *Jack and The War Babies*. Come, join the fun. Urbanites too—we promise you a good read.

I'm infected with wordsmithing. Unlike my friend, Ole' with his Norwegian problem, I don't "take a pill for it." Neither does my mythical friend and storytelling adventurer, Jackson B. Lindquist. It's time to hand him the pen. Yours truly, J. David Erickson.

INTRODUCTION

BY JACKSON B. LINDQUIST

War Babies (1935-1944). Born in 1964, I'm a senior member of a generational grouping called "Baby Boomers." We Boomers are famously numerous, totaling some 75 million litter-mates. We benefited by postwar prosperity, new technologies, and higher education. Some experimented with new social norms, invented rock bands, rode Harleys, and screamed at injustices.

Our grandparents of the Greatest Generation didn't scream or ride rumbling bikes. They earned reputations of tenacity, frugality, and bravery by battling the Great Depression and saving the world from evil dictators. This stoic tribe famously bucked up, no complaints, as did their inscrutable children - our parents - known as the "Silent Generation." Perhaps their propensity for quiet doggedness explains why we've heard little from these self-contained silent ones. But what of other defining markers? Peering through demographic lenses, as if biologists studying bugs, why could historians and social scientists not identify their commonalities beyond simply *silent*? I propose "War Babies" as an alternate description, inasmuch as their childhoods were defined by military fathers, and parents committed to the incessant "War Effort." Before there are no War Babies left to talk with, I aim to interview a random mix to discover what sort of mysterious molecules and hormonal cocktails course the veins of the quiet ones, the War Babies. *Jackson B. Lindquist, Sept 9, 2009.*

Bob, Old Buddy: "This is a preamble to my (our?) pending study. (We'll publish in *The Journal of Demographic Research*.) What do *you* think?" Jack.

Dear Jackson: "No. You cannot begin this way. And no, I should have no part of this. Your colloquial style is not acceptable for research journals. Come to visit. We'll collaborate. We'll establish fundamental guidelines." Robert. P.S. "Where are your citations? You truly want to do this? It's now or never!"

CHAPTER ONE

SYRINGA WOLF

September 16, 2009. Syringa, Idaho. Dr. Robert Hamilton Kerner penned his "Dear Jackson" admonition on his stiff monogrammed stationery. His message was another unwelcomed imperative to life's table of contents, pulling me from my mountainside haven in Syringa. Had not love of my life, Joanie, also been obligated to leave, I'm not sure I would have gone. Why leave paradise?

The Syringa wolf waked me at first light, his howl blowing through our cabin's bedroom curtains. I heard Joanie's sweet song in the shower and threw the covers back from our pine log king bed. I pictured her 115 pounds of shapely strength. The shower stilled. Moments later she landed, seducing me with her joyous chocolate eyes, her long wet raven hair, and everything else in her inventory. Of a million men, I'm the lucky one, living a miracle.

In our glowing aftermath, the marauding Huns wouldn't have bothered to stick a knife in me. Still, I faced duties, the first being not to care so much. Joanie was the stalwart one. She brought our "board meeting" coffee and snuggled in. "You know, Honey-boo, time away only makes our coming home better." In an hour, she'd be gone. After a day's organizing, I'd head east myself. Joanie, the thoughtful, organized one, handed me a list of reminders. The first was underlined: "Two weeks, Glacier Park, we'll meet."

Joanie, a dedicated wildlife biologist, was headed north this morning, bound for the Kaniksu wilderness where she researches grizzly bear migration. My own journey across the northern plains of America would be a scholastic mission for... well, that needs explaining.

Unlike Joanie, I have no professional career. Never did. But my two determined advisors, Joanie and Professor Robert H. Kerner, insist that—at age 45—I should activate my college-informed potential. I chuckle at their well-intended, redundant advice. Long ago a gnarly gnome came to visit. Now he hangs around, nagging *Do something important.* Well, by damn I will.

Hence, my decision to embark on a journey, traveling first to visit Kerner at Great Falls College, where we'd flesh out a concise project plan. Then, with plan in hand—and head—I'd travel east across Montana and North Dakota interviewing a cross section of an overlooked demographic, Americans that Joanie and I call "War Babies." "You'll come home reinvigorated," Joanie promised.

She clasped her hands behind my neck, pulled me in, and planted a warm wet whopper on my lips. She giggled her playful warning, "keep those blue Viking eyes off the coeds." I countered with "keep those gypsy eyes off the lumberjacks." I patted her cute butt as she hopped into her Rover.

Joanie lowered her window for a final word: "Don't forget your razor," her way of reminding me that my week old red beard was not the best image for "literary scholars." You see, I write pulpy fiction without claiming to be either literary or a serious writer earning serious money. Maybe someday. Still, Joanie my love, has impeccable judgment and reminds me, "you want to sell respected books, you'd better look respectable."

At daylight tomorrow Bo and I would embark on a journey with steely determination. After a month on the road interviewing War Babies of regional renown, I'd come home to mine data, marry it with published demographics, record bibliographies, study, publish monographs. Thereafter, job offers would tempt. Ugh! Serious literary work—Ugh! "Shut up, Doubt," I said to myself. "Time's wasting. Steel yourself, get organized."

Joanie tooted, waved, and sped away, heading north to the epicenter of her grizzly bear research in the wild mountains bordering British Columbia. I waved her down the road, after which I began gathering essentials for my own academic safari. Well, 'academic' may be a stretch.

Joanie had remarked, "You 've completed only minimal preliminary research and planning." She cited an expert who'd studied "aficionados of disorder," and I was, quote: "a committed member of the genus *Disorder.*"

She had me dissected and labeled. So did my friend of 18 years, Professor Robert H. Kerner, Joanie's allied advisor. He agreed with her that I thrive on distractions, proven again by choosing this moment to sit down for a creative session with my next "masterpiece," *Blood on her Stilettoes*. If my workplace were Joanie's university apartment in Moscow, Idaho, *Stilettoes* would have been delivered to my small-ball publisher months ago. But our four room Syringa cabin occupies a mountainside above the pristine Clearwater River and is surrounded by a million acres of mountain wonders: crystal brooks hiding jeweled cutthroat trout; dark elk watching from shadowed thickets; musical wind among the pines. My list of un-peopled alpine hideaways remains long... I explore one, add two more.

I gaze past my monitor and down Syringa's slope to the Clearwater. Its waters run high and clear, ready for early-running steelhead. In the morning I'll discipline myself. "Do *not* take steelhead tackle. Follow the gorgeous river to the divide with your mind on the mission."

The pyramid of trip essentials in our cabin's entry grows: a duffel of flannel shirts and Levi's, my virginal laptop, writer's journal number 9, beat up 1952 Fender guitar, and Bo's doggie duffle. She padded along behind me on her thumpy golden Labrador feet. "Yes Bo, I'll grab the 12 gauge, but don't be thinking this is just a hunting trip. It's business, girly dog." With that, I tossed in an extra field notebook and newly gifted cell phone that Joanie said was powerful and convenient (techies had yet to claim "smart"). And I confirmed that my Stetson, "Lucky," was on the peg, ready to go.

Joanie had discovered the hat on a dusty shelf at a good will store, an XX Stetson, no less. But that was fourteen years ago during our second summer together. Recently she remarked that Lucky, the hat that I all but slept in, had organic importance—soft brown felt, medium brimmed, neither Western-slick nor city-cool, more like Indiana Jones. Its brim was ember-burned, its crown pot-holed and streaked with pine sap, but "the damned thing somehow makes you look swashbuckled," Joanie said with her gifted imagination.

"Lucky too, I reminded her. "It helped me catch a world record silver salmon."

Can a man riding his 45th year still swashbuckle? Now in bed and missing Joanie, I recalled our foray into hat psychology. With a minor in psych, Joanie was a nimble muser. She said, "I think I know why you haven't replaced that ratty thing; but it's yours. You ought to be able to articulate why."

"Put me on the couch," I said. "Then do what you want with me."

Tonight I hadn't Joanie intertwined with me in ten percent of our king bed, talking low and sharing the elixir of love. She'd have blotted away a dozen hyperactive worries: this-that-this-that, up and down my scale of uncertainty.

Joanie was right; I'd passed comfortably into middle age without a career focus, or family focus either, for that matter. Fathering a child seemed irresponsible with my career wobbling from one path to the other. And with her commitment and success with biological research, Joanie wasn't ready for motherhood. Thus, our parenting was limited to adopting a succession of Labrador dogs, the latest, Bo, our affectionate golden... and Margaret, Joanie's stuffed puppy Lab, who spends much of her time in the bottom of Joanie's down sleeping bag.

Odd that I longed to talk of our future together now, with her gone traipsing through grizzly bear wilderness armed with pepper spray, while I lay here tossing and turning. Bo too. With every "ah shit" or "damn it anyway," Bo, our beautiful lady Labrador, rises from her bedside rug, huffs disgust, and plops back down.

On top of all that indecision there's always money worries. Fortunately, minimalist Joanie is content nesting in our mountainside cabin. Still, we'd talked of changing course, launching entrepreneurships and traveling, all of which needed money. And now my book royalty income wanes. Bob Kerner, my zany professor friend and satirical critic had predicted so. Ever the realist, Kerner warned me after *Bloody Purple* rolled out hot in '94 that it had no staying power. "It is pulpier than *Pulp Fiction*," he said. My second thriller, *Tall, Dark, and Crimson*, was "vaporous," according to Kerner. I agreed, but rebounded with a counter-punch, reminding him that my publisher paid in real "bread," a throwback to Kerner's brief collegiate foray into hippie-dom.

SYRINGA WOLF

Perhaps more pulpy fiction could boost my spousal income. Besides, my main character, Juneau Sherbinski, has grown on me. I'm his only hope for posterity. How could I abandon him? Maybe I should by-pass *Project War Babies* for now. Why not finish *Blood On her Stilettos?*—let Sherbinski nail the killer and finally bond with my readers. They're already enthralled with Sherbinski's side-kick, Truly North, who is brainy and beautiful. Now she'll inch ever so close to declaring love for him. Honestly? I'm jealous of Sherbie. He has Truly constantly by his side, sharing adventures, while my Joanie is gone half the time.

Damn it! Here I go again, off on a tangent. I'd promised Joanie and myself that I'd write seriously. A solo-authored research study could lead to job offers, nice, but also an imposing proposition. Academic fact finding? Fiction?—Yes, no, yes, no, and why not?—like counting proverbial sheep. Somehow the process worked, rewarding me with a couple hours of post-midnight sleep.

Around 3 A.M. I jerked awake, startled by the Syringa wolf's howl riding a moonbeam through my half-open window. Bo padded to the window and stood with paws and chin resting on the sill, growling. Had the canine challenge come from a cowardly coyote, Bo would have howled back; but since the wolf began patrolling the ridge above town, the coyotes had vamoosed.

After three identical verses of the wolf's lonely song, a cabin owner halfway up the ridge touched off his shotgun and the wolf stopped singing. They had played the same game twice before, all-in-all a gratifying diversion.

Last Sunday afternoon after three days of rain and gloom, the sun broke the clouds. Out of shelters came man and beast, including Syringa Wolf. High on a point of ridge, he stepped out of the woods, shook off, thrust his nose to the sky and howled in celebration.

A half mile below on our sun-warmed porch, Joanie and I passed my binoculars back and forth, punctuated by outbreaks of amazement.

The wolf lay down to nap, a blond-furred curl with ears ever perked. I admired Syringa Wolf. Still do. He's clever, self-reliant, and he knows how to howl.

CHAPTER TWO

THE KING OF HEARTS

Saturday, September 17. Bo lathered my cheek with her warm wet tongue, waking me from a big trout dream. She was decked out in her new pink collar that Joanie had lined with fur from a road killed mink. Six o'clock and time to head out, "Montana, here we come." A final checklist: binocs, camera, extra ammo, nuts and dried fruit, a thermos of strong, creamy hot coffee... . Lastly, I loaded my pine-wood grub box, a treasure chest for life on the road.

I opened my truck door for Bo. Before I could say, "load up," she hopped onto her passenger's blue and gold Montana State University blanket. She bumped her hip against mine, licking my right ear, as if to say, "I'm ready, Boss."

Across Edgewater Lane that we locals call "Main," Mrs. "Eagle Eyes" Pierce watched from her kitchen window. I resolved to creep down Edgewater/Main to Highway 12, honoring her hand-painted 15 miles per hour no-dust speed limit. (Insider information: she secretly likes me for my gifts of cucumbers and flowers, though public knowledge of that would ruin her reputation.)

Below, at the base of our mountain, moonlight mist rose from the Clearwater River. A frigid pre-dawn of frosted windshields and ice covered street puddles. Early risers stoked their iron stoves with pinewood. Ah! pine smoke, nothin' better.

We rolled out of town before the town rooster crowed—a poor decision. The Lochsa Highway is notorious for vehicle/big game collisions, and along 70 miles of winding river highway I played headlight dodge ball with whitetail deer and a bull moose, who turned his butt to us and trotted up the centerline. Despite three cups of strong coffee,

I drove foggy headed with the naked nucleus of a plan spinning in my brain.

I planned to interview real War Babies and consolidate my findings, hoping to formalize a verifiable demographic entity. Who am I kidding? Those were Kerner's words. To provide a concise study plan, I needed Kerner. Fortunately, he had agreed to meet me in Great Falls to collaborate on "actionable strategies"—how to glean information from a generation reluctant to talk about themselves. Kerner would have opinions and advice, that's for sure, maybe help frame a structure for my fact-finding trip across the High-Line region of northern Montana. Perhaps I'd travel as far as Minnesota's Twin Cities, which would please Kerner, the "Prof." He insisted my study would be incomplete without an urban perspective.

15 miles east of Syringa we turned upriver on the Clearwater's left fork, known as the Lochsa River...

I'm a dedicated gawking driver, but needed more light than a pre-dawn September morning offers. A full moon hung low over Freezeout Ridge on the south, although a standing army of pines along the highway corridor blocked all but a few stubborn rays of soft light. But then the highway emerged from the pines, curving to the river's edge where the Lochsa River glittered in gold and silver moonlight. I pulled into a rest-stop, discovering an irresistible moonlit game trail leading to the river.

Bo and I arrived at the edge of a gravel bar where the Lochsa River lapped at our toes and sang gurgling songs. Naturally, Bo waded in, letting the current take her for a swim. Had to happen; my truck cab often smells like wet dog.

On the road again. Mile-by-river mile my attitude improved. I relish traveling when it doesn't include a strict diet of work. I was wheeling Big Red, my Dodge Ram Hemi that had yet to suffer its first backcountry ding. With a mail ordered Montana bird license and my ever-eager pointing Labrador sitting beside me, we were ready. "Don't worry, Bo," I said. "We'll carve out time to hunt a few birds."

Autumn essence flowed down from the high country wilderness and hung over the river. I lowered my window, flooding our truck cab with cool autumn pungency, worthy of a wilderness connoisseur—earthy, musky, eau de camp smoke, wisp of mushroom, essence of elk pee. From a high energy jazz station Poncho Sanchez rumbled with "Cantaloupe Island," perfect for the start of an outrigger paddle across the Caribbean or my pending 2000 mile journey across the North American high plains and back.

In a blush of morning light, the Lochsa's Crooked Fork tumbled and pooled, tumbled and pooled, a trouty looking stream. But, unless you watch carefully, you don't notice how quickly a tributary transitions to a rivulet, to a seep, and a spongy bog. Suddenly, no more Crooked Fork, and Highway 12 crested in a meadow of yellow grass at Lolo summit. I pulled onto a gravel spur road next to a single small fir, just enough cover to hide dog and human pizzlings.

I can pizzle and "hunt" at the same time, in this case the non-lethal variety, known as "spotting." Slanting daylight glinted on a moving something, which turned out to be a bull elk carrying antlers as big as a snag tree. He loped out of the pines and leaped the highway, last seen crossing behind Montana's Lolo Visitor Center.

September, and the elk rut was on. The swaggering bull would soon bellow another challenge. Bo and I stood waiting. Two minutes, three, four, and at five the bull's fearsome bugle echoed from deep in black timber. Bo whined, needing re-assurance. I patted her head, "He can't get us, Bo."

Aside from a few hunters' pickups, Highway 12 was wonderfully devoid of traffic. We descended from Lolo summit through golden aspen and emerald forest into Bitterroot valley. I wore a permanent smile, as did Bo; and don't tell me dogs can't smile. So much wonderment in Montana's golden burnished September... travel cannot be hurried. At 50 miles an hour, we motored up the Blackfoot valley toward the Continental Divide with high volume jazz playing on satellite radio. I hoped to spot an angler with a bowed fly rod fighting a trout in the gunmetal Blackfoot River, *The River That Runs Through It*. Sure enough, at a logjam where Humbug Creek joins the Blackfoot, I stopped to watch a young pony-tailed lady net a whopper trout. I gave her a toot, a thumbs-up, and pulled forward... jumped out and hollered, "Hold on, please, how about a picture?" She froze momentarily before smiling, concluding that I was not the Boston Strangler, because stranglers don't hang out with blond Labradors who come greeting with wagging tails. The trusting lady's picture is secure in my fishing journal, smiling and anonymous, kneeling in a riffle, cradling her 20 inch brown trout.

The Wolf Creek cutoff intersects the Missouri River valley near the village of Craig, a fly fishing Mecca for Missouri River drift fishers and guides. I stopped at The Mayfly Shop managed by Tucker, a college buddy from Montana State. Tucker's a fly rod creature with intimate knowledge of the river culture. We could talk fishing and springboard easily into my concept of War Babies as a demographic entity; alas, I learned that among Tucker's guiding and outfitting cohorts, many were Baby Boomers or younger, but none were War Babies. Not that our visit was a bust, inasmuch as Tucker enlightened me about extraordinary Missouri River rainbow trout migrations documented by microchip implants. I reciprocated with the story of my 10 year old niece catching a 21 pound Kamloops from Lake Pend Oreille. We'd attracted a circle of listeners eager for dueling BS, a fly shop bonus costing nothing.

Tucker and I visited about a tentative date for a late winter fly fishing float after which Bo and I departed Craig with just enough twilight to drive on to Great Falls. Well, not quite. An hour later we reached the *trappings* of town on the outskirts, which by great fortune became War Babies' operational center for 3 days and four nights.

By luck, fate, timing, and perhaps a scintilla of intuition on my part, this first stop of the journey became a well-spring of inspiration, adding a new dimension to this so-called research trip. Unexpected events soon raced like streaking comets, and I came to wonder: how did fate put me in their path?

At the two mile post south of Great Falls, the State of Montana orders drivers to slow to 55. On this Saturday evening, no one actually did so, excepting me, obeying because I needed to scope out the local culture... to think, to plan, and strategize: how do I start the War Baby project and exactly where?

Bo knows the drill: slowing to 40 mph means we might be looking for gamebirds. She slobbed her passenger window, panting. "Sorry, Bo," I said. "We're only looking for a motel."

The city proper, vaguely visible in the distance, appeared as a gray jumble of rooftops tucked beneath a bench-land overlooking the valley.

THE KING OF HEARTS

First impression: by appearance, Great Falls did not brag on itself. By contrast, out here on the prairie THE KING OF HEARTS' giant sign glowed red neon over a cloverleaf settlement, including a collection of brand name gas stations, motels, and hurry-hurry quick stop "convenience," the whole shebang gussied up with blathering signs and pointing arrows telling me where to go.

I crossed onto an off-ramp lane, encountering more of the King's neon- defined purpose: BAR, DINING, DANCING, CASINO... social gatherings, and a good place to begin my informal interviews—testimonials, a living file on a generation of Americans. "Why not? We'll pull in here and ease into the scene, see if I can convince folks to open their lives to a stranger." Bo sat tall and alert, ears lifted, black nose twitching. She'd spotted a cock pheasant sailing into grain stubble on her side. Excitement beamed from her pleading bright eyes.

"Not now, Bo. Sorry, we'll hunt tomorrow," a lame lament for a hunting Labrador. At curbside I tossed her a bacon-flavored doggie treat and cracked her window. She clenched the treat in her jaws. A string of drool swung loose and slimed her blanket. One gulp and Bo returned to a more important task— eyeballing a patch of birdie looking brush behind the parking lot.

Situated at a crossroads, The King of Hearts was likely favored by farm and ranch people, blue collar workers, hunters, and town folks preferring an edge of country life instead of citified Great Falls proper. Anyway, I liked what I saw: pickup trucks, campers, two cattle trucks, and a mix of autos—late models and a few beaters well past their prime, likely akin to their owners.

I perused the low slung Drop Inn Motel bordering the lot, dropped in and registered with Elizabeth, an energetic brunette of, let's say—45, who I later discovered was the younger sister of co-owner, Pearl. Registering Bo required a 20 dollar refundable deposit and a promise: "No, she won't sleep on the bed."

Early on this Saturday evening the casino complex began to stir. A carload of gold uniformed employees unloaded at a side door, and a few customers headed to bar and casino entrances. Some were party dressed ladies accompanied by men wearing clean Wranglers and western hats. Since I would have stood out bareheaded, I let Lucky ride. From the casino's double entry doors I strolled nonchalantly to the bar, as if casino saloons were my everyday hangouts. I noted that the spacious barroom could seat 40 or 50 bar-up sitters and table-gatherings. King's bar was half-filled at six thirty, mostly low energy early-birds hunched over beers, a lull before a storm.

Though not advertised as such, strategically placed televisions indicated a sports bar. And tonight's football broadcast from Bozeman would bring a throng of television football fans to watch a high intensity contest for the Great Divide Trophy featuring the Montana State University Bobcats battling the University of Montana Grizzlies.

I claimed a King's stool at the belly of the bar. Neighbors right and left were potentially good sources of information. The guy on my right was of particular interest. He wore a gray beard and brown bib coveralls, sure signs of certified wisdom. Unfortunately, when pre-game football came blaring from multiple television screens, he and his worker buddy left. Apparently, college football was a poor fit, no match for Sunday's manly NFL.

A blond pony-tailed waitress caught my eye. All business, with quick feet and worn denims, she looked like she'd stepped out of a rodeo. She would be smart about horses and beer. She brought me a draft Stella.

It was a pleasant, 30 minute Stella, space to consider why the hell I was here and how to make the best of it. Let's start with Kerner, my old collegiate friend, and now one third of the War Babies triumvirate, the other two thirds being Joanie and me. Kerner had promised "advisory assistance" under auspices of his administration/teaching position at Great Falls College. My War Babies project needed "a study module, amenable to statistical analyses." Joanie agreed. Citing Kerner's studies of "Aspirational Theory," she worried that I was in danger of slipping into the quagmire of the "Leisure Class."

"So where's the problem?" I said—a flippant counterpoint to her belief, supported by Kerner: I should no longer postpone my return to academia.

The barkeep looked askance at me—a man sitting alone in his casino bar, staring into his beer, perhaps the quintessential sad sack who'd lost a wife or a thousand bucks gambling. He turned from his cash register and stepped my way. Perfect! His blue and gold Montana State jersey made us academic cousins. He hooked a thumb over his shoulder at the TV where players were stretching and warming up. "You came to watch us kick the Griz?"

"How did you know?"

"I just saw you grin when the Cats charged on field."

I offered my handshake, "Jack Lindquist, class of '88."

"Max DeVore, '94," he said amidst his iron grip. "The house likes to buy Bobcat newcomers a beer. " He swiveled his head to scan "the house," perhaps an acknowledgement that house management was not so generous, nor of Bobcat persuasion.

"Well, you're mighty kind, Max; I hope my taste is not too expensive. I'm drinking Stella, this time in the fancy glass please... which Max, a nimble guy, delivered with a rich head of foam."

"You new in town?"

"Temporarily. I have some business here."

Max nodded quizzically. I read him as curious. He'd be back for more. He moved off to confer with a young lady server, his double barreled laugh stamping the saloon with his solid personality. Max would be a treasure trove of information, possibly including friendships with interesting War Babies.

Max was clean shaven, six foot two, square jawed and square cornered, perhaps ex-football. He tethered his long blond hair in a ponytail held by a woven leather band and did so with masculine composure that would not likely be challenged by drunken yokels.

The bar scene was vaguely uncomfortable. Not that I am an expert on watering holes, being so married and out of touch; but during our young carousing days, Kerner and I could walk into saloons and feel at home. And be welcomed, too. On the day I turned 22 we met a rigorous test at a saloon in Twin Bridges, Montana, where we were invited to join a clandestine and technically illegal poker game in a back room. Those old leather skins were planning to fleece a pair of greenhorns, especially Kerner—a skinny Seattleite with blond ringlets escaping his palomino Stetson. Still, I smile at the memory of goofy looking Kerner coughing in his own cigar smoke, then shocking the card-sharks by winning 50 bucks.

Kerner and I found another saloon in Melrose and one in White Sulfur that fit his vision of "Old West." I now resolved to find a remnant old-timey saloon along my War Baby "research trails"—a stale beer-stenchy place where the tender reaches under his bar for a leather dice cup and says, "Double or nothin'?" The game would be "Ship, Captain, and Crew," and onlookers might make side bets.

The King of Hearts would have its regulars as well as local customs. With patience, I'd discover them. Max and his boisterous laugh propelled around his saloon. He was seemingly everywhere at once, at ease in his domain. I expected him to be familiar with a local War Baby or two.

My head buzzed with anticipation, over-amped, I feared. *This project will work out. Relax. People like to talk, especially old Montana guys with time on their hands. I just need to find some.*

Pre-game images of coaches and player-captains fluttered from large flat screens perched in room corners, though Max had yet to activate their audios. At 30 minutes before kick-off, the King's pulse murmured softly. Most customers took either a right turn for the restaurant or a left for the darkened casino and its jingly-jangle machines. A few young bucks came to the bar, probably fans wanting pre-game juice. None took seats next to me.

"*Calm down,*" I counseled myself. Remember advisors from the Writer's League conferences: "Let your mind wander; find your God-given voice." Several suggested as much in scholarly treatises, which offered me a life-raft of confidence, because... I'm pretty damned good at mind wandering. Now if I could just induce a War Baby candidate to let his mind wander through an interview. While waiting for one, I nursed my Stella's as if 50 dollar champagne and reviewed tactics built on Edgewood's invaluable advice.

My friend, William (Bill) Edgewood, has spent nearly 40 years writing military histories. He had listened to my strategic thesis with his laser-like intensity, offering few comments, excepting one word questions. Finally, he said, "I believe I understand your objective. 100 interviews won't be too many."

Bill's dogged persistence teased out a person's essence. I was once a silent listener as Bill dissected a former Wing Commander's boyhood escapades, his formative manhood, and quarterbacking of a critical Korean War campaign. Because this retired military hero became lost in his own story, he ignored my presence. Two jiggers of Bill's single malt Scotch didn't hurt either. Most impressive: this full bird colonel spoke like a spectator to his own life, not once "I this" or "I that" glossed in autobiographical self-congratulations.

Observing Bill on many occasions, probing, probing, poking at folks, peeling away protective layers of privacy, proved he doesn't necessarily need a literary objective. Ordering ice cream at a local dairy or being introduced to a friend of a friend are reasons enough. He nudges: "Why?" or "Damn, nobody knew that!" or "Really!—and you were there?"

"Get him started and keep him going," Edgewood advised. Sitting in the King of Hearts, I waited for that opportunity. Meantime, mind wandering, pondering, I had to admit: never mind an academic abstract, I had no project outline; nor a solid thesis, therefore little for Kerner to work with. If one of his students, he'd flunk me. I coasted along in reverie, when...

"Whop!" Max slapped the bar, "You awake here?" I jolted upright. With mock irritation, Max said, "You want another Stella, you better order quick. The kickoff is in five minutes."

"I'll make it back in four minutes, Max. My lady is waiting in the truck. I need to check on her."

Max stood rooted, wanting assurance that he wasn't dealing with a weirdo. "Your lady?"

"My Lab dog, Max. Hold my place, please." I hustled out to take Bo for a stroll.

Bo Derek Linquist III is my traveling companion, confidante, and security guard. With a single shot glass of exaggeration, I could introduce her as an essential player in a crazy adventure that was about to engulf us. Her name—you'll want to know about her name. A lithe and long-legged golden blond Labrador, Bo is every bit a "10," as was the actress, Bo Derek, in the clever old movie. Like her mama dog before her, my Bo is naturally loved and loving of strangers, an asset in Montana nearly as valuable as a mannered, elegant horse ridden into town. Unsurprisingly, Bo demonstrated her ambassadorial talent on that first evening in Montana.

Bo pattered at heel behind me 'round back of the King of Hearts, where I said "Hunt 'em up;" whereupon she snuff-snuffled up a little brushy draw and flushed a hen pheasant. Curious, but satisfied that I wasn't prepared to kill birds, Bo returned and squatted to pee in the weeds.

A man wearing faded belly-buckled Levis and a battered cowman's hat paused by my truck. He had watched us return across the parking lot, leash-less Bo a precise single step behind my left boot. He waited at curbside next to Big Red. Smiling broadly, he offered: "until a year ago we had a yeller one in the family, same build and coloration as yours. Not as well trained though, I can see that."

"She's a good one," I said, opening my truck door for Bo. "But then, every Lab has been good, all three of them. This girl, though, is a natural pointer. Before her, I'd heard of pointing Labs, but laid it to exaggeration."

"Small world. I heard the same claim, thought it was the beer talkin'." The sun-weathered cowman dawdled about, watching me serve Bo's dinner nuggets and fill her floorboard water dish. The dog-loving stranger was in no hurry to leave.

Copper skinned, brown-eyed, pony-tailed black hair, the man was Native, or mostly so. With hefty muscles on bowed legs and lithe trunk, he could be taken for an Olympic sprinter, retired. With glinty-eyed smile, he said, "No damn back-of-the bus kennel for her, huh."

"Nope. She sits up front so I have someone to talk with." *She perches high on the seat eyeballing the countryside,* I could have added. She'd regained her treasured spot on my truck seat, dark almond eyes gazing, as if to say, "Are you coming, Boss?"

Still, the stranger waited on me. He was friendship-ready, hustling to hold the bar door open. He said, "Looks like you're a serious bird hunter."

"I am, though at present I'm pursuing another passion." I pointed to my bar stool. "How about I buy you a beer?"

He didn't hesitate, joining me stride by stride for our "reserved seating," in Max's words. A fresh glass of Stella graced my "reservation."

"Tall Bud, Jimmy?" Max said, with eyes glued to TV football. "The damn Griz are eating up yardage."

"No glass, just the bottle, Max, and don't charge me. 'Cuz I'll be broke when Grace is finished casino-ing. Besides, this kind gentleman from Idaho offered to buy." Jimmy spoke with rare intonation, each word slicing through background noise as boosted by a throated amplifier.

"We already met. Jack... uh, Lindquist, if I heard right." Max turned and hustled away, practically running now in his effort to serve customers while keeping an eye on the game.

Jimmy nodded at me, proffering a one-finger salute, as if placing an auction bid. He shook my hand, "I'm Jimmy Young Man," he said with a voice deep and guttural. His rough-skinned handshake was but an extension of an arm and shoulder that hadn't an inch of give. I knew that Jimmy could work the ass off town guys half his age.

Jimmy wore his dust colored hat snugged down tight. "The infant has his thumb, the cowman his hat." Did I dream that or read it? Well, this cowman also had his leathered thumb with which he deftly lifted the brim of his hat, the better to turn his square face and intense brown eyes on me, "You here to watch football?"

"Tonight... killing time, mostly. I'm on a business trip, with time out for a little bird hunting. And football? Yeah, I'm a fan; but I don't enjoy watching my Bobcats getting their hinies kicked. How about you?"

"You came to the right place," Jimmy said gesturing at Max. "My friend, Max, played Bobcat football, and my wife was a Bobcat... four years of rodeo." Jimmy nodded at the arched doorway to the casino that my suspicious nature imagined was planned as a subliminal message: *When you enter here, you'll find a kind and spirited place, like a joyous church, one where people smile and sing loud... 'Halleluiah.'* Jimmy laughed, "Soon as the girls come outa' there, we'll go home where I can watch the game on my big screen and *fix my own decent drink.*" Jimmy aimed his deep voice in Max's direction. "*Max,*" he shouted over the swelling din, "you still holding my bet?" Max simply raised his hand like "how" in the old cowboy-Indian movies.

As if there had not been an interlude, Jimmy answered, "Nope, I don't watch football here, or gamble here either. I might place some private bets, is all. That way, when I lose, I lose to my friends, not the house." He nodded at the "church" entry and chuckled, "Now my wife and my sister... that's another story."

I chose silence, thinking Jimmy had cracked the door on a domestic tangle. Jimmy noticed, like he seemed to notice everything, adding, "not that I give a damn—it's Grace's money, and she and my sister only leak quarters and a few paper dollars in there. We may have time for another beer before they wrap up their fun. Max, we're dry," he hollered, and Max—distracted by the Griz scoring on a 40 yard pass—pulled at the tap before I could decline.

You'd think Max was serving dignitaries. He came with a towel neatly draped over his forearm, deftly clunking 16 ouncers on the epoxied pine bar. As part of his waltz, he reached underneath and pulled out a double-shot glass of beer—illegitimately so, I suspected, in a big and formalized establishment like the King of Hearts. "To the Cats," Max said, clonking our glasses. He downed his beer in a single swallow as Jimmy and I echoed: "To the Cats."

Max operated at the top of his profession. I guessed Jimmy did too. Whatever profession that might be, it had something to do with livestock. Minutes later, my observation was confirmed by a wiry, craggy-faced gentleman of about 70, who came out of the restaurant and spotted Jimmy. Jimmy introduced us, and he and this Western-hatted, pearly-buttoned little man named Walker McCloud went to bantering about the price-trend of grass-fattened calves and where it would be next month. All the while, I exchanged small talk with a Grizzly fan who looked 10 years too young to be a War Baby.

McCloud slapped Jimmy's shoulder and headed off. I lodged hope that I'd catch him down the road sometime. I didn't need to make a note. I wouldn't forget a bright-eyed oldster named Walker McCloud who tipped his hat and departed with a little boot ta bop clop across the hardwood floor.

Jimmy Young Man earned my attention, and not entirely for private, scholastic reasons. Jimmy, an intriguing blend of cattleman and Native cultures, was of natural interest, I'd guess a product of about 35 years of Montana adventure. How do I know? Watch him, watch his eyes—as alert as a golden eagle perched on a tall pine, a confident man.

With no reason to question Jimmy Young Man without appearing nosy, I sat quietly, enjoying the grunt, groan, and whoop of football.

With McCloud's departure, an awkward silence divided Jimmy and me. During the interlude, I reflexively pricked up ears at banter from a pair of competing football fans down the bar, young office guys wearing business attire, ties loosened. Half the room tuned in, listening to this ever-louder Griz and 'Cat tongue fight. The scene was an unwelcomed diversion from my game plan. Then, I *jolted*, maybe visibly—

The Game—yes, the game could serve as a smooth lead-in to this interesting character, Jimmy Young Man. I did the math. In his late 30's, add another 30 and his father's generation would have been Native American War Baby, an intriguing prospect. I said, "Jimmy, I understand you're a dedicated Bobcat booster, at least dedicated enough to place bets."

"Yeah, call it loyalty. My wife was a player, if you call college rodeo 'playing.' You and Max toasted to the Bobcats. So, you're a football fan and a bird hunter to boot. Your dog hunt as good as she looks?"

"Not to brag, but she does. She's four years old and in her prime."

"So, you hunt as a twosome?"

"When we have time, we do. As I started to tell Max, this is day one of an over-the-road project."

"Construction, you mean?"

"No, something more complicated—hard to explain." Jimmy held my stare, amending his easy grin with quizzical brown eyes and a wrinkled brow. "But you need a dog on the road for, let's see... protection?"

"No. For companionship. She's never been tested as a guard dog. In Montana though? I won't waste a minute worrying." I meant that; yet a strange and intrusive question circled, refusing to depart: how would loyal and gentle Bo respond to a threatening stranger?

Jimmy and I extended small talk, trading stories of dogs and horses we'd known. But the barroom was filled and noisy. Max boosted the television volume, making conversation difficult. I lost initiative with Jimmy. Fortunately, my mentor's advice was indelible. Edgewood was adamant: "Find your target's passion; he'll want to share it."

Halftime came: Grizzlies 24, Bobcats 3. Max came by and snapped a towel at the TV screen, a mythical enemy. "Max, you have a season of eligibility coming," Jimmy said; "You should go back and show the kids how to play football."

"Or the coaches how to coach," Max said. He went off, shaking his head.

"Jimmy," I said. "Are you okay with me calling you Jimmy? Where I come from we stay with 'Jim' until we know the man well."

"And where would that be, Jack? Where you're from, that is."

"I always say 'Glendive,' though we lived on Whoopup Creek 20 miles south. And you?—you have roots in Great Falls?"

"Naw," he said, angling his iron-jawed face. His dark eyes suggested a hidden smile. In scarcely 30 minutes I had summarized him as extraordinarily intelligent, perceptive, and enjoying a bit of cat and mouse. I thought: I'm not in law enforcement, and he knows it. He's not a lawbreaker, and I know that too. Were Joanie here, she might say, "He's serenely handsome." Ah!—the mystery of her, gaga over swarthy Johnny Depp lookers. So, she marries me—a blond, blue-eyed Scandahoovian.

Back to the present, time to dive in. I raised my voice over Max's television punched high for the second half kickoff, "Jimmy, pardon me for being pushy; but it's time to own up to what I'm doing on the road. I'll keep it short."

"Short is fine, so is long. I'm curious, even nosy, if you don't mind."

"Well, I don't mind, so I'll give you a thumbnail. I'm gathering research for a book, a book that does justice to Americans born in or around the time of World War Two." Jimmy let my question hang while we watched trainers hover over our fallen Bobcat kicker who had tackled their run-back guy at the 50. Their collision and its aftermath suggested a concussion. After a few minutes of hunched over worry, the trainers and coaches helped our wobbly-legged kicker slump to the sidelines. This wasn't the sort of game stopper I wanted, but it allowed me to finish introducing my project.

Jimmy was smart enough to do two things at once. With eyes on the milling, re-organizing teams, he said, "So, you're doing research in a casino bar?"

"Actually, yes—though 'research' is an exaggeration. And this project is not about me. I'm only a vehicle, so to speak, that will carry the assembled stories of War Babies, protect and preserve them. War Babies, I'm guessing, like your parents' generation. They have a story, a legacy, and that would include you."

"Well, my father did serve; he survived the South Pacific island campaign."

Jimmy eyed me; we were on the same wave-length. *Move forward, he'll volunteer more.* "I'd love to interview you and your parents." He didn't flinch, meaning his parents were alive and a possibility.

The Grizzly's tailback barreled up the middle on three consecutive plays. They had a first and 10 on our 15 yard line. The 'Cat's coach called time out, and Jimmy swore, throwing his hands in the air, "We're hopeless."

Following the Grizzlies' TD on a lob pass to their six foot five tight end, the broadcast turned to advertisements. Jimmy seamlessly changed his mood for the better. "Great. Because of birth dates, my parents and I deserve recognition in a book, hey?"

Jimmy was erecting a jousting barricade that I resolved to break through. I said, "Absolutely! Your parent's generation learned about self-sacrifice from your grandparents, members of the Greatest Generation, honored by historians." Whoa! My phrasing was foreign to my ears, like a song out of tune. And the tone was wrong—pedantic, downright Kernian.

The Grizzlies forced a punt and scored quickly. The sour mood among our clustered Bobcat fans was palpable. The Bobcat players were no better. After the Griz kickoff soared through the end zone, the Cat's offensive unit lumbered sluggishly onto the field, beaten. They tried uncreative runs up the middle and punted. Max came to stand by his Bobcat friends, all of us bemoaning our passing attack that failed to show up for the game.

Fading interest marked the beginning of the fourth quarter. The Griz had throttled our offense, intercepted twice and recovered a fumble. Meanwhile, their freshman quarterback was shredding our defense. He and his veteran teammates had us down 31 to 3. Amidst groaning and muttered epithets, our crowd was open to other subjects besides the rout at hand. Max leaned forward over the bar toward Jimmy, a private moment in a public place, "The cookout is on, Jimmy?"

"Yup, 'round noon. We'll whoop it up some. Angus needs it. Hell, we all do."

Jimmy seemed unaware of two quiet ladies behind his back. But he was *not* unaware. He swung around to greet them, "Girls, meet Jack, here. Jack, this is my wife, Grace, and little sis, Summer." I offered my stool and the empty one next to it. Swiftly, athletically—like gymnastic teens—Jimmy's ladies hopped onto bar stools. Though under 40, but topside of youth, these two shared physical verve that belies age. Grace, with her ready laugh and bouncing auburn curls evoked a look of yesteryear. She effused joy of living extending beyond this Saturday night high-jinks casino and "Free Drinks with Coupons."

But "Little Sis," Summer, sat quietly amidst our flock—some sitting, others standing or jostling about. Summer seemed lost in thought. A striking, diminutive beauty with secretive dark eyes, she'd fit the image of a Western movie's demure Indian princess.

The tangle of us with "one more for the road" yelled for the Cats who had just scored with five minutes left.

Abruptly, Jimmy popped from his bar stool and sung out, "On the road again." He turned to go, but paused, remembering something. He extended his hand for his "adios" handshake, then pointed his index finger at me, jabbing it three times: "Come out to the ranch tomorrow. We're cookin' out Sundays, long as the weather holds. If you'd like, come out early with your dog and shotgun. We could use some prairie chickens for the cook-out."

On the go, Jimmy hollered, "Max, draw Jack a map will ya'."

Max nodded confirmation, "I'll do you one better, Jimmy. I'll go along to keep him company."

In the words of Jackie Gleason, "How sweet it is!"—a hunting trip with a savvy bartender and his cranial storehouse of local information.

Max... I'd known him for a couple hours, enough to believe in him as a character, not fictional, but a real life force. Sure, he could be dressed in fiction, the others too—Jimmy Young Man, Walker McCloud, Grace, Summer, and a personage of importance named "Angus." I wrote their names on a paper napkin. Later, I'd organize notes on each. But for once, I wouldn't tarnish them as fictional characters. Their connected story swirled, and it wasn't frivolous. Don't ask how I knew. I just knew.

After learning more, I could write them into a glossy western magazine story for *The Big Sky Journal* or a trade journal... about enterprising ranch families, all buzzing with energy—working livestock, neighboring, romancing, celebrating everlasting "Old West." In other words inspirational models for a troubled world.

How easy it would be to don my reporter's hat, though 16 years had passed since I'd given up journalistic aspirations. I'd kicked about Bozeman and Gallatin Valley for the *Chronicle*, reporting on ag news. But an unwritten rule was frozen in the wind: If you don't have a mainline column or syndication within five years, you have no right to call yourself a journalist. May as well join the corporate mish-mash or—lacking defined objectives—wander aimlessly, toting a vocabulary that a curious employer might find interesting.

I was looking for answers in the bottom of my beer glass when Max came on his refill rounds. As the final football seconds ticked away Max turned off the audio. He said, "You think our Bobcats have any hope this year?"

"The truth, Max: I'm not the sports fan I used to be. I haven't followed football much since moving to Idaho... trying to make a living that doesn't interfere with hunting, fishing, and visiting the hidden treasures of Idaho and Montana."

Final score: University of Montana 36, Montana State 10. An appointed muckety-muck stepped onto the field with the Great Divide Trophy. Out of reverence for the game, Max watched in silence.

Rituals deserve silence. After the trophy presentation speech and the coaches shook hands, I spoke up, "Max, what can you tell me about Jimmy's invite, this ranch where we're going?"

Max wrinkled his brow, as if I'd entered forbidden territory. With conviction, he said, "You'll see." Quickly though, he reverted to his "I've got the world by the tail" demeanor. He jerked his thumb toward the entry to the casino restaurant, "Molly's the best breakfast cook in Montana. I'll meet you there in the morning, 7 bells."

Chapter Three

THE L BAR L

I pulled the key card, stepped in, and flipped a light switch, disappointedly so. Stark room 1 of The Drop Inn Motel looked better with only reflected parking lot light. On a positive note, Bo was content with our place and her bedside blanket. She fluffed it with her nose, turned three times, and plopped down.

Fender, with cold strings and innards, wasn't ready for play. Following Sherbinski's lead, I resorted to television: watch local news, mine for information that may be hidden in plain sight. Even biased and slanted reports may be useful. As Sherbie reminds his assistant, Truly North, "We'll know the culture and observe the actors... every quirk, habit, and tendency. And we'll know the good guys like blood brothers and blood sisters."

Since Sherbinski was my guy, I decided to follow my own advice. I located KFBB Great Falls and relaxed on the bed with a tall necked Budweiser, listening to the 10 o'clock news. Cynically, I hoped for stories of cattle rustling and an interesting crime that needed busting. There wasn't one, only troubling reports of meth usage in the northern High-Line country, accompanied by an uptick in burglaries and car thefts.

Out came Fender. We tinkered with my creation, "Clearwater," the song that changes daily, the song that's never finished.

At straight up midnight I dialed Kerner's number on my weakly charged cell phone. Patience, patience—he'd pick up eventually, because he'd know it was me. I predicted 12 rings, but needed 15 to raise him. Dull as midnight, he mumbled, "Where've you been? You didn't call. Why did you not activate your cell phone?" I explained in schoolboy fashion, a fruitless by-the-numbers exercise, crafting excuses about no cell phone service in the mountains and I only pulled in this afternoon and I'd met some interesting people. With full disclosure I could have admitted that my invitation to hunt new country was not a chit to be used at my discretion, whereas Kerner would cut me slack. Amazing how polar opposites could remain friends all these years. Still, why change the tenor of our friendship? As if we could! I say, "Let our differences tango."

After his obligate moment of pique, Kerner said, "Link"—he's the only one in the world who calls me "Link"—"you and I must confer before you address my Tuesday Lyceum class. We'll do that tomorrow." (Though I had asked three times, he'd still left me in the dark as to how my lecturing *his* class could help *me*.) "You need to know that there's been a change. I've had extensive feedback. My better students are more interested in your techniques for writing fiction than the 'Art of the Interview' as in my proposed outline."

"So, I'll have to wing it, Bob... or we can collaborate on a program the day after tomorrow. We can't meet tomorrow, though. I'm hunting grouse on private property, the L Bar L ranch. It's 40 miles northwest of here."

"And where is 'here'?"

"South of town. A little motel next to The King of Hearts Casino."

I waited, picturing him now fully awake and energized. He'd be pacing the floor, annoyed with me for my midnight intrusion and for hanging about casino culture. Predictable Bob was also an amateur cusser. He uttered a mild gutter word without appropriate passion, his precursor to a lecture: "Link, you know we have an extra bedroom, or if you want your own accommodations there's a Hampton Inn by the campus."

"Bob, you know I don't use chain motels."

Unlike the chains, little independents present opportunities to learn something of the local culture. Bob's town house?—Not a chance, not with "Robert's" obsession with neatness, unmitigated by a wife who had taken a marital "leave of absence." Robert, the nitpicker, could burn an hour discussing Rules of Order, how to hang bath towels, etc., so I decided to turn him in a different direction, "I've apparently messed up our schedule, Bob, so how about we plan on Monday. I'll come out to the college. We'll visit at your discretion."

"And you'll buy me dinner," he said with a lilt in his voice. At that, I grinned out loud, picturing him in his practiced Montana groove, Stetson tipped back, laughing. Suddenly serious, he said, "Are you doing alright, Link?" He shed my "Just fine, old boy," response as if he hadn't heard, assuming the worst. He said, "because if you're not, you and I must save adequate time to discuss your... your situation." Bob didn't know how to sublimate his earnest rescuing mission. Nothing new about that. Besides, Kerner and I never knew for certain who was rescuing whom.

Dumbass, keep it light. I said, "Bob, I gather that you still religiously feed and water your cynicism."

"Why not? I learned from experts like Faulkner and Hemingway. And please don't tell me you're still castigating renowned writers, and..." and 'yaada, yaada.' I'd turned on Kerner's dependable spigot. Not complaining, understand. He could entertain and educate for hours, some of it useful. But during this sleepy time I failed to collect a morsel from his intellectual table. Finally he paused, "Link, you still there?"

"Monday, Bob. See you Monday. We have much to talk about. We'll settle on a format for your Lyceum. Then we'll assemble a design for War Baby strategy."

Kerner agreed to my terms, reminding me that we'd meet in his office at eight o'clock sharp. He said, quite firmly, to come prepared to discuss "real world" fiction, but—in addition—be ready to explore core ideas from our college days, including my infamous essay that ignited student and professorial debates inside and out of our journalism and philosophy classes. I argued, though, that the current academic environment was ill-suited for an unstructured session without a formalized treatise. (Translation: I, the "visiting lecturer," felt woefully out of shape, scholastically speaking.)

"My Lyceum, Link—you must appreciate its historical genesis. Aristotle, Plato, and their Greek compatriots rigorously exercised a free-thinking culture of unmitigated debate."

Never banter with Kerner after dark. Feebly, I said, "Okay, we'll work that out on Monday."

I waited while the phone hummed, about to sign off when Kerner said, "Link, did I hear you say you are invited to hunt on the L Bar L?"

"Yes. I met a fellow named Jimmy Young Man; he extended the invitation."

"That is surprising. Nobody hunts the L Bar L, not anymore."

"And how do you know this?"

"Until recently, I had guest hunting privileges at the ranch. A custodian friend at the college arranged it. The Larigans are fifth generation ranchers and wonderful people. We observed a few simple rules and they responded with kindness and generosity. Not anymore. My friend says they haven't posted their land, but they've taken down their 'Hunting by Permission' signs, something to do with a fatal hunting accident. Still, how could an outsider like you get permission?"

"Well, maybe I'm headed for a snipe hunt," I said. "I'll take my chances."

Leaving Kerner in his puzzled midnight mood, I signed off and dialed Joanie's number, hoping she'd have phone service in remote wilderness. She didn't. Tonight, my guitar would suffice to calm my mind. I lay back on my bed with Fender, and we did our best to copycat George Benson's arrangement of "Arizona Sunrise." I plucked softly, trying for perfection. But I'd chosen a tranquil number. At 2 AM, I woke with Fender on my chest and Bo snoring. I lay awake for a spell, puzzling over conflicting messages emanating from ranch people. Having grown up a nephew of eastern Montana ranchers, I'm familiar with dependable traditions. Established principles run gently meandering courses down through generations. The Larigans, though—consternation had seeped from both Max and Kerner.

Crazy things happen when I head down a road without a firm agenda. What a day! Places, people, and events intervene randomly, running and dancing with abandon. Now, before sleep, contemplation ruled the night. Damn, after tomorrow I'd probably know enough about King of Hearts, Montana and a ranching family to begin a novel. "Naw, no way!" I said to Bo and the darkened room, "For once, stick with a plan. Surprise Joanie. Surprise Kerner. Amaze yourself."

Sunday morning, September 18. The King of Hearts' Blackjack Café. As I slid into a booth at five minutes before 7, the "new guy in town" phenomenon was in play, long looks from guys wearing suspendered work pants, red wool hunting jackets, and a pair of cowmen with sweat-stained Stetsons. Someone said "order out," and a perky blond lady wearing an orange head bandana brought a pair of heaping plates to the pick-up window. "Molly," I heard among the bantering, a perfect target for the movie cliché: "What's a pretty lady like you doing in a place like this?"

As if late for a party, Max rumbled into the Blackjack and strode to the kitchen doorway where he and Molly murmured soft words. Max jabbered his way past counter sitters en route to my booth. He had loosed his rule-bound employee's long pony-tail, allowing his wild yellow hair to flounce and fly. His hair, energy, and athleticism portrayed an untamed soul. "We both want your special," Max told the waitress.

"But you didn't ask me," I said.

"Trust me. You want the special. Nobody doesn't like it"—a quirky, but serviceable double negative fit for Max. He added, "Besides, we don't have time to quibble. The special is quick, and we'll want to catch your prairie chickens while they're still feeding in stubble."

Indeed, the special was special, also quick. I said, "Max, you seem to have pull with Molly, getting our order ahead of everyone else." His wink said enough.

We made quick work of heaped home fries, ham, and eggs smothered in spicy salsa, then out the door and into my truck.

Bo sat tall and alert between Max and me. He said, "I see you have a kennel in the back. Does she ever use it?"

"Rarely," I said. "So where's your shotgun?"

Max nodded at the junction ahead, "Take the I-15 Bypass. Head north; but no—I'm not hunting today." I waited; but he volunteered nothing more, either a slow starter, or deep in thought.

I drove on cruise control at 60 miles per, content to peruse game-bird potential among roadside grain fields and brushy draws. Bo preferred the habitat on Max's side. With forepaws balanced on his thigh, she stared out the window. She glared at Max: *if you'd open your window, I could locate some birds with my powerful sniffer.*

Only after off-ramping at Dutton did Max let his day begin, explaining with a yawn: "Molly kept me up 'till half-past two. She's a sweetheart, but along with the sweet, she insists that I join the gossip club."

"You two married?"

"Naw, she was married at 18, didn't work... says once is enough."
Max waved at the prairie hills ahead, "We're coming into the Teton
Ridge country."

"Well, it's beautiful, Max," I said. "Thanks for guiding me."

"Not me. You can thank Jimmy Young Man. His idea. "We'll see
him in a couple hours."

From Dutton we headed northwest on a narrow gravel road. I
slowed to my customary 20 an hour country speed, while arranging
questions by order of importance. First and foremost: why did a near
stranger nominate me to hunt grouse on prime ranchland? "I'm surprised, Max. I barely know Jimmy and he invites me out to hunt."

Maybe Max had tuned me out, or had reasons not to answer. He
sat with an arm around Bo, scratching her about her mink-lined collar.
When he briefly paused his petting, Bo stretched her neck and nuzzled
him on his cheek. Max, was comically incongruous, his shaggy lion
head cresting thick neck, wrestler shoulders, and barrel chest—rugged
consistency tempered by his instant love affair with a dog.

Last night Max was unguarded, bright, and entertaining. And long
ago I'd discovered that a light touch yields quicker results. With that in
mind, I tried again, "You seem to speak for Jimmy. So why is he so generous with his hunting privileges?"

"They are not his to grant. Not directly."

"So he's inviting me to trespass, or is he an outfitter offering free-
bies?

Max swept his hand across the horizon of grassy hills. "There's not
a simple answer, Jack. We have another 20 miles of slow road out to the
ranch, still not enough time to explain Jimmy and the L Bar L."

Feeling like a nosy newsman again, I said, "So, can we start with
them, the ranching people? Do we have a name for them?"... doggone
Sherbinski lingo slipping out.

Max smiled acceptance of wise guy jargon. He said, "Larigans.
You've already met Jimmy, a son-in-law, and I'll get to the Larigans in
a minute. First, let's resolve something else. And please understand; I
don't mean disrespect. Sorry, but I might sound like a freaked out game
warden."

He surprised me; until this moment, Max had seemed a soul of
cool and easy. I said, "Max, I'm clean as a peeled cucumber as far as

game laws are concerned."

Max grimaced, uncomfortable with his line of questioning.... "Still, we need to know about your hunting habits, uh, how you handle firearms, and how long you've been hunting."

I was surprised by *"We* need to know." I briefly considered the smart-ass retort, "You got a frog in your pocket?" Instead, I said, "Sounds like somebody besides you is concerned about how I handle guns. Jimmy maybe, and where does he fit in?"

"To oversimplify," Max said, "Jimmy and I informally *represent* the ranch family, the Larigans. Jimmy married into the family; you met his wife, Grace. Jimmy's a master cattleman. He says he's a foreman, but he's much more. And being as I'm his friend, the Larigans accepted me like a family member." Max chuckled, "Angus says I'm an orphaned mustang."

"Angus Larigan, right? So Max, let's start with Angus and his tribe, if you don't mind. Sure don't want to cause you and Jimmy problems. But, you can take it to the bank: if I hunt out here, you won't need to worry about gun safety or hunting ethics." He pondered that while we waited for a loose band of open range cows and calves crossing the road.

Max was obviously familiar with the terrain, "These cattle have watered at a stock pond over that hill. Prairie chickens water at the same pond. I've killed a few there myself." With the road finally cleared of livestock, I drove slowly, reflecting. "Prairie chickens," he'd said, rejecting their modern designation as sharptail grouse. They were undoubtedly "chickens" to homesteaders like early day Larigans and certainly for my own ancestors, and that commonality pleased me. I looked forward to meeting the Larigans.

"If you are still in town next weekend, you and I could come out here and hunt this area," Max said.

"Public land, I assume."

"North of the road, yes. BLM manages the rough country on the ridge, all public hunting ground."

"Then why shouldn't we hunt here today?"

Max nodded and pointed down the road. I bumped ahead at 5 miles an hour, hoping that Max would use road time to tell me more.

He grinned, apparently enjoying playing me like a bigmouth bass.

He said, "Stay with me here. I have permission to get you into fantastic gamebird country that hasn't seen hunters in more than a year." My mind roiled: why the hiatus? And why was I chosen to end it? How did Max gain so much leverage? The situation was growing more mysterious and confusing, maybe shaded by obfuscation. Max's next pronouncement only complicated matters—

"If you'll hunt the ranch and come to our cook-out, you'll be doing a big favor for Jimmy and me, not to mention the Larigans. You'll be greeted by some very happy people when they see you bringing prairie chickens. And when they see this sweetheart Labrador dog... I can hardly wait." Bo, with an ear for praise, understood. Max smiled at her, and she stretched to smooch his cheek. Max, bless him, casually wiped away her kiss.

"I get it," I said. "The Larigans are wacko for dogs, and I come as part of the package."

"That's pretty close to the truth," Max said.

"Max, I see that you are wacko for dogs yourself."

"You're right. I enjoy watching a smart dog work as much as the shooting. And you say this retriever actually points birds?"

"She comes by it naturally."

Max shook his head, grinning, "Well, this I gotta see."

Like any experienced bartender, Max was ready with a monologue. I drove slowly along the prairie-bound road, watching for sharptailed chickens stretching their necks, on look-out for danger. Meanwhile, Max carried on about dogs—cow dog heelers and famous retrievers, like Ginger, Charlie Larigan's golden Labrador, who disappeared on the day he died. Before I could ask about Ginger, though, Max changed the subject to a lighter story about a dog he'd seen working on Freezeout Lake. He swore that he'd seen the owner place a duck call in the dog's lips, said his quacks were good enough to bring in mallards.

Not to be outdone, I carried on about Bo's lineage and her breeds' peculiar reluctance to bark. "They subdue canine aggression. Only thing you'll see is amazing intensity in those brown eyes." A little thick, I admit, but appropriate for the time and place.

An image of memoir writer, W. E. Edgewood, appeared in my brain—his wily grin and insistent advice: "You're primary role is to nudge him along, get him started, keep him talking." I did as he advised...

To say that Max rambled would be an understatement. He jabbered in shorthand lingo, covering one hundred and ten years over a few miles of road time. He talked proudly, as if a Larigan himself and a family historian. Max's involvement was surprising, being that he wasn't a Montana native, but a Colorado football jock recruited by Montana State. He told of twin Larigan brothers who emigrated from Iowa in 1900 and proved up on homesteads. Andrew staked a claim north of Shelby, and Charles a few miles up this very road, where he discovered a sweetwater spring. "You'll see just how perfect his claim was," Max said. He boasted of the brothers' progressive visions, developing pasture and hay field irrigation systems for their respective ranches, and—essentially—they each succeeded in romance and marriage shortly after claiming homesteads. The families weathered the Depression and sent boys to war, but never ceased improving operations, their magnificently bred Aberdeen Angus cattle, for example. "Call me weird," Max said; "but I admire passionate settlers naming their son "Angus" after an esteemed breed of cattle."

Max boasted about family females with an equivalent level of exuberance—for instance, Grandma Annie, famous for prowess as an elk hunter and for training champion cow ponies. "The Larigan women were accomplished wranglers, still are to this day," Max said. "Take Grace, Jimmy's wife. She's Angus's daughter, you see, and a rodeo partner with Summer. The two of them..."

"Summer," I interrupted, "Jimmy's sister. She seems downright dour compared to her brother."

"She's not herself now, not since Charlie died; she loved him like crazy. He was a great, great grandson of Charles, the homesteader. Jimmy's still in mourning too, but he hides it. He lost a life-long buddy. The two of them..." Max cut himself off in mid-sentence. We'd come to the end of open range. "Go slow here," he said.

A corner post of a tight four strand fence held a modest board sign announcing simply: "L Bar L South."

"What does the 'South' mean?" I asked.

"Just what it says—the Larigans' south ranch. The north ranch operates under the same brand, managed by the family corporation.

It's a cow-calf operation in the Sweet Grass Hills. Pull over here. We'll hunt the stubble." He showed no signs of moving, however. Something more needed to be said. He wagged his shaggy head, "There was a horrible accident. That changed everything."

"Might help to tell me about it," I said. Bo was crazy with anticipation. Me too, but Max had to get some things off his chest. I refilled our cups with steamy thermos coffee.

Max took a deep breath and began: "Their Sweetgrass ranch foreman quit and Charlie volunteered to move north and take over. It's a simple cow-calf operation, which Charlie and Summer and one hired hand could handle.

They put up a little hay, but used a contract outfit. They'd been settled on the Sweetgrass for six months when the tragedy took Charlie. We'll never know exactly the particulars of his death. He was alone at the time, riding fence lines in the hills. Summer said they'd had some suspicious fence failures."

"Any evidence they were human-caused?"

"Yes, according to Summer. She read the undersheriff's field report and the sheriff's summary."

"What else?"

"Well, Charlie liked to ride fence lines with his shotgun in a scabbard with his Lab dog, Ginger, out front sniffing out birds... sorry, Jack. This isn't the time. Jimmy invited you to hunt."

"No, you go right ahead," I said.

In sparse, painful language, Max told of Charlie's failure to return home, his hired hand's next day discovery of his bloody body... Charlie's inexplicable death by his own shotgun, and the families' shock and disbelief that he'd carelessly lean a shotgun against a fence post. "But that was the sheriff's conclusion," Max said. "Charlie was apparently mending fence when his dog knocked the gun loose. Discharged, killed Charlie and wounded his dog. The dog, Ginger, hasn't been found."

"Sounds too pat to me," I said. "Like a picture puzzle with missing pieces."

"Yeah, can't see how law enforcement can just close the book." With that, Max pulled his door latch, but managed only to open the door and put one foot on the ground. Before exiting, he stared at me, "*Somebody,* must show some leadership."

Max's behavior was transparent, offering me every opportunity to volunteer my assistance. Brilliantly, he had sucked me in. Had I owned a tweedy Sherlock hat, now would be the time to don it and light my briar pipe.

We stepped out into sunshine and bracing September breeze, lingering by Big Red's front fender, eyeballing the land. Bo shook and shimmied, ready to go.

Thick, knee high grain stubble sloped upward toward a ridge covered with knee high yellow grass interspersed with chokecherry and wild rose, habitat savored by prairie chickens. Perfect, except as I suggested to Max: "Two guns with full magazines would be great. We could go to the ranch and recruit Jimmy."

"Not today," Max said. "Far as I know, Jimmy hasn't hunted once since Charlie's death."

"Charlie, I suppose named after Charles, the homesteader."

"Right. Charles was his great grandfather. And now his descendants, born and bred hunters, cannot bear to pick up guns. Same goes for Jimmy, a son-in-law. They've put an honored tradition on hold. Time will tell. I plan to help Jimmy recover, and he wants to do the same for the entire family. Soon as we play out this first hunt, I'll explain the Larigans and their problems."

Bo whined. She'd detected delectable bird scent. She stood close, thumping my shins with her thick tail, waiting for the word. Considering our limited time and Max's state of mind, I said, "Later I'd like to learn about the accident and the dog-loving Larigans, the whole megillah." I figured that after opening the book, Max would finish the story. For now, Bo and I ached to get after these grassland chickens, birds promised for the Sunday cook-out—apparently a very big deal cook-out. I shuffled chapter one of the tragedy into a cranial cubicle. Deal with it later.

Max nodded at the cut grain field, "You and Bo should hunt the stubble toward high ground. I'll bird-dog behind."

I chambered a number four chill and pushed two more into Winchester's magazine. "Okay Bo," I said, "hunt 'em up," and she charged into the stubble, nose skimming earth, zigging, zagging, sniffing, and blowing dirt from her nostrils, hunting hot and too fast. She flushed the first covey 40 yards out. Luckily, I swung long and downed a trailing chicken. Bo made her usual elegant retrieve, then picked up more scent and froze on stragglers from the main covey. What a delight! My pointing-retrieving Lab, a rarity, showed off for Max, the doubter.

Bo had birds pinned in dwarf sage. Over my shoulder, I said, "Max, it's your turn."

He walked up tighter, from behind. Softly, he said, "No thanks, your dog and your birds." I edged forward behind statuesque Bo, whistled, and two birds flushed, illustrating the experts' description of "the sharptail's lumbering take-off." With a count of three, I gave this pair a head start. Easy targets, I dropped both.

At the top of the field, where stubble gave way to brush, Bo turned on scent and locked on point. This time it was a lone flusher, and I needed only a single, easy shot. The count: four shots, four birds. If perfectly honest, I would have admitted to Max that until today I had never limited on chickens without a miss, because once hunted, prairie chickens are notoriously long distance flushers. Today though, hunting naïve birds, I was out to prove perfection, aware that Max and Jimmy had framed me for some sort of evaluation. Something more than Montana hospitality was in play.

As I bagged our fourth bird, Bo lifted her nose into the breeze coming from a chokecherry thicket. "Max, we've got hot scent," I said, "You're welcome to hunt behind Bo with Winchester.

"Winchester?"

"Yeah, my Grampa's gun. He named all of his guns."

Max shook his head and started walking back through the stubble toward my truck. "Come on," he said. "Maybe next time out I'll hunt, hopefully alongside Angus and his tribe."

With Bo following at heel, Max and I sauntered side by side, Max the guide and informant, "For today, well, Angus said you can hunt pheasants too. And Jimmy said chickens and pheasants for his Salish recipe would be perfect."

He said to take you along the crick willows." We stood on a knoll where Max pointed out a meandering creek in the distance. It was lined with willows and knee high grass, perfectly thick cover, ideal for Bo's style of hunting. I paused to choose the ideal point of entry.

"I gather that Angus calls the shots for the operation."

"Right. He's the current family patriarch, though I'd never use the title in his presence. He's a humble man."

"But he's shut down hunting?—or ninety nine percent of it?"

"No, he didn't shut it down. He just lost heart. If he doesn't hunt, nobody else out here will either." Max turned to face me. He closed his eyes and shook his head—"Because Angus lost Charlie, his only son. You know, grief can kill. For a while we all believed Angus would wither away, the man who always seemed to walk with the wind at his back."

"And you said Charlie hunted with a golden Labrador?"

"Right. He named her "Ginger." Charlie and Ginger were constant companions; working cattle; building fence; hunting. She was only five when she ran off. No doubt she's dead. We know she was wounded in the accident." Max scruffed Bo behind her ears. "Ginger and Bo look so much alike they could have been litter mates."

Back at roadside, Max spoke up: "If you don't mind, I'll drive us into position for a pheasant hunt." He pointed down the road toward a willow-lined creek.

Max stopped momentarily alongside the creek to let Bo and me out, explaining how he could hold the birds from running out the far end by singing a "God-awful song that'll freeze them in their tracks."

I've never experienced an easier pheasant hunt. In her predatory groove, Bo quartered three times and froze, picture perfect, canted forward, left paw lifted. I took one small step and the first rooster blew out cackling. He flew vertically to clear the willows, leveled out, flying right to left. Unless there's a pushing wind, I never miss right to left. Birds two and three came out in the same way. All three splashed down in beaver pond shallows. While waiting for Bo's retrieves, I ejected the spent shell and left the chamber open. Max walked up from his station. Like a gun range instructor, he nodded in approval of my gun handling. Fine with me. Like my grandpa said, "If you're insulted by somebody overlooking your gun safety, you shouldn't carry a gun."

Up ahead, the creek curved under a one-lane wooden bridge. As Max drove us across, we cleared the creek's bordering cottonwoods and at last laid eyes on the ranch headquarters lying a half mile up sloping grassland. Beside the lane, a simple "L Bar L South" board sign spoke paragraphs about self-contained pride.

A half-mile up a grassy slope lay a sprawling collection of corrals and low-slung log buildings, all sheltered beneath a protective ridge. From its higher vantage in a flattened depression in the ridge rested a single story home with a wide footprint, clay colored stucco, and three clumped junipers for landscaping. Nice, modern but understated. I asked Max if we'd arrived too early.

"It's never too early or too late for the Larigans. Their visitor shingle is always turned to welcome." Max rested his arms over my steering wheel, grinning broadly, "I've driven up this lane with Jimmy many, many times. I grew up in Colorado ranch country, but I've never seen a more perfect layout. Max slipped my truck into gear, but stopped when we simultaneously noticed a slim figured man emerging from the creek willows. He carried a small-water fly rod of about eight feet and an old fashioned wicker creel slung from his shoulder. "It's Jimmy," Max said, "fishin' brookies on Ruby Crick. We'll park, and walk over, check on his fishin'."

We met Jimmy by a creek-side camp with its fire ring surrounded by weathered sitting logs. Let's take a load off," Jimmy said. "This fishin' is hard work." As we perched on log seats, Jimmy smiled at Bo, and she looked at me for permission. "Okay Bo," I said, and she went to him for pets and kind words. He picked a tiny fluff feather from the corner of her lip. "Ooh, good girl," he said, and to me, "Found some pheasants, I see."

Like any good hunter worth knowing, Jimmy wanted details. My enthusiasm flowed easily in recounting our morning's hunt. I thanked him for the opportunity to hunt "the prettiest bird country in Montana." Just short of embarrassing, Max piled on, boasting of Bo's talent and my shooting. As for "how's the fishin'?" Jimmy opened his creel lid. On a bed of grass lay a mess of brook trout, uniformly 9 to 10 inches, sporting the brookies' fall mating colors: their famous blue and red haloed spotting, shadings of neon greens and oranges—beaver pond "black bellies" dressed now as spawning "blue bellies." Spectacular, a reason we fish them in autumn. The other reason is their perfection as pan fried breakfast. "Cowboy Trout," I call them.

I predicted his answer, but asked anyway: "Jimmy how do you cook your brookies?"

Jimmy jerked his thumb over his shoulder at the delicate little stream. "These beaver ponds are overpopulated with small brook trout, the best for fryin'. Gut 'em 'an leave their heads on. Heat your cast-iron skillet. Not red-hot, but close to it. Fry-crisp your bacon, harvest it, an' leave a nice pool of hot grease. Lay in your peppered and floured brookies. Brown 'em on both sides, real crisp and brittle. That's it. Pick 'em up and eat 'em, bones and all."

"Like a bear," Max said.

"Like a bear," I said. "I've done it."

"Well, let's go gut 'em then; Angus will do the fryin'."

Like a trusted peace pipe, "cowboy trout" cemented a kinship. Now we were a cramped truck-cab foursome—three men and a dog headed to the Larigan gathering. Bo was the innocent one, while Jimmy, Max, and I—conniving missionaries—rode up the amber grassed lane murmuring soft words of hope. I offered, "They just need more time," and Jimmy—"Angus went back to church, you know;" and Max softly urging: "Jimmy, we oughta find you a pointing Labrador, one like Bo here."

"I've already thought about a Labrador pup. Maybe next year... pull in by the old bunkhouse, alongside the crick," Jimmy directed.

"Under the cottonwood?"

"That's it; before Charlie went north, he turned the old bunkhouse into a make-do butcher shop with enamel tables, coolers and freezers, and a smoker."

I lingered on the shaded porch while Max and Jimmy went inside to prepare gamebirds and trout. The ancient log building was the first of several lining the road, including a smithy's shop with forge and shoeing stand out front. Across the road or "street" rested a squatty stable pinned between corrals.

The L Bar L headquarters wafted mystique, like a Western movie town. Not the desperado and gunslinger sheriff sort of place, but a pioneering town where open carriage visitors ride up the center of the street, craning necks, dumbstruck by the myriad of sights and sounds of people going every which-a-way.

And this "Western" had riders. Up the road lay a worn grass field, where a half-dozen barrel racing girls twirled about on horses in front of their barrel triad and their equestrian director, Summer Larigan. I crossed the lane for a closer look.

Summer sat serenely tall and beautiful in her saddle, studying her riders. She was hatless, flowing black hair, copper skin aglow in the sun. She wore a weathered look of internal struggle, perhaps fighting sadness with the magic of horse therapy.

Summer's tall blue roan gelding was a match for her beauty. He stood poised, stock still with his head held high... in a word, regal. Summer dismounted and dropped the reins. The horse's ears perked stiff, but he didn't move, 16 hands of sleek muscle and bone. I wanted to stand next to him and measure him at his withers. I wanted to ask Summer what a long legged traveler was doing on a ranch made for cow ponies; but this wasn't the time. She was surrounded by barrel racer girls, some dismounted, others riding anxious horses, prancing, hot to go. Summer remounted her horse and circled her charges, observing, shouting advice, encouraging.

If this were a team sport, the girls' universal thought would be "I'm ready, coach. Send me in."

I couldn't leave just yet. How can a man not linger to watch pretty, athletic barrel racers? A dustered cowboy standing next to me volunteered: "Summer is good ain't she—a great trainer, youngsters and horses alike."

"No question about it," I said.

We shook hands, "Curly Ledoux," he said his name was.

A door slammed, and I turned to see my companions coming from the old bunkhouse toting an ice chest cooler, explaining that they'd added 20 pounds of bison steaks to our bounty of game birds. In timely fashion, up the road came Walker McCloud, the bison shooter, riding his buckboard's spring bench with his wife alongside. The ancient wagon, "a 1920's model," Jimmy said later, was drawn by a pair of matched black mules, "Molly and Dolly," Jimmy said, recounting how Walker and Annabelle had used a year's worth of spare time "finishing" their mules and refurbishing the buckboard.

Today the McClouds came dressed as pioneers, she with a blue bonnet and long white puffy dress, he as gentleman rancher in a white shirt, velvet gray vest, black trousers, and a "Sunday best" gray cowman's hat. He reined in his mules and invited the three of us and our cooler aboard. "A couple more passengers, Walker," Jimmy hollered, and to me: "Don't forget your Bo."

I brought Bo on her leash. Mrs. McCloud, Annabelle, scooted over and patted the leathered seat. "Okay, Bo," I said, and she vaulted up to her appointed place—a happy show-off. I jumped in the back.

With a "gid-up" and flick of reins, Walker started his team for the gathering cook-out crowd a couple hundred yards up the slope. Smoke curled from their campfires sheltered beneath a sandstone rimrock. Jimmy explained: "On cool fall days we'll have a warming fire plus the cooking pits."

Walker pulled into a lane adjacent to a festive scene of laughing partiers, guitarists, singers, yellers, and firewood pokers.

Using his two fingered whistle, Walker stood from his seat and signaled for help. They had already started for us—a trio of boys in their late teens, but easily judged as men. The lead one, a wide-shouldered fellow of about six foot two helped Annabelle McCloud from the buckboard and took the reins from Walker. "I'll hitch 'em," he said. Another muscular pair—I guessed in their late teens—hefted the cooler from the wagon and toted it to a central fire ring. "They belong to Charlie and Summer," Annabelle informed me.

"Go greet grandpa," somebody yelled, and a half-dozen youngsters took off, running up a rock-lined path. High on the ridge "Grandpa," Angus Larigan, gimped through a cleft in rimrock. Jimmy pulled me aside to explain: all about tradition and the importance of a stalwart figurehead, "When I came to the ranch to ask his permission to marry Grace, Angus said 'Let's think about it,' meaning, 'I—Angus Larigan—want to think about it.' I was between jobs at the time, so he put me to work building fence."

"But he pronounced you 'good to go' for Grace?"

"Eventually, but he left me guessing during two weeks of fence building and another week of elk hunting. Tell you the truth, I respected him for the way he handled the situation."

Jimmy, Walker, and I stood together watching Angus descend the ridge trail. They used the occasion and later campfire time to describe the guts of Larigan leadership...

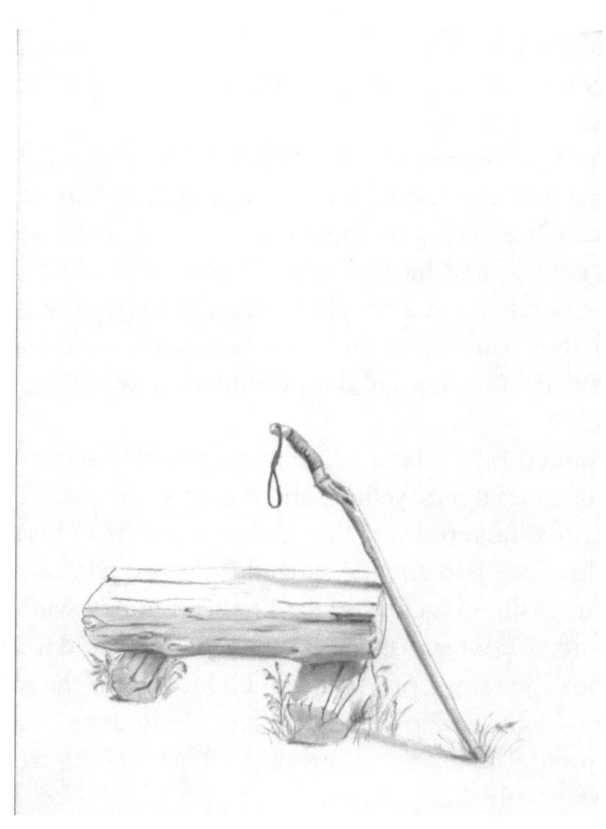

With each painful step, Angus planted his special diamond willow walking stick, a gift from his son, Charlie. Today he gimped down the trail even slower than his bad hip would allow, stretching his usual 10 minute walk to 20—time to think, time to bolster his courage.

Angus could have fired up his new red ATV and driven comfortably from his ridgetop home to the firepit gathering. 25 kinfolk had signed his 75th birthday card. Many had chipped in to buy the machine. Angus knew that now, more than ever, they depended on him. He'd often reminisce about Great Grandfather Charles, so chipper and bright at 85, twice a day walking this same trail to the milking barn and back. Angus's father trod those footsteps too, until the day that pneumonia took him.

Angus needed to show by example. A couple dozen family members and neighbors looked up to see him coming. All but the youngest know: leave an old mountain horse home from a hunting trip and he'd mope about, give up on himself, maybe never climb a mountain again. But Angus plodded steadily. Stopping near the trail's end, he waved, laughing, "Start the music."

Max, having cook-fire duties, turned me over to Walker, who took me by the elbow, "Bring yer dog along. I'll be showin' you two around." He sensed my uneasiness. No, he *saw* it. How *not* to see? About thirty pairs of inquisitive eyes examined me, the newcomer. I'm sure rumors floated about as partiers gathered in threes and fours, sorted mostly by gender and age. Walker nodded, howdied, and joked as we passed amongst them. He took me to the center cooking pit where Angus sat on a flat slabbed log. He stood as Walker began with introductions. Angus's squinted gray eyes began at my middle, ending at my eyes, I suppose similar to his quick study of a prize heifer. He grasped my hand in a strong handshake, all the while nodding approvingly. Well, that's how I saw it anyway.

I said, "Mr. Larigan, you have the biggest, healthiest prairie chickens I've had the privilege to hunt."

He grinned, "Yessir, my outfit seems to spill a lot of grain."

Angus was about to turn 76, Max had said. He wore a weary but indestructible gray Stetson that had been stomped, muddied, and crapped on by countless roped calves and probably a few range bulls that came close to being shot between the eyes. Men like Angus fight age with nobility. He illustrated the principle with his ramrod posture, like Abe Lincoln's. Built like him too, slender with sinewy muscle. About six feet of him, convenient for lasering his gunmetal eyes into mine. His grin burst through thick, gray-black whiskers. "How goes the huntin'?" he started; but before I could answer, he stooped to greet and pet Bo, "You're a pretty one," he murmured, letting his hand rest on her head. A crowd closed around, singling out first Bo, me second, then family chatter with Angus. Hopefully, he and I would talk later.

With Bo as icebreaker and Walker ambassador, stiffness of first time meetings eased before us. Jimmy led, I brought Bo on her leash, and we made the rounds, greeting most of 30 odd cook-out participants. We visited a wood splitting party, a horseshoe game, and Dutch oven pie makers around a second fire. Another crowd of young folks gathered around a pair of guitarists and a white-bearded fellow plunking on an amplified tub.

With Walker at his elbow, Jimmy grasped my elbow, "Let's go sit a minute, ya' don't mind. In the cove there, it's quieter—a place to visit." He led Walker and me away from the campfires, up a rise and into a nook beneath a sandstone escarpment.

Three empty chairs waited. They were cleverly designed with frames of springy pine limbs overlaid with cowhide strapping. I fell into one, thinking—if not for an obviously pre-arranged conference, I could easily take a 15 minute snooze in this idyllic setting. Bo did exactly that, on a bed of straw apparently left by a previous dog person. Walker leaned forward. He said, "Jack, we're grateful for ya' comin' out today; but now it's high time we come clean, Jimmy an' me. We gotta tell you, we done some connivin'."

Aha, Walker—another colorful character added to a roster that made this story writer grin. Jimmy Young man and Grace, his horse-trainer wife; Max, a colorful bartender; lovely Summer and her charismatic husband who died under questionable circumstances in the presence of his magnificent horse and faithful dog, who is missing and possibly dead. And now I'm about to become acquainted with Angus who rules the territory by heritage and wisdom. I could change their names and move this glorious setting to a mythical grassy ridge in Wyoming, a home for my newfound, appealing characters, and an emerging plot. No villain?—no problem. I can write villains in my sleep.

"So, whada ya" think Jack? Kin ya' hep us?"

"Oh... sorry Walker. I drifted off there wondering just how I could do that."

Walker McCloud had taken a chance on Montana back in 1982; then for several years he regretted his decision to move here from his Tennessee hill country. He'd sold his land and 200 head of Scottish breed cattle. Still, he incurred inordinate debt to buy 3000 acres of dry Montana grassland and a couple hundred acres of irrigated pasture. He invested in ranging cattle that called for skills he hadn't learned among lush Tennessee pastures. To compound his problems, Annabelle was blue. She had never set foot outside Tennessee and grieved over leaving her parents and sisters behind.

By great fortune Walker and Annabelle bought a ranch adjoining the Larigan's. Without exaggeration, Walker credited the Larigans for helping him hold on to his Montana treasure and befriending Annabelle. She and Walker grew to love the Larigans like family.

Walker sat quartering me while Jimmy stood digging a boot toe in gravel. Walker started, "Mister Jack, you need ta know how we put ya' in a pickle. It's only right yer told how folks, us included, done some schemin'. We conjured up a job fer you. Sorry, but you kin quit any time a' yer choosin'."

"It's about Charlie isn't it? ... and Angus. And no, I won't butt out until I'm asked."

Walker exhaled audibly, gathering thoughts. The oversized, leather-slung chair made him look Lilliputian. Maybe he sensed it wasn't right for him, because he decided to spring out of it. And boy did he spring, like a man of 20, not 70. He stepped close to Jimmy, purposely—so as to speak on behalf of them both. To put me at ease, Walker extended his strong hand for a goodwill shake and to help pull me from my chair, "Jack, we're mighty grateful; that's what we was hopin', Jimmy an' me. That you would hep us, I mean."

What they were hoping for, I surmised, was a moneyless Montana contract, a currency of commitment—a man's word; if possible to help, he'll do so.

"We need to go back a ways on what happened up-country." Jimmy said. Now we three gathered in a confabular circle shaded by the sandstone rim. Without anyone suggesting so, we drifted from the chilly shade into the slight warmth of afternoon sun, and I thought of the band of elk on Syringa's winter mountain. Wait for the slanted afternoon sun and grab the binoculars; the elk would be there, warming winter hides.

With my two "connivers" standing close, I detected horse sweat fragrance to compliment noteworthy features of dress and manner, both men potential models for my forthcoming western mystery, *The Bloody Buzzard*.

Walker was a study in contradiction. His hat-crowned noggin only came to Jimmy's chin and less so on my six one frame; but I knew he didn't stick with Montana ranching by being little in gumption. He hooked his thumbs into belt loops and tilted his weathered face up at me. "Jimmy an' me been considerin'. We're the ones runnin' the plannin' fer now. We was countin' on Angus to take it on upcountry. Hain't ready, not yet."

"Upcountry. You mean the L Bar L North?"

"Yessir," Jimmy said, "you'll hear it called the 'Sweetgrass Ranch.' Max was s'posed ta fill ya in." Jimmy faced me squarely and lifted his black hat brim with a thumb. The sun brightened his copper face. He stared into my eyes with his intense brown ones. He said, "Jack, to my way of thinking, you've come along just perfect. But we're not pushin' you for an answer, not 'till you're good an' ready."

"An answer for... ?"

"For... could a man in your position be persuaded to donate some precious time? Max says you're traveling on a serious business deal... 'as a professional writer,' he says."

Walker took a half-step forward, "Today yer travelin' with Max. He's ta be trusted. Won't talk outa' line in that damned saloon a' his. He could hep ya' in decidin'.."

"Deciding?"

"Decidin' are ya' in or aint-cha."

Bo rose from her butt-plant on my feet. She paced, studying troubled faces.

Jimmy stepped forward, "What we mean is... uh, we can't pay you, wouldn't be right; and we wouldn't want you to make money sellin' Charlie's tragedy either, with your book writin' I mean."

Walker was all but dancing now, "Ya' wanna hear more don't-cha?"

"Sure. If I'm going to help, there's no better time to learn." As these weasel words crossed my lips, I regretted them. I hadn't committed: "in or ain't." Jimmy sensed my uneasiness. He folded his arms, gazing down upon the curling smoke and the Sunday people, and Angus's small cluster where nobody laughed. Jimmy turned to face me...

"We'll wrap this up, Jack. Walker, I'll start and you jump in when you want." Jimmy drew a deep breath, "Jack, you know by now that Charlie was a horseman and hunter, damn good at both. Angus trained him to handle guns like he did with most all the youngsters hereabouts. Charlie told me he was allowed to carry a .22 when he was 8 and a 20 gauge at 9. He'd bring home rabbits an' grouse."

Walker's arms and hands flew as he talked ... "Handy with guns, Charlie was, same as little whippers down in Tennessee where I come from." Walker studied me, measured me. "Bout livin' off the country, like Jimmy here and his people in the Flathead country knowed about, unnerstan'? Growin' up that-a-way would teach a person not to kill hisself by bein stupid about rifle guns or shotguns, either one. See what we mean, dontcha?"

We stood on a tiny knob-hill overlooking the cookout festivities. Somebody had drug a peeled ponderosa log onto the knob. We took seats, three abreast.

Walker nodded at Jimmy, a signal to jump in: "Walker and I were appointed, more or less, to ask you. Word came out from the King of Hearts, Max and Pearl mostly, about your bein' a detective writer and a journalist to boot."

"An' yer journlist job 'specially," Walker interrupted. "Goin' along the High-Line, we heard, talkin' to the old-timers. That's what got us thinkin'. You could spend a bit of time 'round Shelby an' the Sweetgrass country, maybe learn a whole lot more about all a' the missin' parts of the shurriff's report.

I felt crowded sitting pinned between them, with Bo's butt planted on my feet. Their eyes swung from the festivities back to me, like bankers waiting for me to sign the mortgage.

I longed for a respite, time to contemplate. Not even in Sherbinski's wild and crazy world had I been a party to a richer trove of conjecture. My respite would have to wait. My petitioners looked at me with pleading eyes, like lost puppies. Walker on his feet again, rocked from foot to foot, squinting at me. Jimmy bounced to his feet too, where he dug in the dirt with his booted toe. Repeatedly, Jimmy glanced from dirt to me, eyes of a skeptic. Bo too, bumped my leg and looked up, glaring, "When are we gonna do something?"

I drew a big breath and began, "Here's how I see it: Angus is too downhearted to push for an official resolution of Charlie's death that you all can believe in. Might be one of the few times in 70 years he's faced something he couldn't beat. He might be losing a fight with depression. But you can't wait on Angus. Somebody must step up to the plate: a digger, somebody aggressive and persistent." 'Like Sherbinski,' I almost said.

There wasn't a decent stander among the three of us. We swirled about on the dusty knob, back, forth, and around like players in a primitive ceremony. At the foot of our little hill, curious lookers around the fire rings lifted chins and froze eyes upon us. "Let's go get us a beer," Jimmy said.

Walker braced a hand against my shoulder, "We'll do that, Jimmy... jus' one more thing. I think ya' know the deal Mister Jack. Angus cain't lead out no more. Been lower'n a snake for most of a year. A-fore losin' Charlie, nobody knew a happier man; nuthin' much ever knocked 'im off balance."

"You'd never know it now," Jimmy said. "Grief took 'im down. That and guilt."

The guilt part needed explanation. Angus's guilt? How about Jimmy's? For the third time he said morosely, "I shoulda' gone north."

Jimmy plopped on the log again, as if defeated. Walker joined him, an undeclared counselor. I stood over them, feeling like an intruder.

Walker sighed, "You could read Angus like a book. Specially how he refused goin' ta' elk camp last fall... first time in 40 years. I stayed behind in home country so's I cud look after 'im."

"Says he's skippin' again this year," Jimmy added on.

"Unless I can talk him into huntin' elk with a longbow," Walker countered.

A spring-legged young man bounded up the hill to us, with three cans of Coors trapped before his chest. With a build like an NFL cornerback, he flattened the hill in seconds. He handed over the beers and whirled away without an introduction. "My kid, Stevie," Jimmy said. He knows thirst when he sees it."

Jimmy and Walker exchanged glances, each hoping the other would cut in to another festering wound. Walker, in all but blood a family member, was the one. With a shake of head he said, "Charlie dint want no part a' goin' north."

Jimmy's turn. He looked at me earnestly, "No, and I should have spoke up louder. Angus would have been open to Grace and me moving north to the Sweetgrass. If only I insisted, Charlie would be squattin' down there next to Angus, grilling buffalo steaks and prairie chickens. "

Walker addressed me—seriously addressed me—in the manner of a lawyer trying to persuade a judge. The man to be granted clemency was Jimmy. Walker touched a hand to his back, "Jimmy wants to redo history. I tol' 'im, cain't go back, drives a man bat-crazy. An' there's mor'n enuff 'what-ifs' to pass amongst us."

I broke in, "Go north, Jimmy? What do you mean, 'go north?'"

Whereupon they double-teamed me, explaining how Angus's brother died in January of '07, leaving the Sweetgrass without an operating manager. "It's a simple cow-calf operation," Jimmy explained, "a boss, one hired hand, and one extra for summer."

"Mostly," Walker corrected; "but if a man shows up at brandin' time like I did once-t, ya' learn how the High-Line neighbors come ridin' in ta hep out.... Well, I take that one back. All the neighbors came 'cept them Slimanns—thet peckerwood outfit borderin' the Sweetgrass operation." I salted that away for now, a colorful judgment, but worth remembering. Sherbinski would call it a pregnant lead.

Jimmy and Walker had started in the middle of the recounting, not so logical, not so perfect; but intuition said *let them talk*. In time we'd fill in the holes. In hindsight, I'm glad I just sat there petting Bo, nursing my beer, and smoking one of Jimmy's Rico Rum cigars. 20 minutes of their soul searching revealed the "plot." Except it wasn't a plot. It was real life pathos to which I had been introduced as some kind of soothsaying savior. I didn't ask for this. Or did I? I'm a curious man.

Curious: an apt word for what came next.... In a grass field adjacent to the campfire festivities, Summer paced circles around her tall blue roan, name of Duke, Walker informed me. We, the connivers, shambled down from our knob hill to watch. Bo came along at heel.

Duke held his head lower than proud, subdued, reins hanging to the ground. Summer circled the horse, carrying a long quirt. On alternate steps she slapped the ground with it. Duke twitched his ears, but didn't move. After 5 minutes of this challenge, Summer waved and Scotty, her 16 year old, moved in from the rear with a pump shotgun. He stood about three horse-lengths behind the tall gelding. Summer stood with the gun bearer as he chambered a round, pointed the gun skyward south, and pulled the trigger. Duke startled but didn't move from his tracks.

Walker, standing next to me, smiled approvingly. "Walker," I said— "that is an impressive showing and a striking animal. Who's the lucky owner?"

Suddenly sober-faced, Walker said "Summer is now. 'Long with Summer, Duke was Charlie's pride 'n joy. He run off an' come back to the barn the night of Charlie's accident or whatever the goddam hell it was. Duke musta' been skeered shitless by the gun blast. Charlie an' me had figured he was solid foolproof. Same for Ginger, his Lab dog, but she I unnerstan; poor girl, so mortal wounded she didn't stay by Charlie's side. Hate ta think on it, but mor'n likely the wuffs or coyotes kilt her after she wuz wounded."

At an hour after noon somebody banged on a kettle, and Angus stood tall on a flat-sawn log, hollering, "soup's on."

The crowd stirred and began shuffling toward fire pits. Pinewood serving tables, stump perches, and log seats were arranged in a broad semi-circle about the central fire pit. A bevy of cooks, including Angus, served from iron bar grills, Dutch ovens, and steaming pots. Wearing roper's gloves, Max man-handled a giant black coffee pot.

We'll hol' back on the food line," Walker advised. He led Bo and me to a long, pinewood trestle table, "Angus's place; we'll join 'im," Walker said. Jimmy detoured to a cooler and came with a six pack of Silver Bullet Coors.

We three sat watching and sipping, waiting for Angus. Hopefully, I would discover some sort of reckoning... in vain, as it turned out. Angus chose a seat opposite me, drank a beer with us. But talk was stilted and small, restricted to lighthearted dog and horse stories.

Nor did conversation reach a higher rung throughout a feast of buffalo steaks, spicy breasts of prairie chicken and pheasant, Dutch oven spuds, and Angus's barbecued side-pork. And Max brought me a crispy brook trout. Angus grinned, crinkle-eyed, watching me chomp the trout—fried bones and all. That was the apex of our table merriment. Puzzling... or was it?

I've been to equivalent cookouts in the Clearwater country and on Hell's Canyon ranches. Word travels, neighbors show up with food and sometimes dazzled relatives from a city. We celebrate for any excuse, including the end of winter, a 90th birthday, or birth of a baby. The Larigan gathering should have buzzed with similar energy, but didn't. After filling bellies, our crowd broke into two's and three's, drifting off without a finale of any sort.

I could have drifted away myself, detached from the Larigan's tragedy: Strong people with a proud legacy, they'd heal.

If only life could be so tidy—

Angus leaned to pet Bo. "You come back, Bo. Before the season's over we'll hunt some birds." He turned to me with three quarters of a perfect smile. Gripping my shoulder with his left hand, he grasped my right firmly, locking onto my eyes with his steel gray ones. He said, "Bo, you bring your Ideeho man along." I nodded in acknowledgement and not only to be polite. As certain as the bang of a judge's gavel, Angus had just complicated my War Baby mission.

Max insisted on driving us back to the King of Hearts, explaining: "We have time before dark to show you more country."

At the bottom of the Larigan's lane, Max turned right, headed south. Thus began a 100 mile loop south and east again, driving secondary roads to places like Freezeout Lake, Sun River, Fort Shaw, and Buffalo Jump. On any other day I could have turned my curiosity on each of these places and the expansive land in between. Today however, I intended to use my time to probe Max about Charlie's death.

First stop: an old paint-peeled, broken-windowed country school. Max, in tour guide mode, explained: "A couple dozen Larigans were educated here; three of them came back to teach."

"Did I meet any teachers today?"

"No, unfortunately they've passed on. Charlie was the latest."

Aha!—a shoe horn to my chosen subject. I spoke casually, "Max, about Charlie, the accident, and how he died. Can you share details? Or, is it too gruesome or perhaps restricted to family?"

"Gruesome, yes; but I need to respect the family's privacy. You spoke with Jimmy and Angus today. I thought they would fill you in."

"They talked at the margins. They seem reluctant to dwell on tragedy... too painful. They'd like to lay it to rest, but can't. Too many unanswered questions. So, I'm to be sort of a delegate, Bo too. Angus invited us to come back and hunt with him."

"Really!" Max slapped the steering wheel. "You have no idea what a breakthrough that is." I asked why; but Max seemed relieved to change the subject. We had arrived at Pishkun Park and Buffalo Jump, where we read the signboards, and Max added narrative to sketchy historical accounts.

Max promised one more attraction, showing off the Larigan's feedlot on a bench above the Missouri bottoms. We had it in sight when he took his foot from the accelerator, coasting down a grade. He was deep in thought, something singular. As if picking it from the sky, he said, "Can you believe that an experienced hunter like Charlie would lean a loaded gun against a fence"—not a question begging for an answer, but a statement of fact. He laid that egg, then another: "I love to drive out here this time of year."

"And why would that be?"

"Bird music." Max stopped on the graveled road shoulder and asked me to roll down my window. From my side, on the north, a rooster pheasant crowed from a patch of buckbrush, then another crowing cackle and a third from tall grass on the hillside. From Max's downhill side, bawling feedlot cattle added bass to the concert. He said, "The pheasants are dependable here. They sneak in to steal bunkered grain and pick corn from the silage."

Bo stood with her paws on my lap, nose out the window, softly whining. That's when Max surprised me. He said, "I'd like to ask a favor."

"Name it," I said. "You've been a terrific guide today."

"I'd love to hunt a few minutes behind Bo."

"Fine with me. Winchester is modified, throws a generous pattern."

Max smiled as he stepped out with Winchester, "Wouldn't you like to know how many thousand rounds she's fired?"

Ten minutes, two shots, two rooster pheasants. What a fabulous ending to a power packed day! Only in my cobwebbed mind rested doubt, doubt from a voice that said, *wasn't Angus to be a War Baby candidate?*

A second round of questioning wasn't mine. As I drove into The King of Hearts complex, Max said, "Jack, you need to know the accident scene was trampled by cattle, a real mess, and an extraordinary challenge for the Toole County sheriff's department. Furthermore, a horse blew up on the sheriff the day before Charlie's death. Tossed him, broke his leg. So the sheriff sent out his undersheriff and a deputy from Shelby. Neither had adequate training or experience to investigate an incident of such complexity."

I drove into the Blackjack's parking lot. Max said he was to meet Molly. I again thanked him for guiding me, a wrap on the evening, so I thought.

Max made no move to leave, something more on his mind. Hoping to pry it loose, I said, "But how about the undersheriff's report? Any specific questions left unanswered?"

"Too many to count."

"Then how about this one?—Who had a motive to harm Charlie?" The lingo just spilled melodramatically, like Sherbinski's... out of place, and I wished I could take it back. *Dumbass, this is no place for two-bit fiction. This is real life drama; and you're in over your boots.*

CHAPTER FOUR

LOBBY SOUP

At eight o'clock on Sunday evening the King of Hearts slumbered. Max asked me to park and wait while he went to collect Molly in the Blackjack. "Molly is coming off duty. We'll invite her for a beer," Max said.

Which turned out to be two beers around without a single boring drop. Molly shared her rich inventory of gossip and laugh-a-minute banter. I begged off on a third beer. A long-legged Carol Burnett-ish blond came by to yuk it up with Molly. Max nodded towards the door.

I followed him out to the sidewalk, thanking him for the chicken hunt and a great day. He held my smile without one of his own, knowing that it wasn't about chicken hunting or a so-called "great day." The day was ragged at its edges, unfinished. We shook hands, but not with expected vigor. "Jack," he said, "I hope we haven't unfairly imposed on you. Nobody would blame you if you decide to move on."

"I might blame myself, Max... if I walked away."

He smiled, waving me off, "In that case, Jack, you aren't done with me."

Across the lot, the Drop Inn lobby was still lighted. Maybe there'd be a message from Joanie. Looking through the old style picture window, I saw a lady behind the check-in counter with her nose in a book. I knocked before entering to let her know I wasn't a staggering drunk or a guy with a gun (having read too many Lee Child's thrillers). I walked in and met sister version number two, who looked over her reading glasses, smiling softly. She was an angular, pretty brunette, I guessed a Boomer like me.

"I'm Pearl," she said, dropping her glasses. She offered her hand,

"You must be Jack Lindquist. Elizabeth said you might be coming in late. You have a message from your wife." With a twinkle that indicated my message from Joanie was as promising as this pretty lady's romance novel, Pearl handed me a folded note, "I wrote it down verbatim. Message notes are unusual now with the world of cell telephones, nice though in an old-timey way."

I said, "Well, I'm an old-timey guy and stubborn. I won't text, tweet, or twitter."

Pearl laughed, "Okay by me. At first I thought my caller had the wrong guy in mind. She called you 'Rusty.' "

I laughed; "if we knew each other better, Miss Pearl, I would explain the Rusty business, how 'Rusty' came to be."...

On my 35th birthday I was between jobs, had time, a little cash, and three buddies—Larry, Keith, and Terry—all employed by the Bureau of Fisheries in Seattle. They'd accumulated sick leave, compensated leave, and an alphabetic leave—ABTG something—altogether averaging about 20 days left to goof off. We flew to Yakutat, Alaska and spent two and a half weeks fishing tide water and coastal rivers for silvers and kings. Our daily routine was simple: 14 hours fly-rodding and 3 or 4 more in a beer bar sipping on-tap Alaska Amber and nibbling beer-battered seafood. I came home to Joanie looking as bedraggled as a muddied black Lab at the end of a swampy duck shoot. After three weeks 'without', Joanie and I raced for our pine log four poster. As always, we joyously cavorted, though without the stringed orchestra, roaring rockets, or yodels. She teased, "Jackson, you're rusty." I said, "Yes, I know. Rusty only takes a week. I've been gone three." Thereupon, 'Rusty' became our intimate joke. When I leave for more than a week, she calls me "Rusty."

I pocketed my transcribed note from Joanie, thanked Pearl, and turned to leave, but pulled up short, overcome by eau de carnivore. Pearl confirmed what my nose told me,

"That's our lobby soup there on the corner table. It's hot and waiting: garden vegetable and braised venison soup; you'll like it." Seven hours had slipped past since the Larigan cook-out. I picked up a soup bowl as Pearl came walking confidently across the lobby, knowing that any healthy middle aged man—even a monogamatrite—would appreciate her attractiveness. She poured herself a cup of Joe, flashing a di-amond and silver band on her marriage finger. She also flashed a dark-eyed smile, "Do you mind if I join you?"

"Please do," I welcomed her, and not just to be polite.

The lobby chairs were straight-backed, moderately cushioned un-der leather, hybrid chairs, designed neither for lasting comfort or strict-ly business. Pearl chose one across the low table from mine. She settled in with a smooth twitch of fanny, like a barnyard duck settling on her eggs.

She smiled, "Well thank you so much. I'm normally not forward with our guests, but you're, uh, a little different." I slurped soup and waited. Pearl spoke affably, as if visiting with a neighbor, "It's Eliza-beth's venison soup recipe. She shot Bambi on day one of bow season."

"The best kind, mighty tender," I said.

She shed her smile, mulling something. I grinned encouragement, and she went on, "Molly gave me the lowdown. You're a bit of a celeb-rity around here, you know."

What? Pearl's interest struck me as peculiar, but familiar. Like Sherbinski, buying a stranger a drink, ulterior purpose notwithstand-ing. Like Sherbinski, I managed a casual tone, "Just because I hang with the prettiest dog in America?"

"Well, that's part of the equation, for sure. We host armies of bird hunters. There's lots of public land with four varieties of upland game birds and three mountain species. Sorry, my Chamber of Commerce spiel sometimes just spills out; but in truth, private ground offers the best hunting. Molly says Max DeVore took you out to the Larigan Ranch to hunt. I wondered"—

"By what sort of magic did a stranger manage immediate consid-eration? Kind of a class C mystery isn't it?" I teased, "Class C celebrity too."

I had learned early on about Class C celebrity. Between my freshman and sophomore years at Montana State, I rented a furnished roadside cabin in a little cow town in central Montana where I had a summer job on a highway survey crew. Took to dining a block down the road at Judith Gap's only café, owned and operated by Brandon, a bleached out, butch-cut fellow. Young, about 30, Brandon was skinny and pale. He sat at the counter smoking cigarettes in that peculiar left-handed way. He didn't need to "come out." He was "there" already. At the end of my first week in town, having dinner in goofy Brandon's café, he said, "You're good for business, you know, in case you haven't noticed. Look around. They come in to learn about the new guy in town." His earnest inquiries of me were born of curiosity and boredom, like "Drop Inn Pearl," across the table, ready with more questions.

"If you'll indulge me, Mr. Lindquist; I may be a little meddlesome."

"Jack," I said. "And I don't mind at all."

"Well, don't let me keep you. You must be tired."

"Not too tired for soup and sassy," I said.

A ready laugher, she did so again, her eyes a-light. Her infectious laugh spilled across the coffee table. "You're a funny man, Mr. Lindquist, I mean Jack. I'm glad you found our piece of the world."

"The piece called "King of Hearts," you mean?"

"No, the King only rests on the edge of the real world. My business is here, but my heart is out on Teton Ridge with the country people you visited today." Drawing a deep breath, she said, "Sorry, I'm unduly emotional. You see, Elizabeth and I grew up on a ranch neighboring the Larigans. Our dad sold out to Walker McCloud in 1991."

"Walker! He's a genuine relic isn't he?"

"I'm sure you mean that as a compliment. He's like an uncle to Elizabeth and me. After our mother died, he and the Larigans practically raised us."

"Easy to understand. I never found a friendlier bunch. Bo and I happened to arrive when they needed a hunter and his dog."

"An incredible dog, I'm told. May I meet her?"

"Bo would love to meet you; at the moment she's sleeping in my pickup cab. She's had a big day. We both did. The cook-out was a traditional country celebration like I haven't seen since childhood... music, a ton of neighborly good will, great food, and a bit of drama that could not be ignored."

"I'm sure. Elizabeth and I have been to dozens of Larigan gatherings, cattle ones and people ones. But the drama? Perhaps you'll decide to share it."

Pearl cradled her cup in both hands, studying her coffee. With troubled face, she had arrived at an emotional hurdle. I helped myself to more soup, believing that I was better at silence than she. Correctly so. After a minute of reflection, her floodgates opened, all about growing up "a-horseback," country schooled, dating Larigan boys. "Charlie was my favorite," she said. She mouthed "Charlie" softly, confirming the obvious. "Everybody believed he and I were in love. We were, but in a strange way—too much like cousins."

"Spoils a good romance," I said, just to keep her going.

"Yes, but I shouldn't blather on like a soap opera hussy. It's just that this time of night it's good to find somebody to talk with besides myself.

Night can bring on the lonesome blues you know."

"It happens to everybody at times. But, at least I have Bo." I pointed at Pearl's ring finger, "and you have your man."

"I do, a lawman, and he's a great talker at two A.M. when he comes in after his own late shift. Oh well." She exhaled brilliantly, as if blowing out a candle, ready to change the subject. A smart woman with smart emotions, I liked her quickly and properly, could imagine liking her improperly, if I hadn't already discovered gold, marriage-wise, and she didn't have a night talking husband. She waited until I spooned the last of her lobby soup.

"You have business down the road, huh? ... Sorry, none of my business." She'd lost her smile. "I'm a pushy type, my sister reminds me. But I'd like to know: since you were smack dab in the midst of the Larigan tribe, what did you learn about Charlie's death? Max and Jimmy, Walker too—they must have prepped you."

"Some, though reluctantly. The subject seemed too painful to explore the way I would have liked. "

"Anybody else?"

"Opening up about Charlie, you mean?"

"I was hoping. The family has always been very private. In a perverse way, though, they're more likely to share delicate subjects with designated strangers."

"Like me."

"Like you." Pearl didn't seem the gossipy type, looking for tidbits to pass along, but she did display a fevered case of curiosity. She waited respectfully for me to volunteer something. When I didn't, she said, "The accident—any speculation that it wasn't one?"

"Yes."

"Who's speculation?"

"Mine."

Her jaw dropped. She dinged her coffee cup on the glass table top. "Based on what?" she stammered. "Sorry. Elizabeth is right. I can be nosy. I hardly know you. So please, tell me if I'm out of line." She began to rise from her chair. I motioned her to stay.

"Miss Pearl, my speculation is based on listening—a piece here, a piece there. Now my speculation is seconded by your speculation. But I can't assemble the puzzle until the missing parts are identified. Until that happens, I assume the worst."

Pearl arched her eyebrows and gathered her breath, taken aback. "So, do you have a plan?"

"Wouldn't call it exactly a plan. I'll keep my eyes and ears open. Then build on what I learn. I'm leaving soon anyway, hadn't planned to stay more than two or three days. Before leaving town, though, I'd like to ask a favor."

She frowned, "Certainly."

"We should stay in touch. A voice in my head says I can't let Charlie's death go unexplained. Max feels the same. And you?—You could gather facts from this end if you believe appropriate."

"It *is* appropriate; I'm glad you came along. The Larigans have always been terrific people, but delicate family stuff is closed to outsiders. You've apparently opened the door."

"To some extent, if I read Jimmy and Angus correctly. But I don't know—does the green light include more than morale building? If it does, nosing around some could prove helpful. I'm a stubborn cuss."

She inched forward on her cushioned chair. "How will you proceed? Like an investigator or something?"

"The question is: how will *you and I* proceed."

"Meaning?"

"Meaning I won't go it alone. Jimmy and Walker; possibly Angus too... they're savvy enough to know law enforcement has been too passive. If investigators have leads, we need to know. Give us more to go on so we can re-open an investigation, unofficial and unannounced, of course."

"You seem to know a lot about investigating crime."

"Theoretically, yes; but untested in the real world."

"Molly says you write murder mysteries."

"Molly, yeah—the town crier. But writing crime fiction is pain free. Fiction doesn't levy consequences on the writer and his reckless imagination. I read that someplace, but it's true."

"Sorry, Jack. We're not really gossiping about you; we're curious. Put yourself in my shoes: a strange and... I must say, somewhat mysterious man comes to town—a fellow who steps willingly into a family turmoil. In all fairness, we must do all we can to help." Pearl smiled, "You can count on me, Jack. I trust that we are friends, even on short notice."

Coming up on ten o'clock, time to say goodnight and call Joanie. Hopefully, she'd trundled back to civilization. I said, "Pearl, we'll sit on this for now. Before leaving Great Falls, though, we'll have a plan... maybe... I hope. Our suspicions may be wrong, but the sheriff's "accident" explanation is facile. Still, if Charlie's death proves to be a freak accident, my obligation stands: helping Angus and his family regain their well-being. He's asked me to come back and hunt with him."

"What? Well, that is incredible, a breakthrough."

"I'll be back. I'll call you for a reservation. You serve Montana's best soup spiced with great conversation. "

Pearl followed me to the door where she took my hand in both of hers. She said, "Our talk has been more than interesting, Jack. I'll keep in touch and be alert for helpful information."

"We've got a deal Pearl; you're very kind." I handed her a ragged-edged writer's business card with my phone number. "Oh, one more thing—I think it is best to cut Molly's jungle drum telegraph for now."

I left Pearl with her puzzling face. My Molly advice was based on flickering instinct. I liked the jungle drum line, though: something detective Juneau Sherbinski would say.

A dozen easy steps took me to my truck where I rescued Bo from its chilly cab and took her to our room where she followed me about, bumping my leg, pushing for pets. "Okay Bo—I know I'm late with your supper and late with our call to Joanie."

I unfolded Joanie's note kindly transcribed by my new friend, Pearl, and hence to me. In neat, slanted script Pearl had written—Dear Rusty: Check your phone, you fool. If you're lucky you may find a proposition that will curl your toes. Love you—Babe in the woods, Joanie.

I poked requisite buttons and on the third try found Joanie's message on my antique cell phone. She said, *"Ha, gotcha, didn't I? I have a few minutes of cell service... hopefully. I'll be back in Moscow tomorrow evening. We're processing grizzly hair for DNA testing. Call me tomorrow. I'll be heading back to the mountains the day after. I hope to hear that you've located some interesting War Babies. I love you, miss you. Can't wait to see you. How about meeting in West Glacier next weekend? I've been in the woods too long. No lipstick, no girl stuff. I could be mistaken for Sasquatch."* Love, Woods Muffin.

Flushing warm, I said, "We'll meet her. Bo. Detective stuff can wait." Bo arose and stood with her paws on the bed. I said, "Amazing Bo, isn't it, how we love that woman?" She stretched to thrust her muzzle to my cheek. Her surrogate's kiss would have to do for now.

Normally my forever cerebral video of Joanie would plant a smile on my face and I'd fall asleep peacefully. But tonight wasn't normal. I was building a criminal case on thin ice. Why proceed? No one had suggested a motive... which could lead to a perpetrator, which could lead to truth about what happened, then a plan to trap the rotten bastard and squeeze him for a confession. Or maybe all of that in a different sequence. I couldn't just walk away. The best I could do was to suspend amateur detecting until my commitment to Kerner was fulfilled.

Speaking of Professor Grumpy, I called him. He was predictably irritated with my late night call, but fell to curiosity about my mention of DNA. He kept me on the phone for 20 minutes narrating details about a human genome study and its many implications for criminal investigations.

"I've got it, Bob. I have you. Don't need Sherbinski. Besides, Sherbinski is committed. I'm writing him into my current mystery, *Blood on Her Stilettoes*."

"Yes, I know. Very deep, I'm sure. You can write *Stilettoes* before breakfast tomorrow, leaving no excuse warranting tardiness for our meeting."

"With Starbucks and bonbons, I'll be there." I punched "OFF". Honoring a long tradition, savoring the last word.

I needed more than 6 hours sleep, but wouldn't get it tonight. I flopped on my bed, coaxing "All Blue" from Fender, while Bo cradled her nose between outstretched paws, brown eyes watching me. Almost independently of conscious control, my tired brain hummed along reviewing the day that seemed like a week – a rare day highlighted with game-rich, unspoiled countryside, a landmark ranch, and vibrant people in an atmosphere chilled by death. All of this was new, yet unsurprising. In my sleepy condition I felt as if I'd lived it all before, even the magical powers of lobby soup. I hearkened back to my boyhood experience with this small town western phenomenon. Coincidentally, like tonight, I was dabbling at sleuthing back then, 17 and unreasonably idealistic.

A rumor surfaced about a horse thief operating in the Wibaux hill country east of Glendive. Young and naïve, I had John Wayne-like visions of recovering Drifter, my Uncle Pete's stud horse stolen from leased government grazing land. So I borrowed Uncle Pete's '74 Chevy and single-horse trailer and drove 50 miles east to Wibaux. Checked into an appealing western motel with log siding and a hitching rail. From these headquarters, I sleuthed up and down Main Street. Unfortunately, I was too young for bars, where loose lips deal information. But fate being what it is, like the Drop Inn, Wibaux's motel gifted me with lobby soup and a piece of information pie, which I shared in businesses along Main Street. Wearing cowboy boots, a frazzled Levi jacket, and a sweat stained felt Stetson, I felt authentic and walked authentically out to the edge of town where a Saturday livestock auction was in progress. I blabbed about Drifter to the standers and coffee drinkers, anybody willing to talk beyond "howdy." Next day, Drifter miraculously appeared, nibbling grass in a pasture next to the sale yard.

27 years later, I still celebrate the Wibaux incident. When a guy has incredible luck, well, it's okay to brag, if only to himself, his dog, and a motel room. Unfortunately, there's a second chapter to Drifter's story, the unlucky side of the coin that can't be ignored.

After identifying Drifter, I went to see the auction manager, a retired rodeo calf roper named Smitty. He called the sheriff who came immediately. The sheriff and I sat in front of Smitty at his desk, drinking his rot gut bitter coffee. They smoked, I didn't. A smoke might make me look older and wiser, but only if I didn't cough.

Smitty said, "Tell the sheriff what you told me." I did, and added some meat to Uncle Pete's tale of capturing Drifter from a herd of wild horses that had wandered north from Wyoming. "Drifter still had his milk teeth," I explained, implying that Uncle Pete more or less rescued the foal. I intended to go on, making my case, but the sheriff intervened, "That's enough for me." He pulled out an affidavit, I signed it and became Uncle Pete's temporary agent.

"You have 24 hours, young man, to deliver the stud horse to Pete Jardine. Failing that, you'll be known as a horse thief." The sheriff grinned though, and I grinned back. He stood to leave, but paused to shake my hand. He laughed, "I've known your uncle for 30 some years. "Tell Pete, Shemorry says howdy."

Smitty led me from the back door of his office to an irrigated pasture. He said, "Your uncle's horse is actin' flighty."

Smitty was right. Drifter shook his mane and loped to the far end of the pasture. "We'll catch 'im the easy way," Smitty said. He carried a bucket of 'fat barley.' "Rolled it myself, topped it off with a can of premium Grainbelt beer. Otherwise, you and I would have to saddle a couple of auction ponies and run your horse into my trappin' pen."

Drifter grazed alone, nibbling spring-green timothy and sweet clover. Smitty and I approached from his left side, maintaining non-threatening space. We walked alongside at the horse's lip-nibbling speed. Drifter never lifted his head, but his dark eye watched warily. In his uncompromising horse brain, he was thinking, "I won't be caught. I won't be loaded out of this glorious pasture, the likes of which I've never before experienced in my three years on blue clay prairie."

Smitty beckoned me to follow, and we moved upwind of Drifter. Without hesitating, the horse lifted his twitching, blowing nose and walked up to Smitty to lip a few grains of heavenly barley.

"What's his name again?" Smitty says.

"Drifter."

"Come on, Drifter," Smitty said. He began walking toward Uncle Pete's trailer, mumbling nonsense all the way. Drifter followed in his footsteps, stretching his neck to get at Smitty's grain. Smitty never looked back, but continued his relaxed jabbering as he walked up the trailer ramp. Drifter followed into the trailer, and I secured the tailgate chain behind *him. Smitty squiggled from the tail-gate, grinning, "Fat barley, gets 'em every time... that, and my conversation."*

20 years later I watched Robert Redford play a horse whispering role. I wondered: were Redford's horses treated to fat barley with beer?

After circling trailer and truck, inspecting tires, Smitty says, "I'd keep 'er under 45 if I wuz you. He shook my hand, "Tell yer uncle the thief's been identified. He's runnin' for parts unknown."

That was on July first. On September first Drifter died. "At an easy lope through tall grass," Uncle Pete said, "I didn't see the badger hole." Uncle Pete "busted two ribs and a collar bone." Drifter broke a foreleg, had to be "put down."

I learned a hard lesson; sometimes the best intentions backfire, and you must live with "what if?" What if I had taken the rodman job on the county survey crew instead of going to Wibaux? What if the brand inspector had come a week earlier? He could have pronounced Drifter, the young, unbranded stud, "wild and anonymous." Yes, the rustler would have gone free to steal again. But Drifter would likely have been sold at auction to a rancher, thereby providing a stud's good life: a job, good pasture, and pretty mares.

Yes, it is a thin connection, I know—Drifter's story and the Larigan turmoil. But it is my nature to equivocate. I'd come to a fork in the road. "Take it," Yogi Berra said. "Take it"—not so easy, Yogi. A straight, boringly academic road stretched east to Minnesota. It was the "right" road. The "wrong road," loses itself in secluded ravines and nooks of the Sweetgrass Hills, home to unfinished, messy business.

Alert to my sleepless roil, Bo stood from her bedside blanket and licked my hand. I took that to be a vote for the Sweetgrass.

Chapter Five

ROBERT HAMILTON KERNER, ESQ.

Monday, Sept 19, "Obligation Day," as noted in my Road Journal.
No alarm clock necessary. Bo licked me awake at 6 AM, requesting a trip out to a field of weeds. Back in our Drop Inn room, I stood before the bathroom mirror contemplating how to look presentable. "When you try, you can look author-ish." Joanie often teased.

"Contemplating"... yeah, how coincidental, how appropriate. Two days after hearing jazz master McCoy Tyner's arrangement of "Contemplation," it continued playing in my head. Not complaining. Tyner's piano and his accompanied sax, bass, and drums are unhurried and measured, leaving space for reflection.

So, I studied my casual image in the mirror. Joanie would say, "Spruce up, you're not a Crocodile Dundee."

"But, I'm not selling books today."

"Nonsense! You are always selling, either purposely or passively. You can't look like you came in on the midnight bus."

Joanie was right, of course. I trimmed the reddish beard, topped yesterday's denim blue working shirt with a tailored corduroy jacket, and retrieved Lucky, my one and only town and country hat. Perfect. Great Falls College isn't exactly Montana's Harvard.

Kerner studies such things: imagery, group behaviors, incentivizing of envy, always expanding his inventory of humanoidal puzzles. He'd briefly considered pursuing a doctorate in psychology. I remember him being sidetracked in '89, researching the villain called "Envy." That's when he left Bozeman for the University of Montana and a doctoral program within Interdisciplinary Studies. He'd offered a long winded explanation, pitching enough fodder for me to propose that the "dukes" and "earls" at the U *envy* cow college students who actually learn how to produce things. What I didn't say, because at the time Kerner couldn't have handled my hard edge, is that he was the one overloaded with envy. He took to wearing a store-perfect Stetson, pearl button shirts, and boot-cut Levis. Still, his gringoed accouterments could not overcome his lack of a western gizzard. However—a very big however—despite his comic awkwardness, Kerner worked like hell to moderate his urbane Seattle personae. His greenhorn enthusiasm was a kick. That's why during my nine years in Bozeman I'd helped him pursue his quest for westernization. I taught him horsemanship and took him on novice-challenging excursions: rafting the white water canyon stretch of the Yellowstone, chasing blue grouse on 7000 foot ridgetops, fly fishing the Madison's Beartrap Canyon, and hunting November mulies in knee-deep snow. We even tried an unsuccessful six day elk hunt, the worst kind, shivering in icy rain and hunkering in wet snow. Kerner proved awkward, but game, adding fiber to his attitude. That was 14 years ago and our last outdoor excursion together. We'd gone our separate ways, found new digs, wives, and career challenges. And now, in Great Falls, I hoped to discover Montana fit Kerner like an elk skin vest.

At five before eight I parked in my assigned visitor parking slot # 22 next to reserved faculty parking and punctilious Bob's metallic green Silverado. My antennae were tuned for signals, wondering: was this two year college a fit for Kerner?

In front of the Admin building three young men raked leaves. Subduing boredom with raucous banter, they were obviously college-grown workers, a good sign. Frugal Bob would reflexively approve of jobs for scholarship students rather than contracted landscapers.

Sherbinski pauses before entering buildings. I did the same, resting my butt against a paint-splashed commemorative boulder. I liked what I saw: an unpretentious two storied rectangular stack, single colored red brick, a monotonous arrangement of rectangle office windows. No spired towers harboring smoky old professors reading musty manuscripts. The college was too new for musty and too new for copper statue renditions of millionaire benefactors. Perhaps about right for Kerner though—hopefully a place where clawing for tenure and department promotions takes second place to student achievement. Perhaps he'd found a fit, where institutional team play balances personal challenge, comfortable but not soft. Simple contentment was no friend of Kerner's.

Career concerns weren't his only ones. Kerner's recent phone conversations hinted of marital angst. We'd get around to that discussion too.

As I walked into a lobby area, a 20ish, spritely receptionist sprung from her chair and tripped around her desk, sporting a brilliant smile, "Good morning sir. You must be Mr. Lindquist. Dr. Kerner is expecting you." With practiced ease she offered her hand, "I'm Sunny Daniels. I'm honored to be the first to welcome you to Great Falls College." She placed her hand lightly behind my shoulder and walked me to her desk, where she gestured to an open paged registry and gold pen. I signed while she stood close by. Breathing in her rose perfume and her very presence, I thought: *how did I miss this part of my undergraduate education?*

Sunny smiled, measuring me with her exceptionally large turquoise eyes. She was strikingly pretty, with a perfectly tight clipped blond "do," artfully coifed, a professional job. Sunny validated her name, a bundle of vibrant energy complimented by a blue business suit and medium high heels. As a mystery writer, I'm paid to notice such details... others too, like perfectly sun tinted skin and a lithe female figure.

Looking past Sunny's left ear, I saw myself gazing back from a promotion poster. She gestured, "Voila! There you are, Mr. Lindquist."

"Like a wanted man," I said, leaking pride. Never before had I been featured on a professionally printed poster. I felt vaguely uncomfortable.

The college's poster identified me in bold print... **Author Jackson Lindquist, Guest Lecturer, September 20**. Joanie shot the photo for my book signing last winter in Jackson where I posed, squinting against hard snow glare. I sported a reddish-blond winter beard and wore the Filson vest Joanie bought to spruce me up.

Sunny beamed a generous welcome, "Doctor Kerner, all of us— we're so glad you could come. I've been given comp time off to attend your lecture." She pointed to the rear of the atrium, "Doctor Kerner's office is at the top of the staircase, second floor—or, the elevator is..."

"Thanks, I'll hoof it," I said, bounding athletically toward the staircase, proving to her, but mostly me, that at 46 I haven't surrendered to elevators.

Kerner's door stood open. The top of his head showed above an over-sized computer monitor. I knocked and walked in without an invite. "Wake up, Professor," I said.

Bob leaped from his chair, as if catapulted. "Ah, Link, you're here. Come in, come in."

"I'm in, Professor."

No chance for a handshake. He hugged me without hesitation, not a bear hug, more like a Frenchman's backslapping hug, a Kernerian thing that I had previously accommodated, though I'd never been a hugger of men and still wasn't.

Kerner had never been a dawdler. In his black polished Western boots he clipped around his desk to a corner coffee table, returning with the pot and a pair of magnum Montana State cups emblazoned with snarling golden bobcats. As he poured the java, he offered his mea-sured smile and a familiar dig: "Link, you're a never-ending project that only a persistent bulldog can refine. You leave me no choice. I'm your bulldog."

"You and Joanie. She's a bulldog too, but nicer."

Kerner pulled in a worn oak chair for me, probably a hand-me-down from the college's master institution, Montana State U. No ques-tion, this would be a long sit, and Bob's cushioned office chair gave him an advantage. Nevertheless, I liked what I saw—his bolo tie held by a moss agate clasp, earthy corduroy jacket, and wavy blond hair, now sil-vered by mid-life. He'd been joyous and twinkly at our wedding. Joanie remarked that he could be a poor girl's blue-eyed Robert Redford. Now, 13 years later, he wasn't an ounce over a hundred fifty pounds, and his photo on the wall showed him holding the faculty racquetball trophy. I smiled; Kerner's picture was framed in weathered barn-wood, reflect-ing his commitment to westernization.

We began our discussion with a minor dust up about priorities—a predictable set-to. Our friendship had been *built* of dust-ups. I preferred to begin with the here and now, or—more accurately—the now and yesterday, the yesterday of the Larigans. The current drama, so strong on my mind, could use a dose of Kerner's insight, and I told him so.

Not to be; he had prepared for another subject.

Kerner easily morphed into his thinker pose, cradling his chin, busy cobalt- blue eyes examining me. He said, "Link, you look, I would say... well. Are you?"

"Never been better. Why do you ask?"

"Frankly, when you lost your last salaried job, I worried. Remember? You agreed that you needed a semblance of stability. I've read a number of studies. In the absence of stability, many people become unduly stressed. Follow-on maladies have been identified. Symptomatically, you'll want to measure for energy deficiency, sleeplessness, and sudden mood changes."

I smiled, "Yeah? Did you forget to remind me of my overheated id?"

Bob slapped both hands on his desk.... . "Sorry, Link. That won't happen again. Man, it's good to see you. It has been too long. And you must know the truth. My previous Lyceum was less than dynamic. You're input of energy is just what this doctor ordered. Thanks again for agreeing to participate."

"My pleasure, Bob. I've been here only a couple of days and I feel right at home in this town."

"Not in town, Link. Let's face it. You've avoided town, roaming the countryside with your dog and a bartender."

"Not to mention a Salish Indian and his equestrian sister, an ancient mule skinner, and the nominal king of Teton Ridge."

"All of them attending to a lost stranger, and I'm not referencing geography," Kerner countered.

Knowing Bob, knowing myself, we could have spent an hour pursuing the psychological implications of my diversions among the characters of the King of Hearts and Teton Ridge. But cute "Miss Sunbeam Sunny," the receptionist, came to the door. She said, "Excuse me, Dr. Kerner. The lecture hall is ready for you." She handed him a typed sheet, in large font: "9 faculty commits, four observers, approx.. 120 students."

Kerner led me from the Admin building, pointing out an adjacent red brick building, a modern teaching auditorium that he said could accommodate three or four hundred. We walked abreast, both lost in pre-game strategizing. I was gratified to notice Kerner did not resort to his graduate school habit of walking with hands clasped behind his back, Socratic style. He'd replaced his contemplative saunter with an unassuming swagger.

We paused in the empty foyer where Kerner showed me his color coded checklist supported by numbered paragraphs. A useless bystander, I followed him picking his way through color coded desks that he nudged into his perfect, preferred arrangement. He toyed with clip-on mics—"testing, testing." Then he stepped behind the stage curtains where he tweaked the knobs of a lighting panel.

We walked onto the polished hardwood stage spread in an arc in front of audience seating. Kerner took me to center stage where a Power Point projector sat on a podium. He said, "I suppose you're going to tell me you have no Power Point program prepared."

"You know I don't." My voice was surreal, amplified by a powerful P.A. system. We stood on stage in the empty auditorium, like a pair of actors ready for Shakespearian theatre.

Kerner laughed, "For once, your neglect is appropriate. I've discovered Power Point makes their eyes glaze over. I'll introduce you, very briefly, set some ground rules, and step aside."

"And what sort of program are you proposing?"

Bob rubbed his hands together and put a finger to his temple of genius. He pumped his fists, hooray style. "Link you will astound and inspire. I know there are hidden gems among them. You'll love these students, naïve but eager."

Thus began Kerner's frenetic monologue on the subject of higher education. He danced to and fro across the stage, raising his voice until it echoed from the back of the cavernous room. I watched, awestruck by his passionate performance for a one man audience. He made a number of points about inspiring students, always pausing to see if I was properly energized. He finished with a directive, swinging his hands like a band leader, "Link, all you need to do is be yourself."

"If I have to," I said. "But I'd rather be Juneau Sherbinski. And Juneau would have two stiff belts before stepping on this stage tomorrow. Seriously though, what are they expecting? What are *you* expecting?"

"Inspiration, Link. I have a plan. I'll set the tone, but relinquish control to you. My students need a break from conformity, and you love flying without a parachute."

"But not without a flight plan, Professor."

"Ah! But you *have* one. It is lurking deep within your psyche, ready for a break-out, for discovery."

"That's a little heavy, Bob."

"Yes, but you are smiling; you know precisely what I mean."

"That these youngsters are ready for whacky theories?"

"Exactly. I suggest you demonstrate "Theoretical Fiction.""

"If you say so, Bob. My, how far I've come, dredging up my 22 year old term paper from American Lit."

"Not to worry, Link. I've already introduced my students to your basic premise—or should I say premisi'. And I've asked them to bring some of their personal works. The brightest will do so. We'll want their engagement in this Lyceum." He looked at me, urging confirmation.

"I know you, Bob. Not exactly engagement. You expect embroilment. Of that, I'm certain."

"Right. We'll divide them into teams and let their competitive instincts drive them."

"Nothing to lose," I said. I looked at him and laughed, "Whatever happened to 'Art of The Interview,' Professor? I've prepared notes and a delivery."

"Simple," he said. "You exhibit little passion for "how to" lectures. I approve. I won't have my students sleeping through this Lyceum."

Back in Bob's office, he donned his Montana "hat." Not the real one, not the white Stetson with the eye of the peacock feather stuck in the deerskin band. No, I'm referencing his adopted country disposition. He asked, "Do I have a chance to gain hunting access to the L Bar L?"

"Perhaps in due time. They aren't ready for visiting hunters just yet. When they are, I can test the waters."

"But you said the Larigan family is in turmoil."

"I did, and they are."

Bob glanced at the big black and white circular clock above his door, an obnoxious, institutional thing, ticking loudly, relentlessly interfering with conversation. Each tick reminds us: *You have obligations to attend to.*

"Bob, you must have work to do. I'll butt out. I'll pick you up at seven for dinner... on my dime."

"I'm exceedingly expensive," Kerner said. He handed over a note with his townhouse address. "But why are we dining so late?"

"My beautiful blonde awaits. We have an afternoon date."

As I crossed the reception area, I waved good-by to sun-beaming Sunny. She stood with a pair of pale skinned fellows. Sport coats, no ties—probably admin guys. The three of them stared at me. No question, Kerner had oversold.

I opened my truck door and Bo awakened, wiggling, dancing a welcome. "You got it, Bo," I said. "We're goin' hunting." She cuddled close for our ritual love fest. I began by rubbing the loose skin behind her ears. She leaned into me, grinning, eyes half-closed. Next, lift a foreleg... *"Scratch my chest vigorously and work your way down to my hairless tummy while I bump and wiggle. Ah, there—it's never enough, but I'm much happier."*

We headed south, following a secondary road into prairie country. 20 miles of twisting road took us through knobby buttes to a large sweep of public grassland. No cattle in sight; the land was likely locked in official rest-rotation. I stopped where the road gained a rise and stepped out with my binoculars. Bo plopped her butt down on my hunting boots while I scanned the expanse of gold-lit prairie rising to a rocky ridge. (Bo learned as a pup that sitting on my feet insured that she would not be left behind.)

The sweep of prairieland and rock outcrops ran to the southern horizon, all undefiled by human detritus. I recalled taking a cousin from Minneapolis to similar-looking country in North Dakota, where miles of earth greet blue skies. Shaking his head morosely, he said, "What a sad wasteland!" I was sad, not for the "wasteland," but for my cousin.

Light rain had loosed the musty fragrance of buffalo grass. I breathed deeply and smiled at Bo. She smiled in return, drooling.

With sparse cover separating likely bird habitat, we hiked miles, locating few birds; nevertheless our prairie hike refreshed my soul. Bo's too. We returned to The Drop Inn with two Huns and a prairie chicken. Pearl was overjoyed to accept them. I said, "Miss Pearl, perhaps you have a recipe for gamebird lobby soup."

Kerner and I decided on Lazaro's Restaurant, a five star featuring Greek cuisine. I said, "If they have five star beer, I'll be a happy camper."

A skinny, dark eyed fellow with bushy eyebrows delivered beers. What is it with Mediterranean people? Just because they are capable, should they grow a crop of curly black hairs from their ears? I cast this little bow-legged fellow as a latter day Hobbit. He returned twice to take our order, without success. Bob and I needed time, mostly to answer his questions. He wished to analyze the past, waaaay back... all about Joanie and my stint with her dad's wood products company, and my "quotidian life in the village of Syringa." His questions were transparent and familiar. Unsaid but implied: was I sufficiently ambitious to live up to my potential. Two strong Greek beers loosened my tongue, "Bob, you must admit my career-less life is perfect. After I explain how, we'll move on to discuss how you've dealt with semi-bachelorhood."

In a conciliatory mood, I said, "My story is straightforward. Parting ways with my father-in-law's company needs little explanation. We should have a federal law barring a man from working for his father-in-law. For a few months, I did okay as a pseudo HR director. Then, against my better judgment, Pops convinced me to join his management team. After three stressful months we parted amicably, since I didn't fit the job and the job didn't fit me."

Kerner shook his head, "And that comes to—I think I have this right—two attempts at journalism, two in sales, and the aforementioned bout with 'management,' whatever that means. Jack, you read like a bad essay, with no transition between life's paragraphs. But don't let me interrupt. Self-analysis is exactly what a behavioral psychologist would encourage at this moment."

"Shouldn't I be lying on a couch?" Apparently not. Kerner, the doctor of everything, refused to grin. I plunged ahead: "Well, after fleeing Priest River Wood Products, I needed a nine to fiver, because money dribbling in from my first book was embarrassingly insufficient and Joanie made peanuts as a laboratory assistant while she studied for her doctorate. I got wind of an opening in marketing/advertising with a retail food company. Because I can write with exaggeration, I snaked through their paperwork maze and was invited for an interview. Drove to a branch office in Spokane, a formal sort of place in an informal town. A pair of young professionals grilled me... a blonde girl with short-clipped hair and a West Coast accent, and a pudgy guy who mostly deferred to her. I faked an understanding of their marketing lingo which—by her body language—carried little credibility. She clinched her decision to dismiss me with a question: 'Would you agree that you fit the demographic of Western Rustic?' Guessing what she meant, I agreed. Minutes later we shook hands. I put on my Western rustic hat and left. Lucky and I never felt better."

Kerner looked at me with a wry grin, "That, my friend, was a revealing speech, and I must say, refreshing." With that, he began laughing and couldn't quit. Patrons stared. Kerner grabbed his handkerchief and wiped his tears.

"Okay Bob, what's so damned funny? Here I pour out my unemployable soul to you and you laugh."

The Hobbity Greek waiter hovered once again. We'd held his table for nearly an hour without ordering. Kerner lifted an index finger. "Stay right there, sir. This will only take a minute." Kerner turned to me, "Link, you're naiveté is remarkable, delightful too. The lady representing your potential employer had you perfectly identified. There is, in fact, a demographic called Western Rustic. You would do well to know such things. I have some highly acclaimed texts. I'll loan them, one at a time of course—check one in, one out. You will learn how these studies contextualize diversities among the American social experiment."

"I suppose so, I don't know where I am, and don't know where to look."

"Eureka! We're at last getting to the root of your problem," Kerner laughed.

"And my problem?" the waiter said. "I would like to place your order."

We ordered the Greek garlic lamb shanks and a bottle of—in Bob's words—"audacious red wine." No better time in the offing to ask about Bob's marriage situation. He'd hinted that he and Hanna were apart at the moment. "There isn't a marriage problem," he said, while picking at his dinner salad, "only opportunity problems. Mine is here and Hanna's is with her sister on their inherited quarter horse ranch."

"And where's that?"

"South of Havre. She'll be back soon. We talk once a day, sometimes twice."

I waited, expecting more. He threw his hands in the air, dangling a comment: "We part periodically. Call it an equal opportunity marriage."

With Kernian patois, I said, "And you've framed your paradigm of marital dissonance?"

Kerner swirled his wine glass before sipping. "Hanna and I have adopted practicality, a trait that grows with maturity." He stared in his wine, no smile, discussion ended.

"Okay Professor, any qualms about our program tomorrow?"

"You?"

"Not enough to fuss about. Good or bad, pay's the same... zilch."

Kerner laughed again, and I thought: without copious laughter this incongruous friendship dies.

"And after tomorrow, what?"

"After tomorrow I'll be on the road. War Babies, remember?"

He studied me carefully. "Link, since you've been here, you've shown not a scintilla of interest in our—pardon, I mean *your*—project. Gone off... distracted... disengaged from War Babies. The Larigans and their Teton Ridge friends are unsettled. And I know you well enough to predict you'll become involved in some way. When are you going to share the details?"

"Are you through counselor? You're badgering the witness." Which reaped only a chuckle. But, as planned, he salivated with curiosity. I said, "You know when I'm messing with you, Bob. And what I'm about to tell you is not in that category. I'm dead serious."

"And you have good reason to tell me?"

"Yes, because I trust you one hundred percent, and because you may be able to help me investigate the, uh—I hesitate to call it an accident. My information fails to support an accidental cause."

I waited. Kerner formed a ten fingered tent, pursing his lips, nodding, nodding some more. Finally, "It's the Charles Larigan case isn't it?"

"Yes it is; though there is not an active case as far as the family knows. But you *do* remember the news of Charlie's death?"

"Certainly. The Larigans are a well-known, respected family far beyond this community. The breaking *Tribune* story shocked folks from here to the Canadian border. It was written in a style fostering speculation. Follow-ups were buried in back pages of the papers, each new article nearly a repeat of the last. The pattern lasted for more than three months. Investigative reporters—and I use the label loosely—attempted to shore up the sheriff's and coroner's reports, but could find nothing new, or at least nothing that went public. I suppose the dailies from Helena and Great Falls tired of sending reporters to the High-Line on fruitless expeditions, because the story died. Not the rumors, though." Bob enunciated *"rumors"* with his special Kernian inflection, meaning: *take these wild shots seriously.*

I probed, "Rumors, such as... ?"

"About neighboring landowners, said to be long term practitioners of chicanery—shady mineral property dealings... questionable deeds. The lawyer son finally left town, not willingly, I'm told. I'll wager you this: go into any tavern in Cut Bank or Shelby. Wait until the customers are in their cups; then drop the name Slimann. You'll hear about disputes, under-handed dealings, and nit-picky lawsuits."

While we took a needed time out to attack our lamb shanks, I rolled Kerner's information around before depositing it in my cranial vault—'ker-chink, ker-chink.' Puzzling: how could he know so much about High-Line disputes and skullduggery?

"Professor, I'll take your advice and visit some saloons. Nothing to lose. I'm headed north to travel the High-Line anyway... all the way east to Minnesota, just as we planned from the git-go. So what of these disputes and this Slimann character, or are there Slimanns?"

"Slimanns, and their family firm—lawyered land-sharks and one particularly doltish, lawless son still in residence, according to my source."

"A reputable source?"

"Yes, a High-Liner from Cut Bank. She was one of my favorite students, now an employee. Of totally sound character I might add. Her name is Sunny Daniels. She welcomed you this morning in the admin lobby.

"Oh yes, she certainly did—'Sunbeam Sunny,' and she has some inside dope on this Slimann outfit?"

"Perhaps. You see, she is an aspiring writer, and believes she can use the unsolved death of Charlie Larigan as a model for a parallel piece of mystery fiction. I've advised her to be careful. Defamation does not need to rise to a level of legal liability to cause jeopardy... not on the High-Line where rumors grow, mate, and reproduce. To complicate Sunny's ambition, we have the presence of Bennett Slimann, a hardball attorney, watching, like a hunkered vulture."

"Interesting. The Larigans, Max DeVore, Pearl, you, Sunny Daniels—the huckleberry list grows. You all believe there was a crime. You apparently have suspects. Yet, the law is strangely passive."

"As far as the public knows. But law officers must use caution, gather evidence accurately and quietly. We should do the same, move the process a step at a time. Just because the Slimanns are crossways with Toole County landowners doesn't spell motive for harming Charles Larigan. Let me do some additional backgrounder research on the connections. And Link, you'll share everything you learn so we can organize our strategy."

I laughed, "Welcome aboard, Inspector. Unlike me, you don't come with conflicting priorities."

"Other than a teaching professorship on top of administrative duties."

I poured the last of our wine. Kerner had a point. Besides his current assignments, in confidence he'd told me he expected to vie for the retiring president's chair in 2011.

"You've made it clear, Professor, that you've had suspicions of your own about Charlie Larigan's death. Now that you're officially on the case, you can explore your theories."

"Tomorrow, Link, you and I will conduct a blockbuster Lyceum session. Then we'll talk. We'll construct a plan steeped in erudition. Criminology is best done in an orderly fashion—that much I know."

"Like Perry Mason, you mean, or maybe Sherbinski?"

Kerner frowned and exhaled. "Link, you know I'm serious."

"I'm trying my best," I said. I reached for my wallet, pulled out a folded paper, and smoothed it out. You'll remember this, Bob. I thought it was well written, and timely—arriving after I quit my third job inside of 12 months.

I re-read Bob's missive with difficulty, punctuated with laughter. "Bob, you are teaching, administering, writing research papers, and now investigating crime. You would do well to consider your own advice. I pushed the paper across the table.

Kerner nodded as he read. Not unexpectedly, he smiled.

"Life is like a river." Anon. Link, your life is like a particular river in Siberia, The Ludenska. It travels 2000 kilometers across 50 linear

kilometers only to become lost in the brackish lowlands near the Arctic Ocean.

Kerner toasted me, adding, "touché."

We turned down Greekophilic sour plum desert in favor of warmed brandies. Before sipping, Kerner studied me over the brim of his glass, "I was so convinced you would discover true scholastic relevance with your War Baby study. But now, I am enabling you to fly off on the wings of fantasy. I hope that's what it is—fantasy."

"So do I, Professor. So do I."

Kerner raised his glass to mine, "Let's toast to the truth, bon ami, wherever it takes us."

CHAPTER SIX

FICTION, THE IMPOSTER

7 AM, September 20, King of Hearts, Montana. Bo and I stepped out of the Drop Inn Motel to greet a crisp and frosty morning—energizing, but also cruelly conflicting. Bo was invited to a bird hunt, while I faced a duty-bound obligation in Kerner's Lyceum. Pearl came driving her perfectly weathered blue half-ton Ford truck, 1970's vintage. Bo jumped in the cab and sidled up to her. They were headed for the foothills to hunt Huns and chickens. Bo sat proudly in Pearl's passenger seat, puzzling: *aren't you coming Boss?* "Go hunt 'em up, Bo," I said.

On to the Blackjack Restaurant to purge bleary from my sleepy eyes. Molly eyed me quizzically from her order out window. I didn't stop to visit. Just as well. Two Montana counties and the town of Great Falls didn't need to know my business of which I, myself, had sketchy knowledge.

After two cups of high octane coffee, cobwebs parted; I slapped my steno book on the table and smiled at last night's top line entry: "West Glacier, McDonald Hotel, Sunday 25th – *Buy good wine and fresh flowers. Meet Joanie, 4 PM.*" First though, I faced a worrisome onstage presentation.

After printing a bold heading, LYCEUM, I held my pen poised. It refused to write. Less than two hours to organize the brain, and be ready to welcome 120 Lyceum students, 30 of them guests from the local Catholic college's creative writing class, plus a sprinkling of student and faculty visitors. Pressure. I was tempted to break long-standing tradition and follow Kerner's advice. I could filibuster 'till doomsday about what he called my "landmark progressivist paper."

Kerner and I met at Montana State in1983. I was a sophomore, he a senior. Kerner, the Seattleite, and I a Montana country boy, became unofficial debating opponents, permitted to go at it by Dr. McIntosh, our free-wheeling professor of philosophy. With a head full of naiveté, I failed to understand Dr. Mac's motive. Kerner waited until the end of the term to confirm that he *conspired* with Dr. Mac to match the two of us in confrontations, "demonstrating cross-pollination of urban and rural behavioral patterns." Kerner and I hammered each other. American students and Kazakhstanians have smoother cultural exchange programs. Still, our war of words "paid dividends," according to Dr. Mac, as he refereed debates between two teams, including students who moved willy-nilly between Kerners camp and mine.

Robert Hamilton Kerner was a marvel, a whirlwind of energy... humorous, and—God forbid—*forward*. I learned to question convention simply by lounging with Kerner and his worldly friends in our student union where we drank strong, cream-less coffee. I challenged him, starting with his ridiculous garb, "Dump that cashmere cardigan... makes you look old and sleepy." He did that, and more, but couldn't easily decide between city cool and no-nonsense western. He became a hybrid: wearing a white dress shirt with the sleeves folded above his wrists, tight denims, and Tony Lama boots.

Next came Kerner's foray into hippie-dom, though without sufficient anger or angst, and without the weed. From his side of the looking glass, Kerner saw me as an interpreter for Montana's intriguing, foreign culture, although I was initially reluctant to accept a role of cultural guide. Finally, Kerner pronounced me fully credible when I wrote a rebellious take on contemporary American literature, a "progressivist term paper," he said. Searching for rebellion himself, Kerner took up my "cause." We extended our half-baked notions to Philosophy / Sociology II where we were encouraged by "Doc" Hanson, a mop-headed professor, a kook who'd been known to sneak off to the arboretum, where he smoked a pipe with funny tobacco. Kerner, who arrived on campus with a large vocabulary, said Doc was a "legitimate sesquipedalian." I looked up the word, since I arrived on campus with only a large *Unabridged Webster's* and a vacuous brain.

Doc Hanson had earned his medical creds by resuscitating a heart attack victim who happened to be an important university trustee and a generous scholarship donor.

Doc, a popular and eccentric professor, subtitled a course in MSU's catalog "Exercises in Communications and Individual Expression/Expansion of Societal Norms." How's that for a staid cow college? Kerner followed the prof's lead, becoming chief agnostic, with me as his complicit foil.

We argued incessantly, often switching sides on issues. In American Lit, for example, where I challenged convention and Kerner defended an old curmudgeon, "Status Quo." He initially scoffed at my term paper's thesis woven into "Theoretical Fiction," disputing the very notion of fiction, proposing instead, that novelists construct characters and plots from life's indisputable truths. A couple months later Kerner came around, abbreviating my concept as "TF." He enjoyed interrupting classes with this and other exotic theories. As John Denver said, "Far out." Of course, only the bold or naïve would be so reckless before professors who commanded grade books.

Nevertheless, that spring Kerner proved his independence again by clipping off his ponytail, donning a white Stetson, and registering for a non-credit course in horsemanship. A mutual friend and volunteer equestrian instructor told me: "No one tries harder than Bob Kerner; but a diamond-hitched sack of potatoes rides better."

His stubborn diligence defined him; "potato riding" I would overlook. Kerner was inept, but unabashed, like the cute Lab puppy dog appearing at the hunter's back door with a traumatized white chicken in his jaws. His owner accepts the chicken, but doesn't reprimand pup... *Give 'im time, he'll learn.* So would Bob Kerner.

Lyceum day, September 20, 2009, Great Falls College. At ten before ten Kerner greeted me just inside the auditorium foyer, "Thank God you're here. You had me worried." He shook my hand and simultaneously pushed me forward with his left hand, "My colleagues wish to meet you."

Kerner had apparently visited a hair stylist who formalized his blond hay stack. He dressed Saturday night Western: polished cowboy boots, tight Wrangler jeans, wide lapel denim shirt open at the neck, and a slick-sheened cotton sport coat matching his wine colored riding boots. Without his white Stetson, Kerner's "old school" manners prevailed—no headgear indoors.

I figured Kerner's Lyceum was equivalent to book signings, where authors are expected to be quirky and unduly confident. So, I came dressed as the autumn bird hunter that I was—wearing a checkered red wool shirt, khaki trousers, and my field boots; bareheaded, though, and fighting a feeling of nakedness.

Kerner introduced me to a creative writing professor, a pair of teaching assistants, and Dr. Schwartz, honchoing students from the Catholic college. Schwartz was a stooped, skinny man, frumpily dressed in a threadbare jacket, half knotted tie, and owlish eye glasses slipping down his thin nose—a living cliché of disheveled professor. Dr. Schwartz and the others joined in small talk, trying to put me at ease. We watched students of every shape, color, and style stream past, gawking. I had an ironic thought: Would they receive academic credit for attending a fiasco?

"Let's go get 'em Professor," I said, starting for the wide center aisle. Kerner grabbed my arm, "Not yet. Let them settle. They'll mill like corralled mustangs in this captive environment. We'll give them time to wonder and anticipate."

"And what will we deliver?"

Kerner was practically giddy. He said. "Blast them with your TF."

"A ploy from yesteryear, huh?"

"Precisely. With it comes controversy. And we'll use the fail-safe team game to induce participation. We'll form three competitive teams. You'll notice the auditorium seats are divided into color-coded sections—red, white, and blue indicated by colored tape on the back of each seat."

Kerner pulled up his sleeve and watched digital life ticking away. At 10 o'clock sharp he said, "I'll lead out. Dr. Schwartz, follow please. Then you, Link. You are the honored guest. I'll prep the audience for you."

"Thanks, Professor," I said. "Who plays the groom in this line-up?"

Kerner hadn't time for nonsense. He gathered us close, speaking softly, seriously—as if conspiring, "Follow my lead, gentlemen. We'll walk slowly and gaze upon them like naval officers inspecting cadets."

I eased behind Dr. Schwartz, thinking: *this is straight out of Kerner's playbook*. At MSU he had followed his doctoral thesis with a popular article for *Cognitive Frontiers* magazine, a piece titled "Success in Motion," catchy and appealing to lay people, leading to public service TV slots and guest appearances on afternoon talk shows. He'd been testing his theories ever since, about posture, positioning, orchestrated movement—all designed to command an audience with a powerful presence.

Indeed, most of these young Lyceum eyeballs turned on our promenade, Kerner in the lead, waving and helloing left and right, proceeding down the aisle to center stage. Schwartz looked around in wide-eyed wonder. He peeled off in front of the stage, taking a seat with faculty friends. I stayed the course behind Kerner, walking dignified, though an unbiased observer would say "stiffly."

Suddenly, Kerner pivoted at the bottom of the stage stairs. Like a Knight of the Round Table, he bowed and swept his arm before me. He'd have spread the cape if he had one. Gaining the stage, he twirled behind the speaker's podium and motioned me to stand to his right, where he deftly positioned my lapel mic while our audience milled and convened with friends.

Like an orchestra director, Kerner raised both arms high, waiting for his audience to quiet; but just as they settled, he pumped his fists, commanding: "everybody up, everybody up."

Amazing how they behaved. The youngsters arose en masse, laughing, cheering. Apparently they were well acquainted with the prof's eccentric behavior and reveled in it.

Dr. Kerner bowed graciously before his raucous crowd. "Thank you so much, ladies and gentlemen. Now, a round of applause for our honored guest, Mr. Jackson Lindquist." I waved from left to right across the audience, like a politician.

A nutty professor and a wanna-be mystery writer, and we had 90 minutes to inspire 18 and 19 year olds who'd rather be parked in the willows drinking beer and making out. "You first," I whispered to Kerner, a statement right out of third grade when I talked my cousin into an April swim in Magpie Creek among mini-icebergs.

Kerner stepped away from the podium, smiling. He walked to the very edge of the stage. His kids were still standing. He waved them down with a swan-like swoop and stalked several steps to his right, then reversed course leftward, making contact with both sides of the room. "Ladies and gentlemen," he boomed—the PA system was set at mega-decibels—"we are indeed privileged to welcome our guest. He's an innovator and raconteur with a unique concept of fiction... a pioneer, testing boundaries of literary fundamentals." *Jeez, Kerner, lead me to the quicksand why don't you?* Kerner gazed long at me for effect. Turning back to the audience, he swept his arms across the room, "I see potential writers out there. Most of you have yet to discover your innate abilities... to unravel the joys of insightful, powerful writing. Some day you will. Future business writers, research writers, novelists, thinkers, even historians. Did I mention love letters?

Like a seasoned comedian, Kerner let mirth run its course through his audience. Back on track, he said, "Opportunity beckons. Embrace it. You may discover exhilaration inherent in excellent writing... starting today, at this very moment. Accept the challenge." Kerner plunged ahead, voice booming—"*Nothing* is more important for your success and happiness—powerful thinking expressed with passion and purpose. You are privileged now to meet our guest lecturer, Mr. Jackson Lindquist. Listen intently, for he has mastered skills that he generously shares.

I stood three paces away from Kerner, hands clasped below my elk horn belt buckle, nervous and anxious.—*Enough Kerner; put me in the game.*

"...he is noted for entertaining fiction," Kerner exaggerated. "However—stay with me on this—he'll deny his work is fiction. You will shortly discover why. Now, please welcome Jackson Lindquist, novelist and story teller extraordinaire." Kerner motioned me to step forward. He grabbed my hand for an orchestrated handshake, as one would greet the French ambassador. He bowed and gestured flamboyantly, "The stage is yours, Mr. Lindquist."

Kerner had apparently found a new calling as judge of dignitarian creds. Somehow he made himself believable, as his students applauded raucously.

Now I stood vulnerably before an expectant audience, an overly-primed throng buzzing with anticipation.

Speech experts say you should first find an extraordinary, inquisitive face. Connect and all will go well. And there she was, front row central, a natural—Miss Sunny sitting with her dazzling smile. As our eyes met, she held high her copy of *Tall, Dark, and Crimson* with a caricatured Juneau Sherbinski featured on the cover. *"Action, Jack,"* as Kerner would say. *"Keep it moving."* Ginning drama, like a circus master, I said, "Right here—please stand, Miss Sunny Daniels. Ladies and gentlemen, she is your red team leader. Miss Daniels, please note the red tag on each seat in your section." Sunny stood and waved, beaming a generous smile...

"And team white... 'please stand Dr. Schwartz.' " Schwartz hesitated, before standing, as if lost in the woods. "Please welcome Dr. Schwartz, everyone; he's fortunate to draw you clever students in the white section."

I stepped quickly to my right, fronting the blue section, acknowledging them with my overhead clapping and hollering, "Blues, you will be pleased to know that Dr. Kerner gave me the freedom to plan his Lyceum. He may regret his generosity." The audience quieted, wondering...

"Good luck, Dr. Kerner," I said. Welcome to team blue. You are their commander"—which brought hoots and hollers. *Action, Jack—the moment calls for action.*

Most of the students stood and looked to their leaders. *What now?* They looked up at me with questioning faces.... Perfect.

"Teams, please listen carefully. You'll have 30 minutes to complete your assignment." I hollered above the hubbub, my voice reverberating through the PA system, sounding authoritative, yet foreign to my ears... "Here is your challenge: You'll write opening pages for a work of fiction inaugurated on the spot. Collaborate, create, and organize. Find a hook to snag your readers, then go to work building characters. Form personalities you can love, or villains you can hate. Make them walk, scuttle, run, or crawl... talk, pose, smell, bluff, or kill—all of the animal things; and human things, ennobling, clever, comical and—where appropriate—despicable. Your characters will intrigue and seduce. They'll levitate above the pages. When fully formed, your readers will know your characters as you do. You'll have constructed them, all parts coming together—loveable, comical, diabolical—fascinating characters created from people you've known, loved, respected, or hated. A final tip: think of your works not as obtuse and dreamy visions, but life as you know it by heart."

A few mumbled and shuffled feet; but nobody laughed, booed, or walked for the exits. *Start your engines,* instinct said. So I hollered, flinging my hands like a preacher: "Now hop to it, teams. There could be a best seller germinating, right here, today. In 30 minutes, starting"—I checked my watch for effect—"NOW."

I'll confess: hatching mayhem is entertaining. As a bonus, I enjoy throwing curveballs for Kerner, knowing that is when he performs best.

Down from the stage, I circled the team gatherings, observing, enjoying their collective energies. Each group had its shouters, aggressors, and jostlers ... and chroniclers bent on order, tapping laptop keyboards.

I had no idea what would evolve from such disorder. The three separate groupings milled, disorganized, like ships adrift. I worried. Perhaps my experiment was too impulsive.

Kerner wisely excused himself from the fray, letting class leaders fill the void. Dr. Schwartz seemed bothered and bemused. He openly deferred to one of his favorite students, a frail little fellow who pleaded for attention, without effect. Miss Sunny Daniels, though—her charismatic presence would draw crowds in a wilderness. In the auditorium's "wilderness," Sunny's red team people packed in around her, jostling, laughing, shouting.

With 5 minutes left in our allotted 30, Sunny jogged onto the stage, clipped a mic to her collar, and turned to face her audience. The P.A. system deepened her voice. She said, "Everybody, may I have your attention." About half obeyed. Sunny laughed, at ease, as if she routinely managed rowdy crowds. "Team one directs your attention to the whiteboard," she yelled.

The tip section of a two piece fly rod had magically found its way into the Lyceum and into Sunny's hand. She pointed its tip at a large auditorium whiteboard where team one's script appeared, called up by one of her techies. Her teammates formed a loose circle below her. They hooted and cheered, while a few among teams white and blue booed. Their mood was "spring break" without the beer.

Sunny beckoned and a burly guy with buzz cut red hair bounded onto the stage carrying about 250 pounds on thick, bowed legs. His athletic sweatshirt's backside promoted "Choteau Wrestling." He turned to face the audience, revealing his sweatshirt's front side illustration: a caricatured wrestler standing with his foot on the chest of a prostrate bear. With the fly rod piece in hand, Sunny's emissary approached the whiteboard, sweeping the rod across its face. He turned to the audience, bowed, and read the title page written in bold, magnified text: *"Murder on the High-Line, by Sleuthers, Inc."*

"Bear wrestler" read in commanding baritone. With perfect pitch and pace and wielding his fly rod like a conductor's baton, bear wrestler took effortless command of his audience. They were mesmerized. Background interference disappeared and we found ourselves reading each magnified word along with the bear man's narration.

Murder on the High-Line
by Sleuthers Inc.

"You gotta' become invisible on stakeout," my Scottish grandpop told me. In his day he was the smartest and toughest gumshoe in St. Paul. Well, invisible is possible in St. Paul, here only briefly. If here on this quiet main street, Gramps would order me, "move on this guy now, Mac, before your cover gets blown. Everybody knows everybody in this little Montana burg."

I spot Mason "Squeeky" Biggerstaff stepping out the front door of the Mint Bar. Time to make my move. Squeeky pauses as if lookin' for a familiar face. He squints in the bright light, lights a smoke, and turns left, lurching down the sidewalk toward me. I reach for my phony subpoena in the inside pocket of my phony investigator's tweed. I step in front of him. He tries goin' around, so I ram my shoulder into him. He throws his cigarette at my feet and cocks a fat fist, but wisely holds fire. I'm six-two and work out three-four times a week and just last January won a pair of three-rounders in Spokane's mid-senior division. Squeeky Biggerstaff's a twerpy five and a half feet of pale flab, soft as the baker's doughboy. He's wobbly an' bleary-eyed, boozed already at half past four. You'd a thought he'd eaten rotten meat, the way he scowls, peerin' from them black hole eyes. Looks like a goddam cornered badger. With the first words out of his sour mouth I know why they call him Squeeky. He manages "watch it asshole," a pissed-off whine, snivelin', a country mile short a' tough.
I figure he was just the type to pull off the killin', how it was done—a sneakin' ambush.

I open my jacket, showing my badge, "I'd be careful, 'Punk,' who you threaten. I have a subpoena here. Afore I serve it on you, you have a chance to go visit the shuriff. Tell 'im what you know... could save you from hangin'."

Seein' Squeeky an' me toe to toe, town people gather 'round. A guy drivin' a cement truck stops to watch, his tumbler of live cement goin' "whumpa whumpa." His truck is blockin' the main drag. He don't care. Like all the rest a' the gatherin' crowd, the cement guy's hopin' Biggerstaff will lip-off so's I kin

col-cock the bastard. No such luck. I slap my fake subpoena in 'is hand, an' he flips it aside, an' goes off a- mumblin' to hisself. Perfect. A-fore tomorrow word'll travel up the High-Line to Squeeky's shyster dad in Glasgow that the law is closin' in on his no good kid. All the High-Line towns will know, git to their rumorin', stirrin' the boilin' pot, maybe bring witnesses outa' the woodworks. The shuriff was one smart cookie to hire me. Undercover this way, I got more done the first day than the law did in three months. Huh! I'll bet Biggerstaff is nervous as a fart in a skillet. He's primed to make a big mistake.

Bear Wrestler stepped back, raising his arms, "Do you want me to go on?" The audience cheered, hollering out, "yeah, yeah—go for it," many overlooking team loyalty. In the interest of time, though, I seated Sunny's bear guy.

Sunny and her narrator had supercharged the room. As in the aftermath of lightening, I smelled ozone. On second thought, more likely pheromones.

Sunny and her Reds had hatched a damn good story, and impossible, team-wise. I guessed correctly, verifying later that Sunny had midwifed the infant draft, providing her team an advantage. I wouldn't intervene. Didn't Kerner ask his students to bring samples of their writing? Later, Sunny gave me the first three chapters of her novel, thinking I would offer to edit. I made no such offering, reasoning that any further investigation of Charlie Larigan's death would be jeopardized by her dabbling in a parallel piece of High-Line fiction.

"All of the Montana High-Line towns will know," Sunny's undercover gumshoe character had said, and I thought: *so would real life culprit 250 miles up the line in Shelby.* Nothing stays put on one end of the High-Line

for more than a day. The perpetrator would learn that a novice mystery writer had identified him as a suspect. Or maybe Sunny would implicate the entire sleazy Slimann family along with the half-crazy son. Her moving the location and changing names would fool nobody. Furthermore, Kerner had learned from Sunny that the nut-case younger son was lawless, reckless, and sometimes dangerously whiskey drunk or blitzed with marijuana. Sunny could be in physical danger.

A student brought me a note from Kerner. I spotted him surrounded by his Team Blue students. He pointed a worry finger at me. I glanced at his note, which included a concern echoing my own: never let your suspect know you are on his tail unless you've run out of standard options and believe you can squeeze him into doing something stupid. Kerner's note ended with: "Don't worry, Sunny Daniels is a reasonable person. I'll talk with her."

Stunned and worthless as a facilitator for the remainder of Lyceum, I simply sat back and let teams White and Blue compete for attention and approval. My addled mind absorbed little of their scrappy stories.

With Lyceum's allotted time ending, Professor Kerner scurried to the stage. He compressed his concluding remarks and quickly adjourned Lyceum. But many of his students milled about, bantering about their projects, asking questions. First time I'd seen a professor anxious to leave while students were anxious to stay.

A trio of girls twittered up to me. One extended a copy of *Bloody Purple*, asking for a signing. The three girls hung around, giggling like a fan club, inquiring about Truly North and what is she doing in my next book and does Juneau really love her and..." Kerner came to interrupt, "Excuse me, ladies; but Mr. Lindquist and I have business."

As the girls trundled off, Kerner said, "You should not humor them, Link. They are half your age, but they think you may be fishing."

"As in 'me man, you woman?' You're the anthropologist. You would know the signs. But, if I'm fishing, I'm fishing barbless."

"Hopelessly too. Follow me." He led me behind a side stage curtain.

Expecting a lecture, I beat him to the punch, "You're note says you are going to muzzle Sunny, an aspiring author. Don't you preach about the evils of censorship?"

He smiled, "I do; but in this case I will not censor. Bribe perhaps. I have a plan. It begins with inviting her to dinner, which I already have. 'No boyfriend this time,' I told her. By the way, Link, I suggest you invite Max DeVore to join our team."

"*Our* team, you say. The team that takes on the Charlie Larigan investigation, or would you call it a case?

"Yes, I believe we'll find our collective understanding of the outstanding questions justify calling it a case."

Professor Robert Hamilton Kerner never ceases to amaze: administrator, professor, researcher, and advisor; does he ever sleep? He interjected his deep and persistent belief in demographic analysis. He said, "Miss Daniels has convinced me the High-Line is defined by near-universal principles. You'd best study them before traveling there."

I said, "I'll do that, Bob. At the moment Joanie is chasing bears, so I only need to answer to you and Bo. And she is anxious to see me. You'll also be anxious to see me at 7, at the King of Hearts."

"The reason for that escapes me."

"Simple... For the price of dinner, I'm helping you launch a new career as a P.I."

CHAPTER SEVEN

THE HIGH-LINE

*Historians are at odds when defining the High-Line. **What** is it? **Where** is it? One notion with historical roots identifies the High-Line as America's northernmost railway route from Minneapolis to Seattle. But try that concept on a fourth generation Montana High-Liner. He'll scoff, probably in the manner of a Texan when the Oklahoman says, "Amarillo and the Panhandle really should belong to Oklahoma." Or, ask North Dakotans living hard by the Great Northern tracks in Stanley or Devil's Lake to identify the High-Line. They'll puzzle, "Isn't that somewhere in Montana?" And it is, since Montanans staked claim to the concept without reservation. By custom, culture, and common interests, the High-Line is one 300 mile string of kissin' cousin communities from Cut Bank on the west to the North Dakota border on the east. As to defining the High-Line, you'll never learn from Google. Better to go there. Find work on a High-Line farm, or in Chinook or Shelby, Rudyard or Culbertson. Hang with the folks in hardware stores or Polly's café in Havre. In time you'll discover what the High-Line is all about. In my considered opinion, Jackson Lindquist— (Excerpt from my writer's journal # 9, October 21, 2009.)*

I first encountered the High-Line from the back seat of my dad's 1970 V-8 Oldsmobile. We were headed across Montana to visit Glacier Park and the Rockies. I understood "High-Line" referred to parallel modes of transportation: the Great Northern Railway and two-laned Highway 2 running alongside. About every 50 or 60 miles the rails and highway sliced through a small town with an imported name—Glasgow, Tampico, Malta, Harlem, Zurich, Kremlin, Joplin...

Mom, a history teacher, argued that the High-Line was misnamed. "It should be called Immigrant Road."

Sept 20, King of Hearts. Tomorrow I would drive north to intersect the High-Line. Tonight, Kerner and I nursed beers in The King of Hearts Saloon while waiting for three more members of our so-called investigative "team." The prof was in a giddy mood in the aftermath of his harum-scarum Lyceum. Proving my point, he ordered a pitcher of Max's premium ale delivered by the man himself, pronouncing himself "off duty."

Speaking of giddiness, Sunny Daniels came dancing across the floor to join us. She had evidently hustled home after Lyceum, performed a pretty girl tune-up topped by a silky blue dress decorated with red hibiscus. I stood for her as she handed me a manila envelope. "For you, Jack, three chapters of my novel in draft form. I promise that none of it will be released in an untimely fashion."

Sunny's arrival *was* timely, in the midst of Kerner's lecture on the essence of High-Line culture. Sunny joked, "We High-Liners are thick as thieves."

Sunny and Kerner understood my dilemma: I had a choice to make, and soon. Either get on with my nominally scholastic War Babies mission or launch an amateur crime investigation. Regardless, both required understanding High-Line sensibilities. I could only speculate: Loyalty? Heritage? Community identity?... Something binds kindred spirits along that long, latitudinal band of grain and prairie; a wise person would research the culture, as you would before traveling to Ukraine or Latvia.

Max came in from behind and touched Sunny lightly on her shoulder, "How's my favorite girlfriend?"—the crazy uncle and foxy lady routine. I was not surprised that they were acquainted, even in Great Falls, which by Montana population standards qualifies as a big city. Swashbuckling Max, razor sharp and quick-witted behind his bar, connected with locals and strangers at once, like the barkeep in Dodge City's Long Branch. Prettily audacious Sunny lacked Max's ready-made stage. Still, she was a natural charmer. She could marry a governor or space jockey someday, but only after she'd ripped some turf on her own.

Kerner, Max, Sunny, and I... nobody wanted to spoil the ambiance of beery conversation, old jokes, and Montana country stories. Pearl was the one to walk in and change our mood. She stopped inside the double pine doors just long enough to be noticed by every able bodied man in the room. She was effortlessly pretty, wearing a white blouse with a generous V, tight horse-worn denims, worn-heeled boots, silver-dangly earrings, and a confident smile. She spotted us, walked over and splatted a manila envelope on the table. Max pulled a chair for her. He said, "Listen up everybody. We're gonna get some inside dope."

Before sitting, Pearl addressed me across the table, "Jack, I brought you a summary of events. Sorry, it's so sparse, only a start." In turn, she looked at Max, Sunny, and Kerner. "I'm sure the rest of you can add to these points."

All eyes were upon me as I extracted an 8 by 10 photograph and three pages of notes with bulleted items. I speed-read Pearl's first bullet from a newspaper account:

- *October 22, 2006. Fraud charges were lodged today by three Toole County landowners against Bennett J. Slimann. His Republican opponent for the Montana Senate, Alexander Sinclair, has been recently criticized for using Mr. Slimann's demeaning nickname, Sly. Nevertheless, Slimann's fraud charges are expected to seriously hamper his chances to win a Senate seat.*

That's when our little confab's blizzard of what-ifs and maybes began. Kerner led out: "I have researched Bennett Slimann's history documenting his unbridled ambition, aggressiveness, and political ruthlessness—in other words—his dynasty complex. But let's dig in here: How does any of this relate to a neighbor's purported accidental death? Anybody know?"–which brought the party to a jolting stop.

Finally, Max broke the impasse: "motives, Dr. Kerner. We know that Charlie openly opposed Sly in a mineral rights dispute. And Charlie confronted the youngest son, the crazy one called "Stump," about broken fences, missing cattle, and... well, the Slimanns were just untrustworthy neighbors."

"Unsavory," Sunny added, "or, in plain English, crooked."

From there talk drifted to Sly's self-serving politics morphing into prairie politics in general and small time media's efforts for clarity. Sunny joined in with High-Line gossip and local wisdom: who was straight up honest and who was not. Sunny's passing remark registered, "My dad reads horses and people as well as anyone. He says Sly bought a prestigious Rolex when he ran for the legislature. It didn't help. For the second time, he was easily defeated."

Jotted in my notebook: "B J Slimann – Slimey," along with Pearl's quote: "Charlie's family chose cremation. He was too beautiful to be viewed in a casket."

"Don't believe anyone wanted to see him," Max said. "A shotgun at close range, you know. Now before we forget, everybody write phone numbers and e-mail addresses in Jack's notebook."

I stared at the photo of Charlie before me. "His final image, a month before he died," Max said. Charlie stood at the neck of Duke, the rangy roan that Summer had handled at Larigans' cookout. Max nodded at the photo, "Those three traveled a thousand miles together." The third character, I noted, was Ginger, Charlie's golden Labrador posing by his left leg. She looked so much like Bo, even sat like her.

Charlie, wearing an easy smile, posed for the photographer. He was a handsome man, with straw-blond hair spilling from under his bill cap. Relaxed and jaunty, standing about 6 feet tall, his working man's muscle stretched against his denim shirt. You can read a man like Charlie who openly displays his accessible personality, the sort of guy who knows how to blend work and play.

I studied the picture while the others waited expectantly. Crazy as it sounds, writing Sherbinski's stories had taught me to go slow with potential evidence that you hold in your hands. So I said, "hmm," and scrutinized the photo of this man, Charlie, who I would undoubtedly have enjoyed knowing. I noticed something worthy of questioning. Why did Charlie wear a bill cap instead of a cowman's brimmed hat? And what of the large white lettered "10" adorning its crown? "The '10,' I said. What is that about?"

I waited while they struggled, conflicted. Finally, Pearl volunteered, "Fish and Game honors volunteers who teach gun safety. That's a raggedy old cap in the picture. Charlie received it for 10 years of service; but he taught gun safety classes for close to 15 years."

More than irony froze conversation. How could a serious instructor of gun safety ignore cardinal rules? You never leave an unsecured firearm where it can fall. And an unsecured firearm should never, ever hold a chambered round.

I listened as they echoed Jimmy Young Man's accounting of the sheriff's reconstructed accident scene: Duke ground-tied, disciplined, waiting while Charlie repaired fence, but blowing up and running off at the shotgun blast—the single shot that mortally wounded Charlie and—more than likely—his dog, Ginger. Both Charlie's and Ginger's blood were found splattered on fence wire and the rocky ground. No other clues. Cattle had trampled the area. Max explained, "Jimmy said the cattle travel the ridgeline going for water. Charlie built a stock pond a mile northwest of the fence corner."

An awkward silence descended. They needed me, the outsider, to move the discussion. I offered the obvious, "Did anybody challenge the sheriff's conclusions?"

Max glanced at Pearl, confirming she was too distraught to answer. He picked up the slack, "More than anybody, Jimmy questioned the law. Hell, he did more than question. He went up there on a rampage. He took Angus along, but they came home a week later with nothing more than Charlie's ashes. Jimmy's a tormented soul. He's quit talking about it and most everything else."

"He couldn't talk at the funeral either," Pearl said.

Max chipped in, "Later, Jimmy described the awful details he heard from the undersheriff who covered the crime scene. Anyway, Jimmy was disgusted; he said the undersheriff kept quoting confidentiality rules. Jimmy 'had to walk out,' he said, or he might have slugged the guy."

"Mourning and anger, a bad combination," Pearl said.

"Yes, and anger grows out of proportion when law enforcement fails," Max added.

Being a semi-trained investigator, I wanted specifics. I said, "You mean the Toole County Sheriff's Department?"

That seemed to annoy Max. He said, "Obviously, Toole County. The inexperienced undersheriff found Charlie's body. The sheriff was in the hospital at the time with a busted leg, so he was forced to assemble his reports from second-hand notes. The coroner was new to his job too. All-in-all, the reports were so poorly done that the State Police Special Investigation team took over."

"And?"

"And they found nothing more, or if they did, kept it from the public." With that Max glugged about 8 ounces from his 16 ounce mug, which acted as a sort of trigger for Pearl and Sunny to slug beer too, whereupon the three of them turned to me, wide-eyed and expectant, as if I were a miracle from Nirvana. Maybe Kerner could bail me out—

"What do *you* think Dr. Kerner?" I said. "A second team of professional investigators from the state arrived on the scene, albeit five days late." They added nothing substantial beyond the sheriff's report. After a year, how do you think we could uncover anything new?"

Kerner cut me off with a raised palm and furrowed brow. He stood abruptly, walking deliberatively, pensively, pacing behind our chairs and around our circular table. I recognized his practiced orchestration lifted from his self-help book, *Success in Motion*. Completing his promenade, he stood with hands grasping the back of his chair, making contact with all eyes around our table. People at surrounding tables turned to stare. Kerner ignored them. After a deliberative pause, he said, "I sense a lack of motivation among local and state law enforcement, and little movement toward a factual resolution. You people, however, have motivation and vision. You knew Charlie intimately. He must not remain a simple statistic to fill official files. So I ask, 'who has the energy and means to drive an investigation?'"

I was seated to Kerner's immediate right. He put his hand firmly on my shoulder, "Mr. Lindquist?"

"I, uh... I'd like to believe we could do that," I stammered. "I mean, drive an investigation. At this point, I'm certain of only one thing." I paused, and didn't need advice from Kerner's book to do so. Locking eyes with each newfound friend, I said, "I'm convinced that we shouldn't quit, and I emphasize *we*. I'll head for the High-Line tomorrow and keep you all informed of progress through Dr. Kerner... Bob. And he'll provide feedback from each of you." I waited for confirmation which came with cold-eyed stares and nodding of heads. Strategically, we needed something more, a pledge all 'round to see the mission through. I said, "To be fair, you must know that an in-depth investigation requires a longer term commitment than I can offer."

Our drama was playing in public, an uncomfortable situation. I said, "Anybody hungry?"

We moved to a corner restaurant table where I tried, without success, to lighten the subject over burghers and brews. But, our newly formed "investigative team" couldn't leave it alone. With burgeoning passions, they talked over one another. I wondered: why now? Why wait a year to take action?

For a few minutes, I wasn't a part of the discussion. I can't remember what was said; it wasn't worth remembering. They turned to me with questioning faces. "Jack, how will you go about... ?" Max started.

We're a weird species aren't we? We go along living within a circle of work, family, and friends. Trouble brews; but nobody steps forward to rally the populace. Then a hair-brained stranger comes along. They call him Possible. "Hey, let's bet on Possible, give him the job." So Possible drinks a cocktail mix of whimsy, mystery, naiveté, and ego.

I said, "Max, I can handle the job." My words escaped like a slick skinned trout... impossible to recapture.

Fortunately, Bo and I were headed north, out of town. My mind drifted ahead. The map showed hundreds of square miles of public land between Great Falls and the High-Line—gamebird country, resting peacefully, waiting. Bo and I would find solace before confronting the daunting task ahead.

As if waking from a dream, I heard voices. I said, "Sorry, Bob, I didn't catch all of that."

Damn it all! I'd rolled into the King of Hearts three nights ago as a free man, but now felt like a just married groom fidgeting in the hot sun practicing nicey talk, while my getaway car sits gassed and ready.

Kerner grabbed my wrist (Humphery Bogart would have slapped my face). "Jack, if you were listening, you'd know we have all agreed, and your daily reports from the High-Line are in order." *Order*. Now I was taking *orders*... from four people at once. Strangely enough (I said we are a strange species), part of me enjoyed this foray, a new guy growing within old skin. I liked *them*, too. They rose as if commanded and came around for a *bon voyage*, a little too gleefully, I thought, as if sending me off to Disneyland. Max gave a vice-grip handshake, "You catch the gunzel bastard; we'll hang him." Sunny used both delicate hands to enclose mine, smiled in my eyes, and slipped her writer's business card into my shirt pocket. Pearl waited for Kerner to move. When he didn't, she stepped up to me, rather stepped *into* me for a chest to chest hug, which I knew meant only that her spontaneous, open self had happily joined the team.

Max offered to buy nightcaps, which I declined, explaining that "my lady friend is waiting," that I would keep in touch. I headed for the door.

"Hold on Jack; we're not finished," Kerner—the detail man—insisted.

"Outside," I said. "Bo needs to visit the weeds." I waited on the sidewalk, my head in a whirl. Pearl's fragrance wafted from my shirt collar, and I thought: *I'll pray for an early winter. The grizzlies will den early, and Joanie will come down from the mountains.*

Kerner, bless him, operates simultaneously on multiple missions: thinker-planner-organizer-director. And he wasn't finished there on The King of Hearts' sidewalk. "Remember, use my cell number," Kerner said. "Around 5 in the afternoons will be a good time. Currently, I'm reviewing a number of court records and press reports on the Slimann family—people with an aggressive, rapacious history; and they happen to share property lines with the Larigans. You'll want to download my reports frequently to stay abreast of our research."

"I'll do that, Bob. Call me Mr. Diligence. I'll go home to Joanie a reformed man."

"Humph," Bob managed, followed by a strained silence. Finally, he muttered, "Link?"

"Yah?"

"Be careful."

"Of what?"

"Just be careful, Link. I've consulted with my friend who practices criminal law."

"And?"

"And he said Charles Larigan's death could be a piece in a larger puzzle. He knows of unpublicized state and Federal investigations in that part of Montana."

I made light of it, "So, maybe we'll complete the puzzle. Meanwhile, Bob, my girlfriend there in my truck—you're making her jealous." Bo's dark form shadowed Big Red's rear seat window. With her nose on the window, she had me spotted.

Kerner hugged me, his traditional sendoff—expected, and no longer an odd thing to do. He followed the hug, however, with a stiff cuff to the shoulder, cowboy style. He said, "Good luck Podner." I liked that... a countrified gesture. Give him a few more years and he could be mistaken for a native species. He'd hung his dust-colored Stetson on the saloon's peg wall, now had pulled it down low over his brow, appropriate for the dogged and wiry little man that he was. Robert Duvall in "Durango Kid" comes to mind.

Claiming the last word, I said, "Bob, I have some advice for you too."

He grinned, "You always do."

"Okay, this time pay attention. You need more sun. Surprisingly, as a college professor, you wear your hat well. But then you remove it."

"And?"

I relished his puzzled look, teed up perfectly, "Bob, you remove the hat and there goes your authenticity. You had all summer to whiten your scalp and tan your neck."

Kerner froze, smiled, and melted, laughing from the gut at himself. *At last, at last Bob, you're walking the walk.*

CHAPTER EIGHT

RESPLENDENT LIGHT

Wednesday, Sept. 21. I left a note for Pearl and checked out of the Drop Inn: "We'll be back in a couple weeks. Keep the light on and the lobby soup ready. Thanks, Jack L. & Bo" P.S. – I have your number. You have mine. We'll be in touch.

Bo sat rump by rump with me as we crossed over the Interstate following the same secondary route we'd driven with Max three days earlier. This morning we could have zoomed the Interstate, reaching Highway 2 and the High-Line in less than two hours. But, Bo deserved better. Her bright-eyed pleading would soften the heart of any hunter worth owning a scattergun. Staring at the distant grassy ridge, I swear she remembered its gamebird nirvana holding hundreds of dumb, un-hunted chickens.

After Joanie called, Bo and I had the luxury of time to explore the High-Line country. Our weekend rendezvous was off. With an early snowstorm advancing, she needed to hurry back into the Kaniksus to inspect grizzly hair sampling sites before they were covered deep in snow. Rats! If not chasing across Montana on a pair of poorly con-ceived, unpaid missions, I could be camp-tending for Joanie and keep-ing her sleeping bag warm.

But I'm stubbornly positive. Frosty Montana mornings are serene and precious. I drove slowly, windows lowered, with tastes of country-side riches pouring in. We savored fragrances of grain stubble, musty prairie grass, wild-rose, musky mule deer, and—according to Bo—gamebirds. She paced back and forth to the passenger window, sniffing the air. When she'd reached her frustration limit, I stopped and let her out. Nose on the ground, she zigged and zagged 20 paces into a field, where she froze on point.

No hurry. The birds would hold, hunkering in tall frosted grass, their scent pungent-strong for Bo. I loaded a magnum number 5 in the chamber, two more in the magazine, and walked in behind her, watching her vibrating tail. As always, Bo was as solid as that bronze spaniel pointing imaginary birds in Cabela's showroom.

I whistled and a dense covey of Hungarian partridge rocketed. I dropped the lead bird and another peeling away from the main covey.

Bo quartered across the top end of the same field and locked up. Heads popped up—prairie chickens shivery with damp chill, reluctant to fly. They ducked heads, allowing me to move to tail-booting closeness before flushing. Compared to Huns, the chickens were slow and easy targets, almost too easy. I gave them a 30 yard head start, took long leads, and dropped both stone dead. Bo needed about two minutes to deliver the birds. She sat on my feet and turned her smiling eyes on me, "Ain't we good boss?" If unbridled happiness is what counts, then I want to try a second life as a Labrador retriever.

With two chickens and three Huns in the bag, we drove the twisting gravel track to Ruby Springs Creek where a rooster pheasant scurried off the road from grit gathering. We didn't bother with him, "seed stock" as they say.

Looking up the L Bar L lane, I saw little activity: no horsemen, machines, or people moving about. So Max was right. The Larigans had gone to elk camp for an early bow hunt. I pulled in to ranch headquarters. Behind a barn, dust swirled in a round horse corral. Through the rails I saw a bowlegged cowboy working a buckskin on a long lead. I stepped from Big Red and went to the rails for a better view. It was Curly Ledoux, one of the whoopers at the cookout. He left the horse standing, came to his side of the fence, and shook my hand through the rails. "Glad to see you came back, Jack." With a grin and twinkle he said, "If it's work you're lookin' for, we got plenty."

"Sorry to disappoint you, Curly. It's trouble I'm looking for."

"Waal, Jimmy said you'd be stoppin' by. 'Headed to the Sweetgrass,' he said."

He was a dusty stub of a man with Frenchie brown eyes and graying hedgerow sideburns. Later on, I confirmed my suspicion. Beneath his battered horseman's hat, Curly was bald as a cue ball.

"Hold on a minute," Curly said, "I'm comin' out." He snubbed his horse to the center post and pushed through the gate. On this breezy-cool September day, instincts moved us out of the partial shade of the corral. With Curly's scruffy heeler dog sniffing at my boots, we drifted to the solarized snout of my truck. Bo stood perky-tall, paws on my dashboard. Ladylike and trusting, she woofed gently.

"Jasper's okay if you want yer dog out," Curly said. He chose a comfortable rest, back to the sun and butt against a fender, as if he'd done this a thousand times. His countenance spoke wordless acceptance: *I like your truck, your 'office,'—a good place to talk.*

"Bo might be coming in heat," I explained. "Best to leave her be."

With practical cowboy abruptness, Curly volunteered: "They left me in charge. They're off huntin' elk the hard way—bows an' arrows. Got mine in the freezer. Thirty ought six, steel-jacket."

"220 grain, I'll bet."

"Yup, drops 'em quick, almost too quick. My hunt was over at daybreak on day one of the Sun River hunt."

"Not a bad place to spend a few days, though. I've heard cutthroat fishing is terrific in the Sun River country.

"I ain't much of a fisherman."... Nor much of a visitor, either. He'd left us in a vacuum, so I pointed him in the direction of emotion-free topics, things we could do nothing about, like the drought and Curly's take on the "goddam govmint's" ever-changing rules of the range. Turns out Curly had worked two summers on the Sweetgrass ranch. He volunteered: "Charlie was good as they come, give a guy the shirt off'n his back."

"So he wouldn't have a feud with anybody?"

"Nope. Not Charlie. Din't like a man, he ignored him. Din't have time for feuds..." With that, Curly pushed away from my truck and reached for a handshake - "Well, better git back to work. I got a stubborn bronc on my hands."

... and Charlie's death is too painful to discuss, I could have added.

After turning down my offering of prairie chickens, Curly advised, "McCloud'll take chickns, do 'em justice. Ha—then I'll finagle an invite to his barbecue. "

Curly tipped his hat, and punched me on the shoulder. "Watch yer back up there in the Sweetgrass." He wasn't smiling.

I left Curly with a promise that I'd try to make it back for next year's Teton Ridge July 4th rodeo and, "Be sure to let the Larigans know I stopped by."

I drove west a couple miles to the McCloud's lane identified by their mailbox, a miniaturized replica of a log cabin. And here came Walker driving his team to collect his mail. Walker's private lane was a perfect place for a road conference from my open truck window to his wagon seat. Master teamster that he was, Walker enjoyed showing command over his matching pair of black mules. He made them stand quietly, interjecting "easy girls" into our conversation. I offered the prairie chickens.

"Sure," he said, "toss them birds in the back there, ya' don't mind. Here, here, girls—settle," he ordered his mules.

Walker was all smiles, "Angus took the whole tribe to elk camp, includin' Summer. They need her, ya' know. She's the best bow hunter in the bunch. She punched a bull through 'is heart couple a' years back."

"So, no rifles this year?"

Walker shook his head, resolutely so. "Nope, Charlie's youngest said he wouldn't go on a gun hunt. Cain't blame 'im."

"Well, the mountains are good for whatever ails them," I said.

"Yup, better'n shine from the 10 year barrl."

"I'll take your word for that."

Walker chuckled, "Jimmy had you figured fer a savvy dude. Expected you'd be comin' by. Said ta give you his map... take ya' right to the place Jimmy tol' about."

Walker's "girls" grew restless, shaking harnesses. "Quit," he gruffed with a warning tug on the lines. He reached into a satchel under his wagon seat and retrieved a rolled map, unfurled it, and held it in front of his chest. "Jimmy said to tell ya' jus' follow these directions. You'll be comin' to the place up in the Sweetgrass Hills where..." Walker's voice trailed off.

From a few feet away I could see that Jimmy had drawn the map's features crudely, but definitively, using a heavy marker pen. Walker rolled the map and stretched out his arm, handing it over.

"Wish I could come 'long. Yup, sure do." Walker nodded, tipping the brim of his hat, "Be mighty keerful, Mr. Jack." He leaned forward and lifted his chin, man to man talk finished. He slapped his reins, "Giddup."

Clearly, Walker was anxious for me to get on with my mission. The entire population of Teton Ridge was anxious and hopeful, like Tucson's town-folk sending the sheriff off to catch Jack Palance's Black Bart, the bad man with the sinister grin.

10 miles west of McCloud's place I crossed Teton River and intercepted State Highway 89. My *Gazetteer* promised an interesting drive through sparsely settled ranch country lying beneath the cusp of the majestic Rockies. 89 would take me northwest to Browning, my definition of the High-Line's western terminus and a good place to ease into the scene.

Nap time for Bo, music time for me. No concert hall could surpass the great sweep of prairieland descending from the Rocky Mountain foothills. An early fall rain shower had passed, leaving remnant blue-black clouds racing eastward over sunlit prairie. I let a drift of piney mountain air flow into my open window and turned my radio to stomach drumming volume. Craig Chaquico and his Latin guitar were coaxing wondrous emotion from his famous rendition of "Luminosa."

At Badger Creek's country store, I stopped for "wake-um" coffee topped with fresh cream from "Gramma Sharon's personal Guernseys." Gramma," the proud milk maid, commanded a corner coffee bar complimented by shelves holding fishing supplies. Her spinners, hooks, leaders, and a neat corkboard arrangement of trout flies was framed by a pair of white mini-refrigerators identified by black script: DAIRY, the other: WORMS.

"Gramma Sharon" stood smiling behind her counter, tanned, of proud posture, and vibrant. Looked to be in her mid-80s. Her wise blue eyes, I noticed, were lifted to Lucky's hat band where I kept a "Streaker," an elongated version of the Stayner Ducktail streamer. She nodded, "If you're fishin' the Two Medicine, sir, that streamer might be the ticket for a big brookie. They feed on sculpins. Fish the deep pools for them. Otherwise, you may want to try my hopper pattern... perfect for rainbows this time of year."

"Unfortunately, I'm on business. Next time through, though, I'll give Two Medicine a try."

We talked flies in the dialect that unites trout fishermen across most of North America. Some like 'Rembrandt' flies, others 'Rockwells', 'Warhols' or 'Emersons'. I bought a half-dozen of Gramma Sharon's bright yellow foam hoppers that dedicated purists would vote to ban. I caught Gramma again staring at my hat-bound Streaker. She said, "Mind if I have a look?"

"My pleasure," I said, handing Lucky across... "Be back in a jiffy." I hustled to Big Red and collected a box of well-used flies, including a frazzled Streaker.

Gramma Sharon stood waiting, my go-cup re-filled with her premium coffee and famous cream. Guessing she wouldn't mind cheeky, I said, "Gramma," I see you have a tying vise on your desk. Handing her my beat up fly, I said, "This baby has seen better days; but it's good enough to be copied. Hope you know a duck hunter. The chief ingredient is the flank feather from a drake mallard."

Her blue eyes twinkled. "I'm the best duck hunter around. And thank you so much, uh..."

"Jack. Jack Lindquist. Next time, I'll schedule a longer stop."

Though we could have easily visited another hour, I bid Gramma Sharon adieu. At our current pace of travel and talk, Bo and I would possibly reach Minnesota by Christmas.

As Grandma Sharon stepped from the door to wave good-by, I remembered Chaquico's CD in my special caddy. Pulling away from Grandma's, I was set with Chaquico's "Luminosa" blazing away, a perfect destination song, good for 50 miles or more of replays.

Does the Almighty send music to clear out mind debris? "Luminosa" is translated from Spanish as "resplendent light." Imagining a spiritual message, I drifted through reverie, replaying the last three days, unable to shake an ongoing conflict between my original War Babies mission, an obligation, or investigating a bewildering gunshot death, another growing obligation. Indecision ruled. Driving a road of freedom, I wasn't free. Then, suddenly came the light, "Resplendent Light."

"Hey Bo." She awakened and stretched to lick my cheek. "We need a cover, Bo girl. How about presenting myself on the High-Line as a serious journalist researching War Babies while we investigate what really happened to Charlie Larigan?" She whimpered, unconvinced. "Okay

Bo, when the need arises we can play serious hunters too. Before we get to the High-Line, we'll practice."

A side road along Two Medicine River took us to an unimproved overlook among sage and fescue. Bo danced, whimpered and nosed saliva on her passenger window. We both knew... the river's brushy little canyon would hold game birds.

Standing on a flat rock with Winchester, I said, "Hunt 'em up, Bo," and she plunged from the canyon rim, crashing through chokecherry and buckbrush. Wings fluttered, and a single prairie chicken burst out over the canyon where I took a long lead and dumped him. Bo huffed and snorted, rattling brush, zig-zagging amongst dozens of competing animal scents. I could have kissed her when she popped over the rim, carrying our bird. Instead, she savored a half-stick of venison jerky.

Lunchtime. Bo and I perched on a hilltop slab-rock overlooking the Two Medicine, where I swazeled our skinned chicken with huckleberry chipotle and roasted him on my hibachi.

Our lunchtime vista featured immense contrast: majestic crags of the Rocky Mountain Front blotted out half of the western sky, while directly below us the rocky canyon cradled the river's placid pools and delicate riffles. My fishing journal includes directions to a "secret" stretch of Two Medicine reputed to hold a few giant brook trout. They would have to wait for another day. Bo announced naptime with her "whuff," and plopped in the dry grass. I lay back on slab rock and pulled Lucky over my face. The river whispered and tinkled through its boulders. We'd found a perfect place for reflection.

Joanie and Kerner worked parallel tracks to move me in the direction of scholastic importance, and I had begun this trip determined to follow through. Then I stumbled upon the Larigan story, more correctly an unfinished mystery, one fit for fact or fiction. I yearned for its fictional promise so loaded with vital elements... complicated and conflicted characters, unusual setting, and a burgeoning plot populated by white hat characters headed for an heroic ending. White hats—folks like Angus, Jimmy Young Man, Grace, Summer, Pearl; friends on the fringes like Max and Walker. And Sunny—young and naive, but with an insider's knowledge of the setting and the central characters. From this point forward, the plot would nearly write itself. Like Sunny with her Lyceum story, I could simply change names and places and let 'er rip.

"Dumbass," I said to me and the world. "I can't fictionalize. Not this time. I won't build a tale when only the truth will do."

Bo rose and put her chin upon my knee. I said, "Holy hen shit, Bo. We're toast. We've got a real job to do." Bo's bright brown-eyed countenance changed not a whit. She stood tall and raised a paw to my knee. I stroked her forehead, "Yeah, Bo. We'll chase a few birds too. Won't hurt our image."

I pointed Big Red toward Browning, but did not immediately pull out, resisting the worldly clock and its contrived urgency. "I'm a stubborn bugger, Bo," I said. "We'll take our time at this detective business. If we want to hunt birds, we'll hunt birds."

The Two Medicine hill had treated us well, a respite for contemplation. I remembered Sunny's business card and pulled it from my shirt pocket. Her card's simple sales pitch and her photo (wearing a smile and a ball cap with a grizzly bear logo), her phone number, and web page address. In script, she claimed—"Full of fire, pen name for hire, puns of fun. Sunny Daniels, professional writer."I dropped her card in my briefcase.

My briefcase holding Jimmy's map rested on the seat between Bo and me. A leather craftsman had made it from one-half of my granddad's old saddlebag. It wafted a faint elixir of horse sweat and polished old leather, a solid reason to grant my saddlebag briefcase residence in my truck, and a pleasant remembrance of my fun-loving Gramp.

I spread Jimmy's crude map against my steering wheel. If not directing me to the Sweetgrass tragedy, the map could have been a delight, like a 9 year old's secret map, his arrow pointing the way through labeled "FOREST" to a SECRET CLUBHOUSE that "you can't see 'cuz it's camouflaged." Regardless, Jimmy's map was one I could follow, both by arrowed and jigged and jagged symbols and by his attached description, scribble-printed in ink: *Head north on 15 out of Shelby 'till you come to Sunburst. Take a right, east on Ninemile. Ignore the 9. Go 18 miles to the end of the road. Dead ahead is a fenced lane. You'll see the Sweetgrass Ranch barn roof. The old ranch house is tucked behind the cottonwoods. Check in with our tenant, Chet, or leave him a note. He knows you'll be coming. Follow the map's marked trail up Yucca Ridge, and you'll find the PLACE. Jimmy underlined his final sentence: The last mile is really rough. Suggest shank's mare.*

"Yah, Bo," I said. "We'll check with Chet; and we'll take the gun and walk the last leg."

"Use public libraries for Wi-Fi," Kerner had suggested. Fine, except community libraries in Browning and Cut Bank were overcrowded with schoolchildren. I drove on to Shelby, found their library, and schmoozed the blue-haired 70ish librarian, who fortuitously had two of my titles in her paperback collection. She provided a quiet corner with Wi-Fi connection. She seemed unduly curious about my presence, circling behind my chair twice during my 30 minute stay to glance at my laptop screen.

Five o'clock—time to call Kerner. He picked up on the second ring, like a 9th grade girl waiting for a date call. He began by rattling off relevant names and places along the High-Line between Cut Bank and Havre—"Gifford Lorraine, sheriff of Hill County; Jarvis Kelley, police chief in Cutbank; and Buck Cowan, sheriff of Toole County."

"Hold on, Bob . Did you notice your list singles out officers of the law?

"You're a dinosaur, Link," he said. "Access your laptop. You'll discover that my targeted peace officers are also of War Baby vintage. Check out Buck Cowan, for instance. I'd begin with him. He's a decorated Vietnam vet, and the best crime-stopper on the High-Line, according to my sources."

"Great. But do I disguise my unofficial Sweetgrass investigation? I mean, cops don't often take kindly to amateurs snooping about or trespassing about their jurisdictions. "

"Again, access your laptop. You'll find a write-up by Sunny Daniels. She says mentioning your acquaintanceship with her will ease your way with Cowan. The Daniels and Cowan families farm in the same township south of Chester. She also suggests you don't initially expose your investigative mission. Sheriff Cowan is shrewd and careful, not easily won over."

"You forget, Professor, I said. "I've sent Sherbinski off on similar assignments. Relax. Trust me; I know what to do."

"I'm so happy you reminded me. Yesterday I picked up your first draft of *Jugular Smith*. Remember?—where you began introducing first time readers to Juneau Sherbinski? Your theme was sound, and your plot intriguing. Yet, your un-edited *Jugular Smith* manuscript gathers nothing but dust."

"All true... I think." No use arguing. Perversely, I enjoy sending Kerner off on tangential journeys. I held my hand over my cell phone speaker and sniggled. I'm supposed to be the flighty one. Now, I'm out-lasting him through an interlude of impotent nothingness on an open link coming from outer space to me, an invitation to say something clever. I had nothing, so I left clever for Kerner's delivery...

"As I was saying, Link—you should restart your one conceptual plot that has promise. Now when you're finished in Montana..."

"Yes, I know. The question is: finished with what?" and I wasn't be-ing a wise-guy when I said that. I closed with "Stay tuned, Professor," which didn't work.

"Not so fast, Link. I'm reminding you again. My best student has agreed to a literature search of demographic parameters for War Ba-bies. His bibliography will be ready for your download by the end of the month. And don't forget; you'll have to cite him."

"Extracurricular work," I assume. "Let me know what I owe."

I'd follow Kerner's advice and contact Sheriff Cowan, but not just yet. Not how I do things. First, comes a day or two of getting acquaint-ed with a few townfolk and their surroundings.

I left Bo in our truck and checked into a low-slung stucco motel at the edge of town, a weathered independent, unsurprisingly named "The Glacier Motel." Since Bo and I had time for one short hunt be-fore dark, I drove north out of town, where I found an expanse of live-stock-free BLM prairie threaded with shallow coulees. We enjoyed a bird-less hike, but worthwhile in another way.

We were about ready to pull out when a rancher in a mud encrust-ed three quarter ton Chevy flat-bed pulled in next to Big Red. His leash-less Australian Shephard in the back made eyes with panting Bo. Emo-tionally secure, neither barked.

The rancher smiled: a measured smile, reserving judgment on a stranger with Idaho plates. I understood; a local couldn't simply drive past without knowing more. Through lowered windows, we made small talk about bird hunting, the year's grain crop, and the weather—

in northern Montana you cannot talk about crops and neglect weather. I mentioned the Sweet Grass Hills property owned by my friends, the Larigans.

"Yessir!—my neighbors. Great people, up against hard luck," he said. "If you head that way, you're welcome to hunt the school section west of their mail box. I hold that grazing lease. At present, I have only a pair of mares with colts in there."

He tipped his hat and backed out, leaving me without a name or a chance to thank him properly. Still, his High-Liner attitude portended cooperation, an open road to discovery. My spirits soared. Yessir, a man can live comfortably on false hope... for a while at least.

CHAPTER NINE

DEMPSEYTOWN

Evening time, September 24th. Glacier Motel, Shelby. I asked the "glacial" lady if she'd rent weekly, hoping to trigger her interest in my purpose for staying in Shelby. Like Sherbie says, "Give 'em reason to talk." No luck. She was all smugly business. Furthermore, she charged Bo ten bucks a night to come in and keep me company.

No luck with the bustling waitress at the burgher joint across the street either. She just smiled, took my order, and delivered my hamburger steak on a hot plate, good enough reasons to leave a tip.

I resolved to turn in early, determined to get more than five hours of sleep. First, I was obligated to catch up on "office" work, my desk being the motel's king bed, from where I argued with the confounded cell phone, strangling it to spit out messages: high grade the important ones, like Joanie's incredible response to my love poem; dump junk messages; organize the day's findings, journal them, analyze them; study Kerner's directives that I can't ignore because experience says they matter 9 times out of 10.

When the floodgates open on my miraculous best seller pouring forth a million bucks, I'll hire a go-fer. He'll have huge ears for listening and a small mouth for talking. At this very moment, I would rap on the wall and he'd hustle from the next room. He'd have Kerner's E-mail missive called "The Dempsey Effect" studied and summarized in brief, intelligible form, saving me trouble. In the meantime, reality loomed.

"Crapola!" I was in no mood for a professorial Kernian lecture. His introduction alone filled an entire page. Ready to toss it aside for the night when I came to a hook that should have been in paragraph one, all about Shelby's "90 year hang-over, a bilking that transcends generations." When you come to this town, the premise asserts, expect to be eyed with suspicion. Kerner coupled this concept with unstudied opinion, a rare, but pleasing diversion. He wrote, "The following bizarre history may be important in the context of your investigative phase. We cannot predict how."

I summarized Kerner's "Dempsey Effect" in my notebook and dropped the rest in my memory, specifically: *In 1922 a wildcat driller discovered oil near Shelby. "Oil fever" fired imaginations. While a spurt of oil money came to the region directly, local promoters dreamed magnanimously, even recklessly. They aggressively promoted a plan that gained credence and energy with each passing day. But the agrarian population was ill-prepared to deal with overblown promises by a local real estate promoter, Loy J. Molumby, and Jack Dempsey's shyster manager, "Doc" Kearns. The upshot of their dealings was that Dempsey, an American superhero, would come to the tiny rail town of Shelby (no paved streets, population 500) on July 4th 1923 to face a fledgling challenger, Tommy Gibbons, for the world heavyweight boxing championship. Shelby would benefit by enormous publicity leading to tourism ("the Gateway to Glacier Park"), and big money would come to invest in oil exploration. The catch? Locals must commit to $400,000 in purse guarantees. They did so, and also built an outdoor arena with seating for 40000. Sadly, only 7000 paying customers found their way to Shelby to spectate, Dempsey won in 15 rounds, and four Shelby banks immediately went broke on a lousy scam investment.*

Jack Dempsey, a National hero and contemporary of Babe Ruth, was unsullied by the scandalous fleecing of Toole County, Montana. In the Glacier Motel lobby, a bare chested Dempsey smiles from an old framed photograph hanging beyond the night clerk's shoulder. With unshakeable conviction, she instructed me, "Jack Dempsey was a good man. He was hoodwinked, along with our entire town."

The motel lady's views reflected Kerner's synopsis: the town accepted Jack Dempsey at face value, the rest of us should expect scrutiny.

The "Dempsey Effect" was apparently in play as I walked into the Pumper Café on Thursday morning. Otherwise, why did the breakfast crowd analyze my walk to the coffee bar? And why did a brown uniformed sheriff's deputy study me?

I tried charming lines on the waitress, all delivered in short phrases as she came and went: *"Best coffee in the state of Montana; beautiful ear-rings—I'll bet they're Montana agate; do you know where a man could catch a catfish around here?"* She'd cock her head and smile, no comment.

Curiously, the deputy stayed for another coffee refill after his civilian acquaintance left. He languidly spooned and stirred sugar, glancing furtively toward me. I steeled myself, a little cynically—I must admit. Stubbornly too, hanging about Shelby and Toole County, allowing the locals to fuss about my presence. In time I'd become part of local décor, like last spring's driftwood on a Marias River sandbar. Meantime, I'd begin with the mayor and Sheriff Buck Cowan, Kerner's picks for War Baby interviews.

A loner, in charge of my timetable now and temporarily account-able only to myself, I walked out of the Pumper Cafe' wearing a grin, feelin' goooo-d, like the day I quit my father-in-law's business. Today, I'd kick about the territory, beginning with the Larigan's L Bar L North, a.k.a. the Sweetgrass Ranch.

JACK AND THE WAR BABIES

126

Chapter Ten

SWEETGRASS AND BONEWOOD

First order of business in the Pumper Café parking lot: I pulled my 12 gauge Winchester from its case and placed it in my rear window rack, lighting Bo's imagination. It was a cruel move, but necessary. I said, "Bo, this is just for display. We're not hunting today." Honestly though, I was thinking: *Jackson, you're kidding yourself. Dempseytowners aren't easily hoodwinked, and their smoke signals will travel the breadth of Toole County before the sun drops behind the Rockies. Somebody will connect me with the Larigans, if they haven't already. And what about Sunny Daniels? She wouldn't need to publish her murder mystery shadowing the real life Sweetgrass killing. Simply talking about her project would plant a seed for a bumper crop of rumor.*

"No, Jackson," I said to Bo and me. "What we do now is simply relax and enjoy this incredible corner of Montana."

Driving north out of Shelby, I find it impossible to keep my eyes on the highway and off the miraculous Sweet Grass Hills. Thousands of poetic pages have been written to describe the three mirage-like buttes rising abruptly and improbably from the prairie. Their snow-crested cones show prominently from 50 miles distance. This morning their snows glow orange, while their shadowed west slopes sleep in deep blue. Since I have little talent for poetry, photos at a roadside stop need to suffice.

Traffic is nearly non-existent on our drive north to the little town of Sunburst. From Sunburst we turn east into the sun rising over the Sweet Grass Hills. Strip farmed grain covers the first few miles; but as the land rises toward the foothills, farmland is replaced by an ocean of grass and bands of antelope, scattered Black Angus, and a few horses. My binoculars confirm that a speck on the horizon is a horse and rider, the only human spotted during our 20 mile drive from Sunburst to the Larigans' Sweetgrass Ranch.

The old-timey place looks inviting, a sun-bleached square-log home and a huge barrel-roof barn. I smile, "Will you look at that, Bo?"... ancient ranch home and barn, pine rail corrals and fences, a smithies shack—as if we'd stepped back 100 years, to 1909.

Nobody home. I found Chet's note under a porch rock and left one of my own, letting him know I was headed into the high country. No urgent need to confer with Chet, a Sweetgrass newcomer. Jimmy said he hired him off a ranch in the Missouri breaks three months after Charlie's death.

Chet's scribbled warning read, *"For Lindquist – 'Don't risk a drive up there without at least 10 ply tires. When you come to Yucca ridge, park and walk.' Chet McCrary."*

I crossed a cattle guard, noting "L BAR L," and "CLOSE GATES" signs. Ahead, the road disappears around a brushy hill at the entrance to a ravine, the kind of road that would tempt me to follow, whether I have business here or not.

I drive up the road in granny gear. Why hurry in the thrall of untrammeled hill country? Around a bend, over the ridge, tucked into creek bottoms, behind the next imposing mountain... I'll discover hidden Montana treasures: biological, geological, historical, and cultural.

I chuckled, remembering how Kerner came to college in '83, so full up with civilities that he had little chance to know Montana and how it should be experienced. Give him credit, though; he was open and anxious to learn, beginning by taming his frenzied pace. Ha! Leave it to me to recalibrate him. On the telephone he'd confessed, "Sometimes my college classroom feels like jail."

Four miles up the drainage, the road climbed out of a coulee and into another that sheltered a beaver-dammed creek. Thickets of dwarf serviceberry and buckbrush filled side draws. Bo gazed longingly and whimpered, *why aren't we stopping, Boss?*

While opening the gate into BLM pastureland, my eye caught a whitish, out of place snag. I grabbed my binoculars, discovering the snag to be a big buck's antler poking above his bed in the boulders. Bo sat on my feet, growling softly.

Jimmy's map was spot on: at a stone pillar I turned onto a 4 wheel drive track, skirted a seep and bog, and parked by a sign—"USDA Grassland Study." USDA's sign listed rules and objectives. At the bottom, larger print warned: "MOTORIZED VEHICLES PROHIBITED BEY0ND THIS SIGN." Beyond the warning, offenders' "in your face" ATV ruts ascended the hill.

I carried Winchester up the ATV trail with no intention of hunting active rangeland. I could have hunted safely among the widely scattered Angus cattle, but not without permission from the head honcho. L Bar L hip brands indicate that would be the Larigan's foreman, Chet McCrary. So, I carried my shotgun without a defined purpose, frustrating Bo. On our half mile climb to the grassy ridge top, she sniffed out two coveys of chickens. As they soared from the ridge, Bo stared me down.

"Bo, we're getting close to the dastardly place, and we're not ready. We'll take a breather." I chose a flat-topped boulder, planted my butt, and watched Bo track a running covey of Huns into a bramble thicket.

After flushing the Huns from the ridge, Bo came to me for a drink of canteen water. Our place was the epitome of Big Sky magnificence. Within a 20 mile circumference there could have been a dozen scattered humans, though hundreds of deer and antelope.

To the north, behind our resting place, grassy sub-ridges steepened against a forested cone-like butte. Spreading to three horizons were a few hundred square miles of wrinkled brown prairie and strip-farmed grain fields.

Bo read my mood and pushed her hip against mine. We shed the west wind with body sharing warmth. A precious vista spreads before us, not still-life, but a flickering patchwork of alternate cloud shadowed and sunny grassland. If a man doesn't contemplate life in such a place, he's a quart low on spirit.

A person feels both insignificant and empowered resting here, a place where lonesomeness nags: Get up, get moving—you might find a sheepherder, a backpacker, anyone: a human to connect with. I resist.

A red-tailed hawk begins his ascent 500 feet below where the ridge lifts from sage and prairie. With a few languid wing beats, the hawk feels up-drafting west winds that lift him above the ridge. He soars in a wide arc, effortlessly gaining altitude. I wonder where pure animal joy fits: Does the red-tail's aeronautical expertise stem from the gene of exhilaration?

Bo stretched her neck, intense brown eyes gazing at the circling hawk. He made a second circle, perhaps waiting for the strange two-legged animal and his coyote-like companion to move off through the tall grass and flush a cottontail rabbit or grouse, meals for a hawk.

Out here the red-tail lives at his consistent, measured pace. Human visitors would do well to follow his lead.

Yucca Ridge, Sweetgrass Hills—solitude, a thinking place. I reflect—for the thousandth time—upon the strong lesson about solitude discovered in a saloon in Circle, Montana.

The year was '84, and I'd just turned 20. I needed money to continue my education, so I dropped out for the spring term to work for a rancher north of Circle. A big part of my job was helping build 10 miles of fence.

On a Saturday night following a long fencing day, I sat at the bar sipping a tall draft in the Circle C Saloon, where one year short of legal was close enough. I perched between my boss, Jules Brackett, and his bony old neighbor, Amos. As a greenhorn, my role was to listen. If they wanted to hear from me, they'd say so. I liked that rule. These well-worn cowboys had wisdom for the taking, if only the listener could rescue wisdom from bull-pucky.

Amos, with a peculiar name, thought Jules was a name unspeakably peculiar. "Brackett," he said, "You're one pig headed son of a bitch... but I kind of like ya'." Jules laughed, knowing the insult was nothing more than a prologue to a debatable subject. Often, their topic was the "know-nothin' gummint."

Amos and Jules Brackett started with the "gummint" that evening, but didn't stay with it. They couldn't find enough disagreement. There came an interlude, waiting for the birth of inspiration.

I gathered that their habit was for Amos to chuck a spear and Brackett to brandish the shield. And I remember well this particular joust in the Circle C Saloon. Amos paused long for effect... then he rapped his knuckles on the bar.

He said, "Brackett, where do you want to die?"

Jules answer came quickly, without a hitch. "At home, I'll die in my sleep with my woman sleeping agin' me. How about you?"

"I finlly decided," Amos said. "Come to me jus' last night. Shouldn't a' took me so goldurn long; but I membered an Indin from way back, a Rikara. Didn't claim any honors like chief, but he did say he wuz carryin' medicine spirits. The Rikara says at me, 'White eyes, has spirits guided ya' proper?' An' I says, 'Hell I don't know. That's for you Indins ta' judge.' So he says, 'Go to sweat lodge, white eyes. Build small bone-wood fire'. "

And that's where Amos took 10 minutes to explain how you find bonewood. Jules and I knew better than to interrupt; it was like a sermon. I boiled it down some, using Amos's lingo: Gesturing for emphasis, he said, "Trail a packhorse into the Missoura Breaks, go in December after the leaves are gone an' you kin dentify the barkless bonewood, only kind thet works. Pack it home an' age it a year. Age it slow and only in the shade. Thet kind a bonewood has special powers, burns bright, puts out green smoke, not too het up, but a-blazin light all the same...

"Hold on," Brackett said. I heard it said that bonewood smoke kin make a guy 'don't give a shit' goofy, like with marweegeewanna. They say that. Don't know my ownself."

"Tain't true," Amos said. "Smoked it, I did. Jus' a little bit, mind ya'. Smoked it in a Rikara clay pipe, so's to git the full effect. Hell, I get a better kick outa' Four Roses, if only I kin afford it... then again, maybe ya' gotta be a Rikara fer bonewood smoke to work, but ya know were gittin' way strayed off the subject... found me a whole forest a bonewood down south a' Poplar...

Unfortunately, Jules Brackett's patience wore out. He inruded on Amos's limitless imagination, slapping a ten dollar bill on the bar. He said, "Amos, sorry to break yer train a thought there; I'll buy another round, dang ya', if you'll tell me where I should lay down an' die."

"Well dang you too, Brackett, I'm gittin' to it. Don't git yer nuts in a pinch." Except Amos didn't 'git to it.' His "medicine man" started again dribbling wisdom. Jules let him go for a while before interrupting.

"Sorry, don't mean to keep breakin' in here," Jules said, "But what was the Indian's name?"

"Why ya' need to ta' know, anyways?"

"Just seems important somehow."

"Well, I never fergit easy names," Amos said. "Name was Peterson."

That was the point where Jules lost his senses, laughing so hard he nearly fell off his stool; and he laughed so well and infectiously that Amos and I caught the laugh bug and we three spread it to the entire bar. Because first the Indian unleashed his shaggy dog, and then Amos set another free to nip at Jules and me.

And that's why I could sit high on this magnificent hill and laugh to the heavens, because I'd practiced the story, had some fun with it, and savored it all in mountain solitude . But now comes running another chapter, and he isn't shaggy.

A half-hour after Amos opened his vault of wisdom, he probed near the bottom. He said, "So, Jules, do ya' wanna hear what the Indin said or doncha'?"

"You think it's too rough fer this young whipper's ears?"

"Time he knowed, Brackett," Amos said. "Ya'' ready?"

"Ready an hour before last," Jules Brackett said.

"Here goes, then." Amos pointed a finger first at Jules, then at me. "Thet Indin says, 'I ride up an' over the mountains, down 'tother side—5, 6 moons, till pony go no more. That be the place."

"Amos, Amos," Jules protested. "Why would a man go to such trouble to die alone."

"He don't," Amos said. "He travels to find the Great Spirit. Then he's ready, he and the Great Spirit. Thet's what the Indin told me anyways."

Amos's crazy story seemed fitting for the Sweetgrass, and perfect for Bo and me perching on Yucca Ridge, just a mile south of the scene of Charlie's death.

The tragedy wasn't so much the place *of* dying; but *why?* That is entirely another matter, "a horse of a different color," Jules Brackett would say.

We hike a rocky cow path up the ridge; top a small rise. There it is: the death scene—a rock cairn supporting the corner fence post, and across the fence, a lightening-blackened snag tree standing like a sentinel—the landmarks, exactly as described.

I take a disciplined seat on a flat-topped boulder. *Slow down*, I remind myself. *Observe everything. Visualize*, the voice said. Bo sat on my feet, sniffing the breeze and scanning the meadow beyond the fence.

Charlie would have ground-tied his horse about where we sat, a stone toss away from the fence corner. To be doubly certain, he could have jammed his lead rope into a crevice in the rock. I imagined the scene, as if a movie.

Jules Brackett and his fencing gear came to mind. His saddlebags carried a roll of barbed wire wrapped in canvas... and leather gloves, a wire stretcher, fencing pliers, a hammer, and a can full of staples. Charlie would have had those things, and hopefully the sheriff's file cataloged them. Something not yet considered would be important. Sherbinski would dig dirt, reconstruct the scene. With patience, he'd discover a furtive creature called "cold evidence."

Winchester's magazine held two shells, the barrel empty. The inviolable rule demands "check it anyway." I verified its empty barrel and rested the gun against the corner post as postulated by the sheriff's report. I beckoned Bo to my side and encouraged a small game of chase to emulate a playing Ginger, who conceivably knocked Charlie's gun loose. Bo never came close to simulating such a doubtful outcome. I stared at my gun, thinking that a blow to its barrel would likely knock it sideways, not to the rear. To the great outdoors and Bo, I said, "None of this makes sense." And at that very moment, my eyes widened to an anomaly demanding an answer. All four strands of barb wire had been spliced. Charlie had not discovered an accidental break made by a tree limb or a bull's horn. Maybe that someone caught Charlie in the act of repairing it. So, why wasn't the wire splicing mentioned in the sheriff's report? I had to know. A heart-to-heart with the sheriff was imperative.

Knowing not what else to look for, I wandered along the fence line kicking stones and thinking, while Bo wandered the brushy terrain to the east, sniffing old bird scent. I crawled under the fence and followed ATV ruts headed northeast around the hip of West Butte; but with daylight waning, I returned to the death scene. An hour at this chilling place was 50 minutes too long. Bo and I turned and trotted away.

As Sherbinski says, "The setting for a crime scene is bigger than a room, a street, or sometimes even a town." With that in mind, I led Bo on a circuitous route, doubling the mileage to my truck. Rats! Unlike me, Sherbinski would have discovered some infinitesimal clue during his trek off the mountain. All we found was a covey of 20 or so prairie chickens, clucking comically as they sailed away.

Chet hadn't returned. From an outlying corral a trio of replacement bulls complained of empty bellies. Chet's rock message center was undisturbed. I scribbled a note: "Chet - Been there, found the place, have questions. I'll spend some time in Shelby. Won't leave the Sweetgrass country until we visit. Jack Lindquist."

Friday morning, 8 AM. I called the sheriff's office, offering only my name and request to meet with him. "Sheriff Cowan will be unavailable today," the lady deputy said. "If you will explain the exact nature of your call, I could reach him on the radiophone, depending on the, ah, importance of your purpose." She waited; I stalled, reluctant to play a card... "Mr. Lindquist?" she said.

"Sorry. Yes, please tell Sheriff Cowan that I am a journalist and I'm working on a story that should interest him."

"I'll pass that along," she said, dismissively. "I'll need to know where you may be reached." I gave her the info and returned to the Glacier. I didn't expect a call and didn't receive one. I lounged around my room making notes and playing an old embedded number on Fender. On the third rendition, Bo poked my leg... hard. Time to pee. We drove to the weed field behind the city limits sign. Coming back down Main, I took the side street to the sheriff's office and parked next to the stone jailhouse.

I left Bo "guarding" Big Red, walked into the sheriff's office, removed Lucky, and flashed my best smile on the front desk lady. Standing before her and a desktop computer, I held Lucky like the Bible, looking as benign as an Eagle Scout, "I'm Jack Lindquist. I called earlier. I'm hoping you have reached Sheriff Cowan on my behalf."

She was a beefy lady of middle age wearing an ugly brown uniform, a badge, and a brass nametag etched with "E.J. Burns." She wasn't exactly homely or pretty, and apparently not interested in working on pretty. She wore no make-up on a squarish face framed by straight, brown hair... no doubt a diligent all-business assistant busy sheriffs employ to keep offices functioning smoothly and to help sheriffs get re-elected. During my growing up years, she'd be known as a "Girl Friday." Today that would get you a whop upside the head.

"Friday" looked over the top of her blue plastic glasses, inspecting me. "The sheriff is, ah... he's still out on a case. He said if you would care to interview with me, perhaps we could shorten the process, unless—of course—you have a formal charge to make or you know of infractions to be reported."

"It is none of that," I said, handing her my writer's business card. "If the sheriff finds a time slot for me, my number is on this card. I'll be at the Glacier Motel and around town, maybe one more day."

Would a threat of my leaving town move them along? Not likely. Without a smile, Friday Burns, E J, stood to shake my hand. I smiled anyway and wrote her name in my pocket notebook. I said, "I'm sorry Ms. Burns. I have trouble remembering names. May I call you by your first name?"

"Oh," she said, again no smile... "I guess so. My name is Emma."

"Emma Jean, perhaps?"

Long pause and a wisp of smile, "How did you know?"

"An educated guess. Guessing is my hobby."

"Interesting," she said with narrowed eyelids. "Unfortunately, I don't know enough about your purpose to speak on behalf of the sheriff."

I tipped Lucky and smiled, "Thank you for your time, Emma."

I had reason to believe the sheriff was open minded and a good man. He'd eventually call me, out of curiosity if nothing else. While waiting for eventually, I decided to practice my clever detecting in downtown Shelby. Hung a right onto Highway 2, where a head scratcher sign indicates that the next mile of Highway 2/High-Line is a poor stepchild of I-15. I parked, imprisoned Bo in her truck box kennel, and walked three blocks of hybrid state/federal byway to a corner bar and grill. I used the side-street door, pausing inside to adjust my eyes to the dim light.

At mid-day a four man card game and a stout bartender occupied the bar side of the Plainsman B & G. It was late for lunch goers and early for all but problem drinkers. One of those sat slumped at a stool next to the side door exit. He babbled at the bartender, "Come on, Mick, gimme one more shot a' Daniels here. Mick, the tender, faced him with his butt resting against the back bar, thick arms folded. He grimaced, wagging his head, one word...

"Nope."

"Jerk! My money ain't good 'nuff? Asshole!"

Mick stepped forward, looking down on his heckler. He said, "Try that one more time, Stump, and I'll throw you and *your* asshole outa' here."

"The Mick" Mickelby was a big, muscled guy, about 45 with a short clipped dark beard, graying crew cut, and busy brown eyes. His black collared shirt fit tightly around his shoulders and biceps. He didn't seem the sort to drink with the "boys" when business was slow. He nodded at me as I took a seat two bar stools apart from the runty, whiskey-pickled man called "Stump."

Mick studied me, waiting on my drink request. He seemed a perfect fit for Dempseytown, standoffish at first meeting, while buttressing Shelby's hero, Jack Dempsey, by decorating his back wall with old black and white fight photos. Mick stood in front of me with straightened arms extended to the bar. No smile, no frown, as neutral as a vending machine. He had no intention of asking, so I nodded at his line-up of taps. "Bud draft, please, 10 ouncer, room temperature glass." In one fluid, quick-handed motion, he poured, turned and deftly placed my beer in front of me. Mick moved decisively, in command—a master bartender.

Stump-the-drunk stood, wobbling, staggering toward the side door exit. He, in fact, "stumped" across the pine-board floor, perhaps due to an injury or deformity to account for his unfortunate tag. His leaving was no loss for my purpose. He wasn't coherent enough to inform me of anything. Seconds after leaving, he re-opened the door and stuck his head in, "Asshole, Mick. Ya' jus' lost yerself a good cust-mer."

"One can only hope," Mick said to no one in particular, though he stood only a few feet away from me.

Patience, I counseled myself. *Mick practices disinterest, but not convincingly*. I sipped my beer slowly, savoring Budweiser as if it were Big Sky Millennial Blue Ribbon. Mick wiped his bar again, making busy. With thick neck and stout shoulders, everything stout from the waist up, and a face edged in certainty, Mick could have been a retiree from a battered life as a light-heavyweight or a pro linebacker from blue collar Canadian football.

He returned before I'd bottomed my glass, a good sign. On the other hand, he returned without a word. I opened innocuously, gesturing toward four senior-ized men at a card table across the room, "pinochle?"

"Yup, a Montana version with Shelby rules." Mick studied me with brown eyes. He nodded at my glass, "'Nother Bud?"

"No thanks, I have an appointment," I said, swinging onto my feet. I'd leave owning the last word. 'Leave 'em laughing,' as they say in show business. *And wondering, too.*

As I opened the door to depart, Mick said at my back, "Sorry, Mister, 'bout that nut case. He's dependably obnoxious. Unfortunately, he sometimes drives drunk." I waved him off and walked out, almost salivating. Mick Mickelby was now primed and ready, and at this moment going crazy with curiosity. "Who's the semi-tall, semi-bearded stranger and what's he up to?" I'd let him ferment for a day, maybe two. If I owned a "wire," I could return wearing it under my shirt.

Like Sherbie and his habitual detective-ness, out on the street I paused to study the street scene. I smiled; good habits pay off. An over-hanging sign on the next business up the street announced *Slimann and Sons*, words etched in antiqued pine board for "old west" authenticity. Ha! My team's notes suggested this Slimann outfit was anything but authentic. I walked over for a closer look. A gust of wind came up the narrow street and swung the overhead board sign. It creaked like the bank sign in *Tombstone*.

Slimann's agency was shuttered, explained by a notice in a side win-dow: *Closed. Sorry For Any Inconvenience. For your legal and properties assis-tance please call 701-821-7000.* What gives? 701 is a North Dakota prefix. On the front door glass, cracked white paint lettering declared their business services:

Slimann and Sons
Bennett J. Slimann, attn. at law
Legal Assistance
Properties, Mineral Equities
Title Searches

My crew in Great Falls had informed me that Bennett J. was good at shystering. It would be worth knowing what his sons were good at and what they did in their spare time.

After a hard day of detecting, Bo and I needed a place to run. We located Shelby's high school by following big yellow buses. Invited our-selves onto their oval track encircling the football field where Shelby High School was conducting practice.

Three laps in my hunting boots, I figured, was equivalent to a mile workout. Except, damn it!—as I stepped onto the track my cell phone's pheasant crowed. He crowed again on laps two and three. I succumbed to my phone's notion of urgency and took a seat on a hard trackside bench to talk with Urgency H. Kerner.

He barely said hello before plunging to serious business. I was a poor listener, distracted by footballers running drills in the infield. Bo too. She sat beside me on the bench, her big brown eyes tracking holler-ing, hustling players. She stared at me, begging to run and join the fun.

Meanwhile, Kerner peppered me with investigative issues, which I deposited in gray-mattered message recording. I was absorbed with watching Shelby High's six foot five quarterback throwing pinpoint passes to a skinny, but fleet little receiver. He took a pass close by our bench and stepped out of bounds. As he turned away I read his name, "Red Hawk" printed in bold black letters across the back of his practice jersey.

Here came the coach, trotting over to check me out. He moved with the characteristic rolling gait of a thick-legged linebacker. I stood to greet him. He looked warily at Bo, who returned his attention as if he were a triple scoop ice cream cone.

Bob would have to wait. "I'll get back to you ASAP, Bob," I said, punching *end call*. My tone of voice was comically misplaced, remindful of my short-lived salaried importance with my father-in-law's company.

"You must be a parent I haven't met," the coach said. He didn't say it convincingly. We talked football in little circles until he came awkwardly to his real mission, "Any chance you're scouting for Cut Bank?"

"No sir, I'm not. If I scouted for Cut Bank, I'd go back and go tell my boys to blitz your big quarterback on every play, because if he has time to throw it's all over. If I scouted for you, we'd talk about your fast receiver. I've watched him run every route flat out. He could hesitate, a jab step or change of pace before turning on his afterburner. Your rifle-armed quarterback can get him the ball deep."

He looked at me quizzically, "You a coach?"

"No, I'm an observer."

He smiled, "Pretty good at it, too, I must admit."

I handed him my business card. "I'll be in town awhile, long enough to catch a game or two."

"We'll look for you," the coach said. He turned and jogged away at a respectively athletic clip. He identified himself humbly, simply COACH printed across the back of his gray sweatshirt.

Kerner calling again. I resolved to listen this time, though my focus was on a pass-only drill. "COACH" huddled with his quarterback, center, and receivers. His assistant and his defensive backfield gathered across the scrimmage line, strategizing how to stop the next pass play.

Meanwhile, Kerner droned on about building trust with local law enforcement, but "stay undercover best you can" and "don't forget to take plenty of pictures" and "find out who law enforcement interviewed." Lastly, he advised me to await pertinent information being assembled by our team in Great Falls. "Most importantly," he said, "I'm sending our formatted paradigm for investigative procedures."

COACH blew his whistle, the snap came on the second "hut," and Red Hawk sprinted 20 yards, slowed abruptly—looking back for a mythical ball—then dashed for the end zone. His quarterback's rocket pass arced 40 yards, dropping into his hands. As Red Hawk trotted past, heading up-field, he gave me a thumbs-up.

"Link, are you still on?" came Kerner's tinny voice.

"I'm here Doctor,"

"So why are you silent?"

"I'm coaching football practice." Following a confused silence, I thanked him for his painstaking research on public record citations involving the Slimanns.

"You're welcome," Kerner said. "I'll pretend I didn't hear your claim about coaching football. Now, seriously, when do you begin?"

"On what?"

"On... have you listened to a word I've said?"

"With bated breath."

"So, when do you begin?"

"8 AM the day before yesterday, confirming Jimmy Young Man's suspicions and a couple of my own."

"So, we have a putative crime scene?"

"I'm convinced we do."

"What brought you to this assessment?"

"... Bob, can you step back and imagine how this sounds? Like a badgered witness and a prosecuting attorney."

"But, are you alright, Link?"

"No, I'm not. I haven't seen Joanie in a week. And Dempseytown is a lonely place, just as you—in a round-about way—predicted."

"Dempseytown? ... You have apparently found my assessment relevant."

"Yes, and now at the moment when I finally find some folks who are not hopelessly Dempseyfied, you interrupt."

Kerner went silent, mulling our situation. Finally, "I see your point, Link... socially speaking; but you talk of the populace as if they are a homogenous citizenry. They are not. You must seek out the denizens of Shelby with their reservoir of wisdom and truth."

"Denizens? Why not simply citizens?"

"Because denizens are not simple, unlike too many common citizens who invest little emotional energy in bettering their larger community. Too many commoners simply reside. Denizens commit. Think of literature, even pop fiction. How are denizens qualified?—invariably in positive terms: intrepid denizens, magnanimous denizens, selfless and stalwart denizens. And—please—purge your eponymous characterization known as 'Dempseytown.' I doubt the locals will find it edifying."

"I'll take your word for that, Bob; but deep philosophy will have to wait. Football practice, remember?"

"And why? What possibly can a football team offer us in terms of advancing our investigation?"

"Logically?—nothing. Intuitively?—perhaps a crumb. Besides, according to plan, I'm currently chasing after War Babies, not investigating.... Later Bob, gotta run." And I did need to run, literally.

Red Hawk, the classy wide-out, had come to fetch me. He said, "Sir, Coach Latham wants to see you—come-on." Bo and I ran behind him to the 50 yard line, where Coach Latham signaled me to join in their end of practice cheer. Red Hawk grabbed my right hand, the quarterback my left. Bo sat in the center of the team circle as we shouted, "Go, Coyotes, Go. Go Coyotes GO"—an act revealing the key for the Coyotes eight game winning streak. Coach Latham's winning mission was plastered with joy. He made my day joyous as well. Coach and I shook hands, and he said, "Next week, Saturday afternoon, we play Conrad on this field. Hope to see you."

"I'll be here if possible," I said. Latham was looking past my ear,

"I hope you're not getting a ticket."

I turned to see the Toole County Sheriff crew-cab pulling away from the curb. The driver had left a white paper pinned under my windshield wiper. Curiosity tinged with anxiety inspired me to beat-feet over to retrieve the sheriff's missive.

The note was headlined in bold print: *MR. LINDQUIST: APPOINTMENT, 8 A.M, SEPTEMBER 24.* And scrawled in longhand: *Sheriff Cowan would like confirmation that you can meet with him. Deputy E. J. Burns.*

I ordered a take-out sausage pizza at the Plainsman and nursed a Charlie Russell Red while waiting. Since I was the only customer at the counter, using my cell phone to call the sheriff's office was marginally acceptable. Otherwise, I'd have to throw my own butt out of there. I called to confirm tomorrow's meeting with Sheriff Cowan and headed for the Glacier carrying pizza dinner and another cold Charlie Russell.

Bo helped me finish my pizza, high-grading—nosing away the onions in the soggy box.

Telephone time. I called Kerner, a contemporary Ann Landers. As a youngster, I read Lander's column daily, free advice colored with clever sarcasm. Kerner, with peculiar enigmatic style, was also a wise advisor; yet his take on the dichotomy of denizens and ordinary citizens bothered me. I said, "Bob, how can a non-denizen like me be trusted? I'm an 'ordinary' and a stranger to boot."

"Glad you asked," he said. "You can be trusted for the very reason you are now ensconced in foreign territory. You have a knack for being accepted as innocuous, in your vernacular—part of the woodwork."

"I'll take that as a left handed compliment."

Kerner tried to extend the conversation, citing a new book by a psychologist from Harvard School of Medicine. I begged off. Time to check in with Joanie.

Bingo! Joanie answered. She had come from the mountains carrying a packet of bear hair for DNA studies. She detailed high spots of her snowy wilderness trip, and I recounted my dibble-dabbling in a place devoid of welcome mats. We burned an hour of my cell phone budget, including telephonetic romance: innuendoes, maybes, and hints of hard to reach fruit. All of which, doggone # % +^#@ and henshit, came to a dull thudding end when Joanie, having fallen behind on report writing and lab work, said she couldn't come to Montana.

Without using religion to make the case, I say that good news is usually buried in bad; though often buried deeply. Wade in the muck. Feel for something solid. The maxim is illustrated by the joke about the little optimist boy, whose father discovered him wading to his shins in horse manure. His dad was very angry. He said, "What in tarnation are you doing?" The boy says, "With all this manure, there's got to be a pony here somewhere." Well, Joanie and I found "the pony." His name is DNA.

Leave it to a genius like her to get fired up about laboratory work.

That's my Joanie. With only a half–time teaching assignment, she explained: "I'm devoting free time studying DNA processing. In the future my research budgets will not be devoured by lab costs; which brings me to what you call your 'sterile crime scene.'"

"It is," I countered. "Rocks, livestock trampled dirt, and down on Teton Ridge, Charlie's buried ashes. So what could I possibly find as evidence?"

"DNA."

I detest pessimism, yet here I was wallowing in it. I said, "I don't know where to begin to find DNA."

"Nor would I," Joanie said. "Not until I perused the scene. I'd widen the search beyond the obvious. Then, most importantly, you must embrace the very nature of DNA. In a nutshell, think organically. Keep that constantly top of mind."

"Okay, Professor," I said. "I'll never forget. You are organically irresistible."

"And very hard to get, Honey Plumbs."

The getting, we agreed, would take place in two weeks or less.

Back to the unsettled world of law and lawlessness. Tomorrow, Dempseytown would see me transformed... Jekyll today, Hyde tomorrow—an academic missing only the musty tweed.

Tomorrow the sheriff would see me as a middling scholar. Depending on his reception, I could possibly get hooked on interviewing. I buffed my old oxfords and hung my wrinkled corduroy jacket in the steamy shower—a traveling salesman's remedy.

Fender and I finished the day with a slow version of "Willows"—better than a sleeping pill.

Tuesday morning, September 24th. At straight up eight I walked into the Toole County sheriff's office carrying my steno notebook with 10 questions printed as reminders.

This time Deputy Emma Jean Burns greeted me with a glinty-eyed smile. Since she was more or less the sheriff's professional appendage, I could read him by reading her. "Good morning," I said. "I left my recorder in the truck for this initial visit."

"Very considerate, Mr. Lindquist. I'm sure Sheriff Cowan would approve. And the recorder would be for what purpose?"

"Yes. You may recall... when I came in before, we spoke of my demographic project which will chronicle Sheriff Cowan's role within a generational grouping of important American citizens like him." She searched my face for clarity. Finding none, Emma Jean excused herself.

"One moment, please." She walked the few steps to Sheriff Cowan's half open door, where they conferred in low voices. Nice protocol, maybe a little overdone for an office staff of eight or ten, including a street-dressed guy who glanced at me and hurried out the back door carrying a cup of coffee. Emma Jean could have simply hollered, "Sheriff, that writer from out of town wants to see you."

"E J," as the sheriff called her, took me to a 10 by 20 conference room and brought me a cup of creamed Joe in a cracked white ceramic cup and its smudged image of Jack Dempsey. I opened my steno book and waited. Through thin walls I heard Sheriff Cowan speaking on the phone—nothing clear, nothing specific; but I suspected I was a subject under discussion. Call it native intuition endemic to pro investigators like me.

After a half hour of my twiddle-thumbed day dreaming, the sheriff gimped into the conference office, each step punctuated with a thump of his walking stick. I stood to greet him. He reached long for a handshake and leaned his walking stick against the wall. Gazing out the window, he said, "One more month, I'll be good to go."

The sheriff wore his hat, confirming my good decision to let Lucky ride. Nothing says "sheriff" better than the spotless sheriff hat, and Cowan's was no exception, as if crafted by that singular talented hat-maker who churns out buff colored felts... medium brim, modestly cupped, each hat as dependable as its stalwart sheriff owner. This sheriff, Buck Cowan, tugged his hat down a notch and locked onto me with his serious hazel eyes, eyes level with mine, which made him about six one. Gray flecked hair at the temples set off an open, friendly face framed by neat sideburns. Joanie would say handsome. About 210 pounds, flab-free, and proudly postured, I expected that Sheriff Cowan would thump self-proclaimed tough guys who were stupid enough to try him.

He motioned me to sit at the head of the conference table, decorum be damned. He took a chair to my right and tucked his chin sideways, scrutinizing me. After awkward seconds, "I have maybe a half-hour, Mr.

Lindquist, unless something unexpected comes along. Tell me again, how may I help you?"

"Sure. None of my business, Sheriff, but you had a civilian in here, nervous acting. He grabbed a cup of coffee and went out the back door."

"Thanks for your concern, Mr. Lindquist. He's authorized. That's all you need to know." The sheriff grinned, "Now let's see how authorized we can make you. You want my time, why?"

"Sorry. I'll get right to it then. I'm a writer. And an associate of mine has unearthed a concept that needs research, about a chapter of American history..."

I gave it my best, three minutes of contrivance, like crafting good wings for a dodo bird. Cowan nodded along, as if accompanying a song. I fingered my steno book. "I know enough of your history, sheriff, to believe you would be an excellent choice for my first interview. You're about 65, the right age for a demographic group called the 'War Babies.'"

The sheriff wheeled his chair back and swiveled to engage me face on. He laughed warmly, sincerely amused, although with what was to come, a lesser man would have laughed me right out onto the street.

Sheriff Cowan reached into a satchel on the table and pulled out a dog-eared copy of *Tall, Dark, and Crimson*. He tossed it on the table, "When I learned you were coming to town, I requisitioned this from my wife so I could get to know you... if you get my drift."

Without conviction, I said, "I understand."

"Your writing is entertaining—law on the lighter side. But I'm curious. Why does a mystery writer like you suddenly become scholarly?"

"Sheriff Cowan, at this point in my career..."

"Please call me Buck, and I'll call you Jack, if you don't mind."

I nodded, "Agreed."

"Good. Now Jack, I don't mean to be rude, but I don't have much time today."

Thereupon, the sheriff, Buck, embarked on a candid and cerebral discourse about law enforcement among a diverse citizenry and what his patrons expect of him. I hadn't anticipated this side of him. As my dear departed Mom would say, "He let his hair down."

"I understand you're from the Idaho Panhandle," Buck said. "I visited there one time... spectacular mountain country, an extraordinary place to settle. Your people are packed tight in those river canyons. I read them wrong at first, believed them to be provincial, standoffish. Before I left, though, I discovered I'd been too quick to judgement."

I nodded, thanking him—those were my people he was judging; still I wondered about the intent of small talk, where he was going with it.

He grinned easily, wanting to put me at ease. "Jack, I've lived in the High-Line country my whole life, excepting my time in the service. I've seen visitors come along and misread the culture. You see, Montana east of the Rockies is big... wide open, but surprisingly interconnected."

"I know exactly what you mean, Buck. I was born and raised in Dawson County cattle country, sparsely settled—wide open. We knew every neighbor within 20 miles."

"Good, then you'll know exactly how you easily fell into an awkward situation, which happens to complicate my job."

"Can't imagine how, Sheriff." (I could not help myself; in this situation a sheriff should be called Sheriff.) I said no more, as if waiting for an unexploded grenade to coming rolling across the conference table.

He said, "Complicating? Yes. I'll lay it out for you, beginning with my cousin Molly Duboix from Great Falls. She works in the King of Hearts restaurant. You remember her, don't you?"

Cowan paused considerably while I cleared my throat. I mustered, "Yes, I know Molly."

"And her live-in, Max, who squired you out to Larigan's ranch where you were welcomed by the family and Jimmy Young Man? Oh, and we have another mutual friend, name of Sunny Daniels. All this I knew before you drove into town."

"Sure is a small world isn't it?"

"Yes, and ambitious travelers like you make it smaller."

Cowan tried, without success, to maintain professionalism. He laughed, readying another bomb. For me, curiosity and trepidation dueled. I longed to get in at least one lick. I said, "Your network must be Montana's version of the CIA. So, what else do you have?"

"That you *do* get around, Jack. You recently starred in a movie."

"Uh... no, couldn't have been me," I stammered.

He grinned—not cynically, but crafted as good-natured jousting. He said, "Well, let's look at a clip." He flipped open his laptop. While his computer readied itself for computilating, Cowan nervously checked his watch. He would soon dismiss me.

As the laptop monitor's images came into focus, I saw a man and a yellow dog bouncing up a trail, face on to the camera. They came to a flat topped boulder where the man paused before plopping his butt on the boulder. I gulped. *How in hell... ?*

"My trail camera caught you and your Labrador on a nice day in the Sweet Grass Hills. You carried a shotgun, but no game bag, obviously not hunting, though being a friend of the Larigans you could have."

Clearly, Sheriff Cowan had a head start and was uncatchable. I decided to dispense with subtlety: "Sheriff... sorry, Buck. I remember the burnt snag tree. That's where you hid your trail camera, right? You're thinking Charlie Larigan was the victim of foul play. So do I, and so do his family and friends. And you're thinking you might catch the perpetrator returning to the scene for some unknowable reason."

"Meantime, Jack—you believe you could play a part in catching the culprit, right?"

"Yes, though I don't have a defined plan. Not yet."

"All of which is copacetic. Nobody saw you hiking into the Sweet Grass Hills. Well, my trail camera saw you. If your involvement ended with your visit out there—or should I say *investigation* out there—no problem. But you're a curious sort and have apparently learned a thing or two in creating your fiction character, Sherblinski or Shebonski— whatever. So, you nosed around my jurisdiction and happened onto The Mick down at the Plainsman. Not good. Then you latched onto Coach Latham. Not good."

The air in the conference room suddenly smelled dank. I said, "Buck, I respect law enforcement. You have your reasons for reining me in, which I sense you're about to do."

"Jack, you catch on quickly. Thank you. Just for fun, why don't you tell *me* why you must back away."

I took a deep breath and began, "Sure. The big picture is straightforward, lacks only a finish. You have a suspect or suspects, meaning you have uncovered a possible motive. Your endearing friend, 'The Mick,' has radar ears and a sponge for a brain. Out of job necessity he sits at the nexus of underground gossip from customers with lubricated lips. He respects you and shares important tidbits, but will not leak information moving in the other direction... to potential suspects, I mean. The coach isn't so easily explained. He was connected in some way with Charlie Larigan. In any case, if the perpetrator sees me hanging with locals like Coach Latham or Mick Mickelby, he may surmise he isn't home free, that the case is still open. Like you, the bad guy could discover my real reason for coming here. He could cover any untidy tracks or even flee the country."

Cowan chuckled, "Go on."

Returning his grin, I said, "You haven't flinched or twitched, so I think we, sorry—*you*, have a strategy for corralling the culprit... likely a single suspect. Speaking of... a name has surfaced. Just between the two of us, does the name Slimann ring the proverbial bell?" I watched for changes in his droll grin; there were none—a poker player extraordinaire.

Sheriff Cowan closed his laptop and pushed back his chair. He loosed a little throaty laugh, sort of an exclamation point, "Good Jack, *very* good. If you weren't a transient, I could consider hiring you—only, though, after I have the Sweet Grass killer locked in that stone palace in Deer Lodge. Meantime, you and your dog and your red pickup are becoming a bit too newsworthy in this little town."

With that, I stood and stretched. I said, "Buck, I should thank you. In fact, I *do* thank you. Quitting simplifies my life. With contrived conviction, I said, "Now I can move on down the High-Line focusing on my original mission."

Buck stood, grinning, "Good thinking, Jack. Let's shake on it." We did so, both applying strong, but equal pressure, manly, but without chest-thumper's nonsense. "I'll walk you out," he said.

As we neared her desk, E J peered around her computer screen, "Do you want anything written up here, Sheriff?" He slowed only long enough to hold the door for me and instruct his deputy assistant.

Reflexively tipping his hat, he said, "E J, we have nothing new for the record this morning."

The sheriff followed as far as the curb, where he stood with his hands on his pistol packing hips. "There she is, your co-star," he said. Bo, so ever alert, sat tall, nose out my driver's side window. "Mind if I give her a treat?"

"Not a bit. My friends are her friends," I said. He reached into his khaki jacket pocket and pulled out a dog cookie, "I have these ready for the State Police drug sniffer. We never know when she might be needed here."

I slid into my driver's seat and bumped cookie-chomping Bo aside, expecting a parting shot to come. Correctly so. I lowered the window, and Sheriff Cowan leaned over, bracing his big hands against the door sill, "How much longer will you be in town?"

"Maybe 'till tomorrow. Can I assist you in any way?—undercover, of course." It was a one act play, the send-off scene, dismissing me from his lawman's domain.

He slapped the top of my pickup cab, "We have your number, Jack. Don't be surprised if you get a call." I gave the sheriff the Montana index finger salute and pulled away. I had no destination in mind.

How would Sherbie feel? How should I feel? One minute I'm doggedly and happily climbing "Discovery Mountain" turning stones, the next minute I'm plodding downhill without a purpose. And I couldn't even go off to commiserate with The Mick, the single likely commiserator in town. Hey! No joke—this sudden jolt to the psyche could derail a gainfully employed professional adult. If I were a serious drinker, I'd head for the nearest bar—Correction, according to my deal with Sheriff Cowan, bars were off-limits. Matter of fact, he implied *Toole County* was off limits.

With superb timing, Bo whimpered. I replied, "Let's go bust a pheasant, Bo."

South of town in a swampy seep of the Marias bottomlands, Bo flushed two roosters, easy shots. The farmer who gave me hunting permission took one for his neighbor, the other for himself. He said, "I've farmed here for 40 years. You're the first Idahoan ever came to hunt." I wanted to say, *"I damn sure wish that's why I came."*

Back in my unkempt room at the Glacier Motel, I admit to moping about, postponing phoning Joanie and Kerner. Kerner would say "reporting in," and he lives by the clock. He likes five PM. I finally swept my nerves into a pile and, at 10 o'clock picked up the phone. I kept it short—first Kerner, in the barest of details, hoping my mindset, "That's life," would be convincingly translated by Kerner to Sunny, and to Jimmy and the Larigans, Max and Pearl, and especially Walker McCloud. Walker lived optimism to the hilt. I pictured his weathered face beaming confidence, his unspoken belief: *you'll bring justice.* I'd let him down, all the others too... and Joanie, who mattered most of all. Coincidentally, with Fender resting passively on my lap, the pheasant crowed, the bird that Joanie had programmed as the ringer on my cell.

"Hey, Rusty, it's me," Joanie laughed. "Thought you should know I'm back in the mountains... found an old cabin within reach of the Forest Service's repeater signal. It has a decent roof too."

"You're camping out there?"

"No, I'm *living* here, feeling decadent."

"I'd love to share in your decadence."... and so on we went, morphing into our trademark telephonic promises. Unfortunately, real life intervened: my admission of failure and a target of Sheriff Cowan's edict.

Joanie sounded first relieved, reminding me that I was now free to seriously research War Babies. On the other hand... "You're depressed aren't you?" she said.

I managed to reassure her with a "proven fact," of which I couldn't cite the authority, that "despondency must last more than 72 hours to qualify as clinical depression."

Joanie's melodic Lauren Bacall laugh is enough to cure the mopes, if not depression. She said, "Take one aspirin and go to bed. You're still crazy, which means you aren't depressed. You'll be fine in the morning."

"Not quite. I'll be fine when you are close enough to light my fire."

Kerner, however, wouldn't be "fine in the morning," nor convinced that I should fold the tent. He called back with a new take on the situation. He said, "Sheriff Cowan's concerns are understandable; but his timing is terribly unfortunate. You must ask him for a continuance."

"You'd better have a good reason, Professor," I said. "He won't stand still for a debate."

"But he possibly would for a movie."

"What?" I puzzled how Kerner could know about Sheriff Cowan's clever technique. I said, "You're referring to his trail camera."

"No, I'm speaking of a documentary that re-enacts Charlie's demise. Your team has cleverly depicted the death scene: scripted, acted, and filmed. Miss Sunny Daniels and I will finish editing in the morning. After Sheriff Cowan views it, he may want to re-consider his decision."

"You mean to boot me out of town?"

"Jack, I think you underestimate the man. Now, you'll want to access Wi-Fi in the morning, no later than 10 AM."

"Got it, Captain, but don't expect miracles. Over and out." I was in no mood for another missionary diversion.

I pulled out a hard chair and sat down with Fender. My only light came from the soundless TV, and it was just enough.

I seldom play "Willows" without Joanie. But tonight I needed it so bad that my fingers effortlessly opened the melody. After 14 years I didn't need to think it, just play it soft and mellow for me and my waning inner strength... for Bo with her chin on the floor and her bright eyes watching. And I played it for Joanie, the very genesis of "Willows." For the umpteenth time I hearkened back to the time.

We had known each other a month, just enough time to fall in love, not exactly "young love" but young enough for loony-ness, such as Joanie's insistence that she truly enjoyed my messing on Fender. We chose a secluded nook in the willows by the East Gallatin River, where on one remarkable occasion I completed only the opening phrase.

"Our song" was conceived there on the Gallatin, but only the framework; that I filled in while courting Joanie. When we married six months later, Joanie wanted a name. I said, "I can't play it the same twice, so how can it have a name?"

She said, "Because I said so, and I always get what I want."

"So, do I get what I want?"

Ah, memories! Sanity depends on them.

Daybreak, September 25th. I took Bo to the high school track at dawn when chances of bumping into Coach Latham were slim. This time I ran a full mile in my hunting boots. Bo was happy too, permitted to romp without her leash.

I took on biscuits and gravy at the corner café where the chief waitress had set the world record for grumpy. Fortunately, she had the day off. The younger one who served me talked football knowledgeably and emotionally, bragging up the Coyotes who last Saturday "wiped out" Conrad on their home field.

Next stop: the Toole County Sheriff's office. I walked in casually with Bo on her leash, greeting a 20ish blond girl with a brown uniform and no badge. I introduced myself as a "friend of the sheriff," needing to provide him 'an informative CD.' "I'll need to use your internet to download."

She eyed me cautiously, "I'm not sure of my authority to accept items... perhaps evidence? You see, I'm new at this job."

Bo bumped my leg. I said, "No worries, Miss. I'll accept full responsibility with Sheriff Cowan. In the meantime, Bo here, recalls her last visit when she was awarded a dog cookie."

Bo got her cookie, I a clipboard, a form, and a directive: "You're supposed to sign in here and please write in your purpose at the bottom."

Brook was a half-timer, said she "didn't know the rules yet." She poured me coffee, suspending her office's customary two-bit coffee can contribution. Nonchalantly, I said, "Say, when I was in here before I saw a fellow I used to know, gray haired now, about five ten, pudgy. He didn't wear a uniform." Brook didn't hesitate...

"Oh, you mean 2120. He dresses civilian."

"2120—his badge number, right?"

Brook laughed, "I'm surprised you would know that Mr. ... ?"

"Lindquist."

"Yes, Mr. Lindquist. Sheriff Cowan likes to refer to deputies by badge numbers. Jones... they say he tried retirement, but didn't like it."

"Yeah, old Junie, a darned good deputy, I'm told." To myself, I said, *an eclectic name and a mystery man, Juniper Jones has the makings of a great character for my next book.*

Brook offered me a seat in the conference room for movie time. I chuckled cynically. Damn. Just as I'm preparing to vacate Dempsey-town, folks warm to my presence.

To my satisfaction, Brook returned to her telephone and computer. I lit up my laptop and commandeered requisite enters, shifts, highlights, and a palsied touchpad. A few gazillion electrons streamed from satellites, arranging themselves into an opening page image. There stood a windblown Sunny Daniels in front of a four strand fence. Like a blooming rose, Kerner's boundless imagination came into focus. He'd masterminded a movie of homicidal theory.

Sunny stood on the same kind of rocky scab-land as the place where Charlie died. She was dressed simply, ranch-style: worn denims, a red-checkered wool jacket over a Levi shirt, and western felt hat, medium brim.

Wired for recording, Sunny spoke to a camera and its unseen operator—"*Today, September 23rd, 2009, we will re-enact at Teton Ridge the tragic gun-shot death of Charles B. Larigan. He died on September 29th, 2008 in the Sweet Grass Hills, Toole County, Montana. This film will demonstrate how he died. As you will discover, it was not a freak accident or per chance.*"

Nor was the film's setting left to chance. The afternoon sun slanted over Sunny's left shoulder. From her perspective, she faced the corner of a four strand barb wire fence. The terrain and set-up accurately replicated what I'd seen on Yucca Ridge.

Sunny turned west toward a low sun from where she and her movie viewers watched a rider on a blue roan horse and his trailing Labrador dog coming up a grassy ridge crest. The camera-eye view showed the horse, rider, and dogs' methodical approach. As they closed the distance, I recognized the rider, a sober-faced Walker McCloud with an unfamiliar red glad rag and a dented hat that was too large for the little man. The horse was unmistakably Duke, Charlie's extraordinary gelding. I didn't know the dog, but saw in her a likeness to the golden retriever hanging about the Larigan corrals.

Walker dismounted and dropped Duke's reins. He removed a wreath of barb wire from his canvas saddlebag and proceeded to the fence corner.

As Walker assessed the breached fencing, Sunny narrated: "*For months Charlie Larigan had been troubled by cut fences, missing livestock, and trashy 4-wheelers tearing up trails in his grazing allotment.*"

Walker moved close to the cut wires, bent over, pantomiming the splicing. Suddenly he straightened, hearing the engine of an approaching ATV. I was drawn to the drama, but with a sense of foreboding.

A large, noisy ATV came into view, first its roll bars lifting above the rise of hill, then oversized tires and a dark form behind a windshield. The driver drew to a stop side-by-side with Duke. Duke, however—being superbly trained— startled, but did not move. He remained standing only a dozen or so steps from Walker (Charlie) and exactly where he had been commanded to stand. In her narration, Sunny explained that

Charlie had trained the horse to ground tie and would not shy, even from ATVs or rude pedestrian strangers.

Sunny momentarily commanded the scene, standing next to Walker and his actor dog, *"We'll never know exactly what the two men said to each other; but when the suspect who rode the ATV becomes the accused in court, he may talk and plea for leniency."* With that, Sunny stepped from the scene, and "Act 2" began.

The movie bad guy faced off with Walker, shouting cuss words. He wore a straight-brimmed black hat. With bushy eyebrows and sideburns, the actor was easily recognized as Curly, the foreman of L Bar L south. (Later, I learned, Jimmy Young Man first volunteered to play the part, before wisely declining.)

The adversaries' dialogue was convincingly heated, but ad-libbed and not entirely intelligible. Accusations colored with swear words flew in both directions until our good-guy took command, leveling charges of ATV induced erosion, fence destruction, missing livestock, and allegations accusing the fence-cutter of transporting marijuana.

Curly, the intruder, advanced a couple steps toward Walker, i.e. Charlie, hollering about trumped up charges by *"your crooked sheriff friend."* Curly "BAD-GUY" was coming unglued. He retreated a few steps until he was alongside Duke. With eyes locked on his adversary, he reached for Duke's saddle scabbard with a gloved hand and drew out a crude wooden replica of a shotgun.

The finale' was predictable: BAD-GUY advanced toward GOOD-GUY (Charlie) and his dog. Paying no heed to our GOOD-GUY'S plea to "calm down," BAD-GUY leveled the wooden shotgun, and someone off camera shot an actual shotgun. Walker went down clutching his stand-in yellow retriever. BAD-GUY Curly placed the prop shotgun on the ground at the "dead" victim's feet, the "shotgun" muzzle facing his mid-section.

The film ended with a short interview featuring Sunny, who reminded viewers of known facts about the real life dog, Ginger, who ran off after leaving her blood at the scene... and Duke bolting, running five miles, returning to the Larigan barn. Sunny finished with her assertion: *"Nobody who ever watched Charlie Larigan handle a gun or hunted with him believes he was careless enough to accidentally shoot himself and his dog."*

Lastly, the production credits and cast appeared in scrolling style:

SWEETGRASS AND BONEWOOD

Robert Kerner – *cameraman.*
Sunny Daniels – *narrator.*
Pearl Harmon - *script.*
Jimmy Young Man – *production advisor.*
Walker McCloud – *Charlie Larigan.*
Duke – *Duke.*
Peg, the golden retriever – *Ginger, Charlie's Labrador.*
Curly Ledoux - *the shooter.*

I saved the film in two separate files besides the CD copy, which I marked for Sheriff Cowan. I buttoned up my laptop, and took the sheriff's CD to half-time Brook, told her in my hybrid gentle/firm voice, "I'm leaving this CD in your possession. Please get it in Sheriff Cowan's hands as soon as possible."

"Yessir, understood; but you can give it to him yourself if you'd care to wait. He's on his way back from Cut Bank."

"Thank you Miss, but that won't work. I'm overdue for another assignment." Bo sat by my leg, following our conversation, grinning her silly canine smile, meaning: "be nice to her boss; she has dog cookies." Brook, Sheriff Cowan's up and coming halfer, was already reaching for the cookie sack under Bo's watchful gaze.

Mentally speaking, I was already gone, paging ahead.

CHAPTER ELEVEN

U TURN

9 A.M. – I needed to shake off Shelby like Bo sheds dust. Pulled onto Main heading east on the two-laned High-Line—a gateway to my original destination, the one of responsibility and order. At the city limits sign, beckoned by the northerly hills of the Sweet Grass, I stopped on the highway shoulder. The snowy cone mountains gleamed bright below a clear, crystalline sky. An unknowing traveler might guess the mountains were 30 miles distant. They were 70. Last night, their snow line dropped another 1000 feet, and the peaks dominated the center of gray-prairie horizon... cold, pristine sentinels, and—at the moment—tainted.

Next stop, Havre.

My old horse-sweated briefcase lay on the seat beside Bo. It held Kerner's select listing of noteworthy War Baby candidates from "Who's Who," internet searches, and his statewide academic network. Last night I read some of their bios, including that of the western writer, R.. G. Lorraine, who wrote the prize winning historical novel, *The Prairemaster*. Encouraged by Kerner's connection, I planned to garner an interview with R. G. in Havre.

Bo sat tall and alert beside me, her bright eyes staring easterly over the highway, wondering—I wish I knew—but whatever, no less important than my half-hearted ruminations.

Two-laned Highway 2 stretched to a gentle eastern horizon, empty and peaceful as far as I could see. With cruise control set at a languid 60 mph, I checked my rear view. Not a single agitated crazy coming from behind at 80 mph—a mile and one-half per minute. Nice.

I gave in to Poncho Sanchez and his amped Latin energy playing on satellite radio. Poncho hammered on an ironic version of "I Showed Them." Well, obviously I didn't "show them." Yet, this was life as it should sometimes be, sparse but not empty, with failure left behind and a soft challenge ahead. I'd take *War Babies* as far as possible. If inadequate for the makings of a scholastic product, what do I lose? Not a thing. I'd gain the privilege of knowing "Babies" like A. G. Lorraine. If he turns out to be less than inspiring, I'll find others.

Downtown Havre, Timber Motel. Judy, one of three joyful sisters who like dogs, checked me in. Judy needed only my promise: "No, Bo won't sleep on the bed."

After dinner at Champ's, I turned in early to prepare interview questions. Maybe I'd see R. G. tomorrow, maybe not. I'd left my request on his phone recorder.

Joanie needed an update and I needed a long-distance Joanie fix. We were not wholly successful. Poor satellite position, bad weather in the stratosphere, or my outdated cellphone? Don't know. Her voice was weak and electronic; mine was flat, a melancholy byproduct of Sheriff Cowan giving me the boot.

Telephone conversation is sometimes inferior to a well–written e-letter, which I promised Joanie was forthcoming. It would carry upbeat news about meeting R. G. Lorraine and a couple of his adventuresome buddies.

Then came dreaded study time. I'd rather dig ditches. Kerner had sent a thick sheaf of papers encapsulating statistics on our target population. Papers bulged the rear pocket of my brief case. Without my feeble sense of obligation they'd stay there, moldering. As it was, they served a purpose. 30 minutes into perusing charts of average income before and after taxes, percentages grouped as this or that and another, home ownership, public service hours contributed, and... my brain ground to a halt. I fell asleep. At midnight Bo nosed my cheek, notifying me she needed to go. (Confession for Judy: Bo put her front paws on your bed. Her paws were clean.)

Back in bed, wide awake, I stared at Fender resting in a chair in the glow of a night light. I took her in my lap and we cavorted with three versions of "Gypsy Dance."

Bo and I began September 26th, 2009 with a one mile run on Havre's high school track.

Today marked the one year anniversary of Charlie Larigan's death, so noted the *Havre Daily News* in a story about inadequate funding for law enforcement. This wasn't your typical pass-over story on the way to the sports page. I knew so by listening to the cowman seated beside me at Champ's Café breakfast counter. He wore a sweat-stained Stetson canted back, showing a thin crop of gray hair. His lips blubbered, and he mumbled as he read. Noting me as his audience, he said, "Money or not, they botched the Larigan investigation."

I ignored a fourth pocketed cell phone vibration and adjusted my countenance to credulous naiveté, "There wasn't really a case though, was there?"

He eyed me carefully. "Not an official case, no; but I spend a lot of time in the Sweetgrass, and everybody out there thinks Charlie Larigan met foul play."

"And you agree?"

"I'd bet my best horse on it." He shook his head, "Everybody liked Charlie... salt of the earth."

He shook my hand with his big rough skinned one, "Jake" something, volunteering that he was a cattle buyer. I didn't remember or take time to write his surname, because in the next few moments everything changed. In Sherbinski's vernacular, my world broke its gyroscope.

"Sorry Jake," I said. "I have a damned cell phone in my pocket, and it is going crazy. Be right back." I stepped out a side door into the alley and found notification of five messages, two from Kerner, two from Sheriff Cowan, and one from Pearl Harmon. Pearl was first on my call list.

She answered in her immutably chipper voice, "Drop Inn, how may I help you?"

"Jack Lindquist, Pearl, delivering on my promise to keep in touch."

"Jack, I'm so glad you caught me. Hopefully you called to announce that you've changed your mind."

"About what, Pearl?"

"You haven't heard? Heard... sorry, you apparently haven't talked with Professor Kerner. He wants you to return to Shelby. So does Sheriff Cowan."

Stunned and a little put out, I said, "Lay it on me, Pearl. They better have good reasons. I feel like a ping pong ball."

"I understand how you feel, Jack. But I don't want to speak for them... can't take the chance of getting something wrong."

The door opened behind me, and my cattle buyer friend stuck his head out, "Your biscuits and gravy's ready." I waved him off, "please ask them to keep it hot."

"Pearl, thanks for the heads-up," I said. "I didn't mean to be short with you."

"Then please, give me another minute, because I have a clue to pass on. It is crying for discovery."

"Not to be difficult, but if it hasn't been discovered, then it doesn't qualify as a clue."

I regretted my curtness and said so, "Sorry, Miss Pearl. Let's do this methodically. We'll visit later today when I have time and a better place to talk."

"Oh," she said, fizzling like a leaking balloon.

Jake was gone. Just as well. Another country crime-sniffer on the fringe, telling me what to do. I fueled with a big country breakfast, ready to face a long day, an epic day predicted by Pearl's foreshadowing.

Turned west onto the High-Line and drove 20 miles to Kremlin where I stopped at a corner café amongst assorted stock trucks and pickups, several connected to trailers with saddle horses aboard. One guy drove in ensconced in the enclosed cab of a diesel tractor with wheels taller than my truck.

Bought a thermos full of black coffee and filled my tall Jack Dempsey souvenir mug. I punched Kerner's number.

He answered, short of breath, "Where've you been?—thank God you finally returned a call, Pearl needs you I need you and Sheriff Cowan needs you. Call him right away... Link, you still there?"

"Professor, take a deep breath," Back on the job, or high-jinks, whatever, and feeling oddly refreshed, I said, "Bob, I'm listening with rapturous attention."

"Link, Link, this is serious. Where are you?"

"I'm at the Kremlin."

"Sure. Kremlin, Montana. I've got it, the 999th Kremlin joke.

"Well, Pearl says you have news."

"I do. First, what do you think of Pearl's clever investigative tool?"

"You first, Bob."

He started, spinning faster and faster. Twice, I had to ask him to slow down.

The sea change in the Sweetgrass investigation didn't begin with Bob Kerner. To this day I'm not sure of its precise genesis, except to say that gears of three minds meshed. Kerner described an after-hours meeting in the Plainsman Bar. Coach Latham and Mick Mickelby were appropriately lubricated, just enough to loosen tongues. They told Sheriff Cowan of their roguish plan, one that required conniving and guile.

"I'll provide a condensed version," Kerner said. But you must talk to Sheriff Cowan, immediately."

"I will. So what happened?"

"Well, since you left for Havre, the sheriff has been tormenting over this case. He said he's given up on help from the state investigators, but still determined to move forward. So he called a meeting with the two others who know vital particulars of this case."

"Wait a minute, Professor. You keep saying 'case.' Until this morning, nobody admitted that one existed; I thought a case required a suspect."

"And why do you assume there isn't, Link?" Kerner's voice had an edge. "Now if you'll indulge me, we'll advance the discussion."

"Check. I'll consider my ass chewed."

Kerner laughed, "I know you well, Jackson, and your ploys too. You have rhinoceros skin. Just hold your remarks and listen."

"Right."

"So, Sheriff Cowan said the three principles came to an agreement... By the way, I did in-depth research on the sheriff. He has an impeccable record of public service. Shelby and Toole County are fortunate to have him."

"How about his two civilian advisors?"

"Based on the sheriff's judgement, which is sound, I'm convinced they are are trustworthy. They persuaded Sheriff Cowan to change strategies. Cowan approved the plan but says you are the key its successful execution."

"Me? Hell, he kicked me out of town."

"And he now realizes that was a mistake."

"Well, he had me convinced—no solid clues, no suspects."

"You are correct on count one, mistaken on number two."

"So 50 percent adds up to a case worth pursuing?"

"Link, listen to yourself. Since when did you become a pessimist?"

He was right, best to admit it. "Professor, if you were here, you could sit me in the corner. So the suspect? My notebook is ready."

"Not on the phone, Link. Besides, I want you to hear it from Sheriff Cowan."

"And Pearl's pearl of wisdom?"

"Same thing. You'll want to hear it from her."

Kerner, bless him, knew precisely how to wind me up. I said, "Bob, I've got winter meat—a whitetail deer and a couple dozen game birds in my freezer. Joanie has a late season cow elk tag. And the steelhead run is yet to come. I have nothing better to do than to head up the "Crusades for Justice" up here on the High-Line."

"You're a good man, Jackson. Now call Pearl. And you must confer with Sheriff Cowan."

"At your service, Captain."

He didn't fire back. I waited. Finally... "Link?"

"Yeah?"

"Be careful."

"Of what?"

"I'm deadly serious, Link. Don't take anything for granted."

I pulled out, turning west on the High-Line, the last leg of a two day U-turn. I thought: *Saddle up, Cowboy; you're in this until the bitter end.*

Chapter Twelve

THE CONTRACT

In the middle of Shelby I peeled off on Montana Avenue and drove directly to the Toole County Sheriff's office.

Since I was now reporting to the head honcho, I pulled into employee parking.

Bo trotted behind me through the front entrance. As my assistant, she was equally deserving of perquisites.

E J rose to greet me, "It's good to see you, Mr. Lindquist." Curious, E J sporting a smiley face. With freckles and straight cut bangs, she looked like the Dutch boy on the paint can, "The sheriff will be glad to hear you came promptly."

"I always try to please the law." Good. This time she laughed out loud.

"Sheriff Cowan is out of town on, uh... business. He said to give you a temporary place here at Headquarters."

"*Headquarters... yeah,*" I said in a deeper, authoritative voice. No choice, I had to say it, probably a superego thing Kerner warned me about.

E J called for Brooke, her office go-fer, to handle the receptionist desk, and motioned me to follow. Bo and I trooped along behind. Maybe I strutted a little.

E J, a walking yacking machine, barely paused to breathe, "The sheriff said to give you a place to keep your things, and a telephone and stuff. It's sort of in the back, very private and quiet... but the last guy didn't keep things clean... didn't stay long though..."

We passed through the conference room, stopping at a closed door in the corner, where E J announced, "The last guy back here took a police job for a tribe in Alaska." She opened the door and I almost gagged on musty.

"I don't blame him," I said. The cramped office contained a tiny desk, dusty air, and rancid paint. I smiled to soften my comment: "Maybe you should have given the last guy a window with a fan."

"Buck—I mean, the sheriff—said you were a joker. But, he said you'd be useful on a case and to make you feel comfy. I don't know the case; do you know the case?"

"Could be one of several," I said. With furrowed brow, Deputy E J "humphed." She wasn't buying my remarks, but understood that I'd placed nothing of consequence on the sale table.

I swiveled my butt into the worn, squeaking chair and swung my feet up on my desk.

E J lingered at the doorway, "Anything else we can do for you, Mr. Lindquist? Coffee, perhaps?"

"No thank you; but now that we're working together, you may call me Jack." She smiled, acknowledging her newfound admiration for me. I said, "You're very kind, E J. Thank you."

"Well, Emma, will do if you like. We'd like you to feel at home, uh—Jack . Anything else you need, you can call my desk, extension number two."

Bo stood beside my desk watching our conversation, keeping time with her thick metronome tail. I said, "Yes, there is one thing. If you have an extra rug, my assistant is ready for her nap."

"Your big dog, you mean?"

"Yup, name's Bo."

"Funny name for a girl dog."

"Or a lady dog."

Emma was smart and a lady. She smiled, "I'll bring the rug."

As I considered laying my head on my official desk for an unofficial nap, the cock pheasant crowed from my hip pocket... my cell's message from Pearl suggesting now was the time for an uninterrupted discussion.

Pearl picked up before the second ring. "Jack, so glad we connected. This is a good time... no early check-ins coming, and my departures are gone."

"I'm all ears, Pearl; and my notebook is ready."

"Where are you?"

"In my new office near the back door of the Toole County Sheriff's Department."

"What?"

"Never mind."

"So, you talked with Professor Kerner?"

"Sure did, and he's convinced you have a golden nugget."

"Yes, but you know him well. He's—no other way to put it—naïve about the world outside of academia. Am I right?"

"Right you are, Pearl. So, lay it on me —Mister Worldly."

"Promise you won't laugh?"

"Promise."

"Okay, I'll hold you to it... Here goes: I was sitting at this very desk the night before last, had all my customers tucked in. I was absorbed in Tacker Wight's best seller from 2006, *The Grass War*. You heard of it?"

"The book, no. I know about Tacker, the Olympic marksman; but his grass book? I assume it was not about dope grass."

"No, it's a mystery embedded in a story of a modern day range war. You'd like it. Anyway, I was in the middle of the last chapter, hooked on Tacker's story, you know—how you, yourself, capture the reader. And there it was. One wonders how Tacker came up with this. Well, actually, I do know. I read his biography. He grew up on a Wyoming ranch."

"Explaining what, exactly?"

"Explaining how he could dream up a phenomenon called the 'shit print'... come on, you're laughing; you promised you wouldn't laugh."

"I lied. But go ahead."

"Okay, but you should know that your wise professor friend didn't laugh. Nor do I think Sheriff Cowan will when you describe how it works."

"The principles of the 'shit print.' Explain it, and I'll hold myself to a giggle."

"Okay, you'll understand, because you said you grew up in cattle country." She cleared her voice and began, explaining in fine detail how Tacker Wight's story hero hearkened back to childhood, a ranch kid running and riding wild with a brother and a hired hand's son. They did stupid, curious things, like overturning dried cow pies to discover embedded artifacts—preserved beetles, a rare shell casing, and an unshod hoof print of a wild horse. "Best of all—a half-bald tire print on the underside of a dried cow pie. The print was traced to a suspected rustler's stock truck."

"*Tire print?* "Say no more, Pearl. You are brilliant."

"No, Tacker Wight is brilliant. I'm lucky. I bought his paperback at a used book store. Cost me all of 50 cents."

"Well, with your permission, Pearly one, you may one day appear alongside Juneau Sherbinski. He could use a second heroine."

"I'm an expensive character, Jack, and Pearly sounds cheap."

"Name your price, then."

"Easy. You must call me just as soon as you nail something."

"...if we could be so fortunate. Regardless, I'll call. This is crazy good."

Crazy good luck too. Stump's ATV had been impounded for 7 months during the marijuana farm investigation. His tire print morphology should remain essentially unchanged.

With another dose of good luck, I caught Joanie in her lab in Moscow. She picked up after the first ring.

"Joan Lindquist," she said tersely.

"Hey, hot body, it's me. Sounds like you need a day off to go fishin'."

"Or join your Montana posse. But at the moment I'm studying new research on organic chemistry forensics. How about you?"

"Amazingly coincidental. It so happens I've learned some new organic chemistry myself that will fascinate you, all about herbivores and their lasting legacies."

"This had better be good, Jack." She giggled, "You risk becoming a refuge' displaced from the organized world. But go ahead; I have my notebook open."

Thereupon, I dished Pearl's concept, like hors d'oeuvres before the banquet. True love, that's what it is—because she indulged me long enough to become a believer of fecal imprinting and its possibilities for mammalian research. We chewed through a half hour, some of it punctuated by her dismay. She could not be with me in the midst of the action. "Action?" I said. "You mean you're ready to dance and cavort?"

Joanie giggled, "You, a writer, should know better. You ended a sentence with a proposition."

Hearing footsteps, Bo woke from her nap with a soft "woof." Sheriff Cowan appeared in the doorframe, leaning into it with a shoulder, looking remarkably like Gary Cooper. "Coop," I could call him had I known him better. Into my lawman's phone, I said "Gotta go, Baboo. My boss just showed up. Love ya'."

"What? She said. You don't tolerate bosses."

"I'll explain later. Right now I'd like you to find a slot in your calendar for a getaway to our secret camp by the hot springs."

"Sorry to interrupt, Jack." Cowan checked his watch. We've got some business downtown to attend to before the ballgame."

"The Shelby Coyotes' game?"

"I call 'em Latham's Coyotes. He made them winners." Cowan tilted his head, lasering his steely eyes on mine. I gathered that Latham and his team were special, more than small talk. "Let's take a ride," Cowan said.

He paused at the door of his domain, "Headquarters." Over his shoulder, "I'll be back in an hour, E J." She stood, expecting more, receiving nothing. Her face soured. The new guy, a temporary, first day on the job he's privileged to accompany the sheriff on assignment.

Cowan grabbed my elbow as I stepped toward his curbside patrol car. He said, "No, no. I'll ride with you so I can check out your fancy truck."

"It's your call, Buck." Bo watched, irritated—*will one of you guys open the doggone door so I can get in?*

I headed for my driver's side. Again Sheriff Cowan interceded, "I'll drive, you observe."

Bo and I loaded from the passenger side. She pushed against me, asking for attention. I stroked her between her ears.

Reading body language, Bo pronounced the sheriff benign by nuzzling his cheek. He scruffed her in return.

Driving without a word, Sheriff Cowan turned right on Mineral Street, left on Central into the six block area known as Downtown. He parallel parked on the side-street next to the Plainsman and pointed at the sign overhanging my truck: "Slimann and Sons." The sheriff—*the law*—had parked my truck illegally, driver's side left, at the curb. I stared at him critically.

"I'm betting you know exactly why I parked here," he said.

"Something to do with the Slimanns, I'm guessing. This den of coyotes is well known, even down in Great Falls. The question is—why you illegally parked my red beacon of a truck in front of Slimann's office, and with me in it. Remember? Two days ago I threatened your investigation just by being *seen* in town."

"Hold on, Jack. You and I are going to make a deal, unofficially that is. And before you get too worked up, you have my guarantee that we'll break no laws, regulations, arms or legs. Furthermore, you will be privy to everything I know and continue to learn about the issue."

"Issue, huh. May we call it what it is—a homicide?" Sheriff Cowan only nodded. He wasn't to be pressured. I decided that from here on out I'd address him as "Sheriff," never "Buck."

He said, "Jack, first an apology. I'm sorry. I know you came here with good intentions. You had a bunch of fine people urging you on. Still do. I made a poor decision, thinking you were a potential risk to put my suspect on guard, to lawyer up again. So I dismissed you—more or less. Then I saw the little movie produced by your friends on Teton Ridge. I showed it to The Mick and Latham, and we talked ourselves into changing strategies once more. There will be risk; but I like our odds. I say 'we,' because you will be a principle, although a volunteer in the plan. I'm guessing you'll agree." He paused, analyzing my demeanor.

"You mean I'll agree to be a decoy?"

"I wouldn't put it that way. I'd rather say that you'll be the stranger with a reputation. You'll be seen as more knowledgeable than local law enforcement, including yours truly. You'll be a threat to the suspect, who—by the way—could be dangerous. Fortunately for us, he doesn't have smarts to go with dangerous."

" 'Us,' you say?"

"Yes—You and I, Coach Latham, and The Mick. They helped perfect a plan. Mick actually hatched it. He had you pegged that first day, before you dropped your head on a pillow in the Glacier Motel."

"The Toole County telegraph at work, huh?"

"Bigger—the Montana telegraph." As if aiming a pistol, Cowan pointed his index finger toward the Slimann's empty law office. We'll know our plan is working when Daddy Sly comes flying home from

North Dakota to rescue Stump."

"Stump?"

"Yeah, Jonathan B. Slimann, better known as "Stump," Sly's ne're do well son. Mick says you've met him."

"Stump-the-drunk. Yes, I remember. Wouldn't say I actually met him. We locked eyes and decided we didn't like each other."

"Add yourself to a long list. "Stumpy is a sad case, and a mean bastard. He has a juvie record for clobbering a kid with a baseball bat...""

Just then a stylish lady came waltzing down the sidewalk. She was designed to draw looks with her tight stone-washed jeans and medium high heels. A manicured Yorkie tripped along beside her on its leash. Bo jumped into Cowan's lap for a slobbering good look. "Okay Pup," the sheriff said. "I'll take the tall pretty one; you take the little hairy one."

The sheriff seemed in no hurry. He sat petting Bo, his icy blue eyes with a faraway look, "Jack, I'm going to tell you about this nut case, Stump. Mick knows him well from the many hours Stumpy spends in The Plainsman getting snockered. Mick will help, but not until you commit."

"Commit?"

"Yeah... how would you like to be a front man?" I didn't answer right off. "Take your time," the sheriff said. "This is a good place for us to be noticed."

"And become the talk of Dempseytown?"

"Dempseytown, huh? I think I like it. Not sure everyone will."

The looker with her looker dog came back up the street, and Bo stretched across Cowan's lap, staring, whimpering. I said, "Bo likes you, Sheriff, and I think you're alright too. We're in. When do I get my badge?" I knew the badge was entirely out of the question.

"Patience, my man. You may get a badge, but not from me." As he pulled away from the curb, Cowan suggested that time spent next door in the Plainsman Bar could be productive, and that his cohort, Mick, would explain why.

The sheriff drove himself back to his office, talking all the way. He said, "We'll get you up to speed, Jack. I asked E J to give you a boost. She'll copy you with my undersheriff's initial write up, my supplemented version, the coroner's report, and the official report from the state investigators. Keep these documents safe and confidential, especially the state report. If you're ever confronted, you can say somebody was careless with the documents. If under oath, you'll need to admit I was the 'somebody'."

I listened, he talked. I was reminded of a movie scene wherein General Patton and two field generals were crowded into a jeep. Patton did the talking, they the listening. He was explaining his plan to win the Battle of the Bulge.

Sheriff Cowan parked my truck alongside his own in the "Employees Only" lot. He said, "Wait here, I'll be back in a minute." To avoid disturbing Bo's nap, I stepped out and circled around to enter Big Red from the driver's side.

Cowan fortuitously returned just as Brubeck closed out "Take Five" on my jazz station. He bent to my open window, handing me a thick manila envelope bound together with masking tape. He said, "Keep these copies safe at all times. When we have this case wrapped up, or we don't, I want them returned."

"The 'Cowan Report,' huh?"

"Correction, Jack. It's the 'No-Name' report."

As I started my engine, Cowan reached with a ticket. He said, "One more thing. This will get you into this afternoon's football game. Mickelby will find you. Latham knows you're coming too. He'll be in a great mood after his kids mop up Cut Bank. Along about 6 o'clock , you can buy him a tall one at the Plainsman. He and Mick will fill you in from there."

"I've got my marching orders, Sheriff; but you didn't tell me how much beer I can drink on my expense account."

"Get outa' here," he said. "You'll be wise to stay sober and alert."

Chapter Thirteen

STING

I wore my camo hunting jacket and a green wool stocking cap, blending in nicely with the football crowd. Not that dress mattered. When I took my seat next to The Mick Mickelby, heads turned. I'd already been "made," as they say in the detective game.

We were seated in the third row directly behind Coach Latham's bench seat. Mick nodded, but kept his eyes on the field. He smiled, though, as if to say, *I'm glad you showed*. But he said nothing right away, nor did I. We sat watching the Shelby Coyotes run pre-game drills.

Finally, Mick broke the ice, speaking in a near whisper, "I've been told you're a studious football buff."

"I am; but that's only partly why I'm here." We shook hands firmly. "Jackson Lindquist," I said. "We never officially met."

"Unofficially, Mr. Lindquist, we know each other quite well, a matter of mutual interest. So, you apparently met with Sheriff Cowan."

"I did. He signed me on this morning, and by extension I assume you and Coach Latham too. Your role I understand, the coach not so much."

"You will. Before the day is over, we'll have a solid plan. We're going to administer the squeeze." I felt his gray eyes on me. He said, "We're tired of the wheels of justice forever mired in mud."

The Mick wore a maroon University of Montana letterman's jacket, complimenting his maroon U of M stocking cap. His thick chest and wide profile indicated he probably lettered in football. He swung his head left and right, same as I, watching the tall Coyote quarterback sling practice passes downfield to scampering receivers. Mick sported a wide smile, "This Lund kid has immense quarterback potential; but before you get any ideas, he's already committed to the Grizzlies." He said that with a twinkle. For has-been athletes, the games never end.

"You've done your research, Mick, on my background with MSU. I'm at a disadvantage. I have no equivalent information on you, only that you wear a Grizzly letter jacket, football according to those little embroidered pigskins."

"Come on in," Coach Latham hollered. While his players gathered, he turned momentarily, spotting Mick and me. Quickly, he turned thumbs up before returning to the business of coaching.

"Yeah." Mick said. "I played three years, middle linebacker. Played alongside Latham as a senior."

"But here you sit with a hated Bobcat, academic variety."

"Naw, I left that stuff behind."

Player captains, co-captains, and officials gathered for the coin toss at mid-field, the Shelby Coyotes represented by their star quarterback, Lund, and Red Hawk, his favorite receiver. Mick said, "Now there's a pair of future Grizzlies. Lund could have signed with any one of a dozen big time programs." Mick looked past me to his right, cautiously—even furtively. He did the same to his left, before reaching into his inside jacket pocket. He pulled out a thin leather wallet, "Keep this in a safe place. I'll explain later."

Excepting football mutterings, and a few macho outbursts, Mick and I never spoke again for the next hour as Shelby piled up the score. They led 28 to 3 at halftime, scoring twice on long passes to Red Hawk. "Hawk" scored another on a wide-out reverse that went for 60 yards.

Mick had to leave at halftime, but not before adding another set of instructions. He said, "Jack, I'm going to miss the second half; my shift begins at 4 o'clock. You need to come in, say about 6 or 6:30. Come with Latham or separately, either way; it doesn't matter. But I want you to sit next to him. He'll call me over for an introduction, and you reach in your pocket and whip out that badge wallet I gave you. Flash the badge. Stump Slimann will be there watching and eavesdropping. He hasn't missed a Saturday night drunk since forever."

"Hold it Mick," I said. "Won't I be impersonating an officer of the law with the badge?"

"Nope. We checked it out." Mick looked straight ahead, voice held low. "You don't ID yourself as a cop. Just let Stump and his sleeze-ball friends see the badge as you flash it in front of me and Latham. When you are free of prying eyes today, check that badge wallet. You'll find a note outlining our strategy."

"So, who's in the know on this?"

"Latham and I, and a certain officer of the law. And then there's you, a guy you'll hardly recognize by the time we have you re-mastered. You're gonna be a big time detective. Think of yourself as a seasoned Chicago dick who busts the mob."

"You're sure we can pull it off? Dempseytowners seem discerning and skeptical."

The Mick spoke in a near whisper, "Not always, Jack. Take Stump Slimann. He's mean enough to strangle puppies; but he's also a loner, doesn't mix with regular folks, out of touch with them. He's an odd duck, but dangerous... has dangerous friends too."

Mick stood to leave, cuffing me on the shoulder. "See you this evening. It'll be interesting, I promise."

The final: Shelby 49, Cut Bank 10. I stayed put, wondering: what's in store for me? Unlike Sherbie, I no longer call the shots.

Opposing players filed past each other in queues: "good game, good game," after which the Shelby players milled in front of their bench, shouting and fist pumping. As they began breaking out to trot for their locker room, Coach Latham handed a note to Red Hawk and pointed to me. "Hawk," hustled over and handed me the note, "Coach says to give you this."

What Coach said in the note was, "Lindquist, 6:30 at the Plainsman. Wait in your truck. I'll find you. We'll talk." I barely knew the man, but liked him. His style was classic staccato Mickey Spillane.

Back at the Glacier, I took a thinking man's shower. I'd perused Max's offering of questionable booty. The lawman's badge was hefty, real. I didn't need to know its official history and wouldn't ask. The badge's accompanying note was written in tiny detailed print, describing how we'd build my personae from appearances, innuendo, and rumor. Shelby, the heart of Toole County, loved rumor, which would be to our advantage.

Wearing Wranglers, a blue denim work shirt, and Lucky replacing my camo bill cap, I would fit with Kerner's demographic of "Western

Rustic," but simply "Saturday Night" according to nearly everybody else.

I arrived at the Plainsman at six fifteen and took a curbside parallel parking space in front of Slimann's office, parking legally, nose to the south. A few minutes into my "Sherbinski stakeout," I caught motion in my rear view. A guy in a muddy short-bed pickup pulled in behind me and parked. He opened his door, stuck a leg out, and with difficulty straightened to a standing position. He braced against his truck... Jonathan (Stump) Slimann, pathetic, impaired, and vulnerable, like a crippled rabbit hunkering before the hungry fox. Yet, I knew better. Cowan and Mick had warned me.

Wobble-legged Stump passed behind my truck and in front his own, finally gaining the sidewalk. He paused for the briefest moment alongside my truck, proving exactly nothing. My Idaho plates would be enough to cause curiosity.

Stump shuffled toward the Plainsman's side-door entrance, where he stopped briefly to toss the stub of a brown papered cigarillo. Aha! "Organic," Joanie had said, and Stump's smoke butt would have fresh organic, DNA organic. As Stump disappeared into the bar, I stepped out and circled his truck, taking phone camera pictures of his truck with its cargo of a mud-encrusted ATV, including special close-ups of his tires. I slipped on my shooting gloves and searched surroundings for curious eyes that would define me as Shelby's weird visitor. None present, so I retrieved Stump's still-smoldering cigarillo, snuffed it, wrapped it in newspaper, and took it to my truck—my ridiculously red stakeout truck. I took my place behind the wheel.

Bo lurped her lips. I said "Hey, this isn't a treat; it could be the back end of evidence." I closed the smoke in my glove box. "We must believe, Bo. Matching DNA may be lying out in the Sweetgrass." Other than a nicely pitched whimper, Bo didn't talk back. I had time and space for creative thinking. "Tomorrow Bo, we'll visit the Sweetgrass and flip a few cow pods before the snows come." Unsatisfied, she locked her seductive brown eyes on me. I said, "Yah, yah. We'll hunt up a grouse along the way."

Mess with detective characters long enough and you'll know just what to do. On stakeouts Sherbie is always alert to his surroundings. Glancing in my passenger side rear view, I see a tall muscular dude wearing a Shelby Coyotes sweatshirt. Coach Latham. Stooping to check me out, he stepped in, and sat. He shook my hand. Good to see you again, Mr. Lindquist. Your card said you are a writer."

"The card exaggerated. Anyway, just call me Jack. Too bad we can't just talk football. This is messy business we're in." Bo licked his hand and he stroked her head. "You remember my assistant, Bo." Dan smiled at me with an athlete's game face, the deadly serious mission before us be damned.

He chuckled, "When you came to my practice, I suspected you'd come to poach one of my future Grizzlies. The Mick straightened me out."

Latham was square necked and square jawed. No ball cap. Immaculate blond crew cut. Clean, new looking sweatshirt, un-faded Wranglers... dressed perfectly for small town Saturday night. Latham had yet to be adjusted by marriage. I would bet on it.

"Congratulations, Coach," I said. "I've never seen a high school team with better skill sets, especially in the passing game."

"Well, these are rare kids. I came along at the perfect time. They deserve my best." He sobered when he said that.

"Appears that it's happening—your best, I mean."

"I appreciate your observation; but last year I let them down... should have been more alert, more of a father shark, so to speak. Sorry, you can't know what the hell I'm talking about. It has to do with the reason we are here."

"You can fill me in, Dan. We have time. Our suspect went in only 5 minutes ago. He'll get himself blitzed, Mick says, at which time he may become careless. Am I on the right track?"

"Yes, as far as you went. There's more."

I reached under my seat and pulled out my steno pad. Dan stared, wide-eyed, apparently smitten by his first foray into crime fighting. He began talking, as if baring his soul, surprisingly vulnerable for a former collegiate linebacker expected to be stout of heart.

Dan spoke like he'd rehearsed his presentation, delivering economical sentences, chronologically arranged, no theorizing, as if he knew for certain the killer's mind.

I learned that Dan had taken his coaching job three years back. The previous coach, also a former Grizzly, moved up to a bigger program in Helena. He'd been frank with Latham about a couple players, "good kids," caught messing with marijuana. One, Johnny Red Hawk, was the older brother of Latham's current co-captain, the popular and talented receiver called "Hawk," the quicksilver kid with sticky hands.

"Mickelby says Jimmy Red Hawk and your quarterback have scholarships," I said.

"Yes they do. Mick and I aren't going to allow drugged up lizards to mess with them." I sensed where Dan was going. I gave him room.

"The season before last I put Hawk's older brother, Johnny, and his halfback buddy on probation on day one. They hadn't settled with the judge on drug possession charges, needed to complete community services. Between the judge and me and the boy's family, our halfback never strayed again. He's a back-up tailback for the Grizzlies right now. But Johnny Red Hawk didn't cooperate. His probation required him to report to Sheriff Cowan. And Cowan believed Johnny could give us details to nail the dope dealer, how he approached kids and where he delivered."

"And the scumbag dealer turned out to be Stump Slimann?"

"Right. But he's a small time chump. Stump works for a dangerous dude, part of a ring that DEA says imports hard drugs and high potency marijuana. Worked Havre and Great Falls at first; but then they branched out to the Reservation and small towns, too. "

"Including Shelby, right? Dan, I'm in my second week now, sliding around this mud-hole. And from day one the name Slimann has been bantered about. I'm all in, but I need to know the essentials."

"That's why I'm here," Dan said. "And the critical details are straightforward. I remember exactly the summation your friend Doctor Kerner made while Sheriff Cowan had him on the speakerphone."

"Dan, I'm not surprised that Kerner would be digging for details; lay it on me."

"Well, Mick and I were sitting with Sheriff Cowan in his office. He advised us to take Professor Kerner seriously, and to illustrate the fact he dialed the professor's number. Cowan says, 'Just listen in and you'll learn about his mother-lode of research covering all tangents of the Charles Larigan case.' Cowan put his conversation with Professor Kerner on the speakerphone. Boy, he can talk."

"Ha, don't I know it!" I said. "So what did you learn?"

"I'll have to fill you in later. Dr. Kerner went into exhaustive detail, how he found official sources, off the record stuff, and some very unofficial sources. Then he boiled it all down to one thing. He said, 'There's a single suspect of local residence. It is son number two, Jonathan.' Mick and I know him as Stump. Hell, even his brother calls him 'Stump.'"

"I've got a pretty good fix on Stump too," I said. "So what about the rest of his rat pack?"

"Sure. I made notes and converted them to memory. You know Dr. Kerner well. He strikes me as brilliant, with a storehouse of details and a big vocabulary. He said, 'Bennett Slimann and his oldest son, Marcus, are aggressively avaricious'—I looked up the meaning. To quote Dr. Kerner, 'they are cunning and calculating, too smart to resort to personally dealing drugs or committing violence.'"

"So leave Bennett and Marcus aside?"

"For now. They had no overriding motive. Sheriff Cowan and The Mick say Daddy Sly and favorite son number one made a small fortune settling dubious personal injury claims and buying underpriced mineral rights from naïve widows. They're currently in North Dakota scamming new suckers."

"So, we focus on Stump. His motive was... ?"

"Motives, plural—settling scores with Charlie Larigan. Charlie caught him with a dressed out yearling L Bar L Aberdeen Angus in the back of his truck. And Stump rides that damnable ATV willy-nilly, tearing up the countryside, public land where the Larigans have grazing rights. The final straw was Charlie catching him in the act of cutting a fence. He held him at gunpoint. Stump was transporting a stash of marijuana harvested from a plot over on the backside of West Butte. Charlie turned him in to the sheriff, who brought in DEA. He'd have gone to the big house if not for Daddy Slimann's lawyering."

"But despite motive, nobody had evidence to bring Stump in when Charlie died, right?"

"Right. Cowan was not able to question him as a suspect, but simply because the Slimanns were neighbors who might have seen something suspicious. Stump claimed he was staying in a line shack near the Canadian line when Charlie died, and he 'heard it was an accident.' Of course, in that remote area, nobody saw Stump to confirm his where-abouts."

"So, with no evidence, how can the sheriff close on him?"

Dan rubbed his hands together, "That's where we come in, Jack. Rather that's where *you* come in. We'll convince him that you *do* have evidence."

"And I'll be a threat?"

Dan grinned, "We certainly hope so. He may get nervous and do something stupid. So what do you think?"

The idea was crazy, but irresistible. "I think we'll go for it," I said. "But I'm curious, Dan—you seem to be driving hard on this. Why?"

"The Red Hawk boys. I'm coaching the young one, Jimmy, right now. Great kid. But two years ago I coached Johnny, a senior. He was first team All-State as a junior. In mid-season Johnny was acting mopey. A team-mate came to me, said Johnny was smoking dope. Well, you know the score. The kid put me and his team in an impossible position. What could I do? I never had to face a problem like that. And I never had any training or experience with drug usage. So I tried to get him to open up—offered a bargain: only a two week team suspension if he'd help the sheriff nail the dealer. The counselors talked with him too. We got nowhere. He quit football, and a month later Sheriff Cowan had enough to bring him in for questioning. DEA was there waiting. They had Johnny on tape trying to sell dope to an undercover agent. The Feds are serious about nailing the Montana dealers, because their pipeline is connected to an international cartel. A lot of product ends up on the Reservation."

"And Johnny Red Hawk is a tragic example."

"Yes, and nobody suspected he was in such serious trouble. That includes me. Strange, isn't it? He was a model of sportsmanship on the football field, always a team player, helping opposing players to their feet and so forth. Dope messed with his head, the way I see it."

"What a waste! So what about Stump?"

"Johnny testified Stump could have been a supplier, but 'maybe not,' claiming it was 'always dark' at the drop off. Stump's old man—his attorney—successfully shielded Stump from testifying... technicalities and diversions galore. Stump got away clean. Johnny is serving a two year term in the Deer Lodge pen instead of moving up in life with a college scholarship."

"And justice says Stump needs to pay a price."

"We're going to see that happens. The Larigans deserve a resolution. And this town needs a good clean-up and disinfection."

"Then let's go in there and go to work," I said.

Dan reached to shake my hand, "That's the plan, Jack. A little show and tell."

With Dan leading, we entered the side door of the Plainsman saloon. We passed behind Stump and chose bar stools, but separated by five empty stools from him and his cohorts, two guys sporting narrow brimmed hats and long black leather jackets that came down over their butts. May as well wear a sign: "Not From Around Here." On Stump's left sat a bullish guy with muscle on top of muscle. He had an uneven black beard, looked like it had been cut with dull scissors. His greasy black hair spilled over his ears. The other guy was puny with a skinny face and bony shoulders. All three had hard drinks in tall glasses, dark amber, no ice. The big guy wore thick, heavy rings on three middle fingers—both hands—probably as effective as brass knuckles.

The Mick casually nodded at us, as if strangers. He served another customer first, taking his time before sauntering our way. Dan and I ordered Hi-Liner Drafts—amber, lots of foam. We sat waiting, without talking. Mick came with the beers, at which point I dropped a twenty on the counter along with my orphaned wallet badge. "What's this?" Mick said. He stepped back under the bar lights and flipped open the leather flap, pretending to scrutinize the badge.

The three rats turned, watching with hardened eyes. I studied them purposely, and they stared back. Stump tapped the gorilla's forearm, mumbling something unintelligible.

I flashed Mick a left-eyed wink. Leaning toward him, I spoke loudly, "Mister, I'm looking for a fella named Slimann. The guy walks with a gimp, goes by the name of 'Stump.'" Mick's bar patrons were beehive buzzing over a loud broadcast of TV rodeo, so I wasn't sure our marks heard. No matter. What mattered was how Mick turned and looked directly at Stump, nodding, "That's him."

Stump half-turned on his stool, fumbling, preparing to stand; but the little weasel guy grabbed him by the forearm, holding him in place.

The trio hunkered, heads together, like twittering rats.

I stood, took two steps to my right toward the rat trio. Mick leaned over the bar, and I did the same from my side. He pushed the wallet across the bar to me—opened to show off the badge. We faked a whispered conference, apparently convincingly, because the scummers stood as one and thumped out the side door. They left no tip.

Mick untied his apron and nodded to his assistant, "She's all yours, Peggy." He signaled, and we three connivers moved to a small table in a back corner.

"What happens now?" I said.

Mick waited until his beer jockey left ... "It's up to Sheriff Cowan and his retired lieutenant, Juniper Jones. He's a clever old codger. Cowan re-deputized him. Junie's out there right now, tailing those three weasels."

"So, Mick, how do you see this playing out," I said.

The Mick nodded, "I'll go along with Cowan's assessment. He says the cartel's enforcers could rid themselves of Stump, or they could scare hell out of him. In that case he might try to run or come to the law for protection."

"So, my job is done?"

"I wish," Dan said. "You'll need to have a presence for two or three more days to convince them you are real. Hopefully, they'll assume you are DEA or a state investigator before a gang honcho does research on you."

"Meanwhile, stay alert," Mick said. "You're a shotgunner, Cowan says."

"Close range, big target. I won't miss."

"Yeah, I'd like your chances."

"You mean if one of those dirt bags come looking for me?"

"Or all three," Dan said.

Mick spoke with authority, like a lawman, "Go nowhere alone. Bolt your motel door and keep your ears open."

"I'm not worried. My Labrador is better than any alarm system. Besides, "I'll bring my Winchester 12 into the Glacier Motel tonight. And Bo, she's with me every night anyway."

"Good," Mick said. "But, as a precaution, I'll ask Cowan's deputy to swing by the Glacier a few times tonight. He drives a white crew-cab Chevy, though it won't show much white through the mud. Now tomorrow, we'll meet here again, around six o'clock. I'd bet the farm those dopers come back. They need to keep track of their enemies."

"And we need to keep track of them."

Mick chuckled, "According to plan, they'll be tracking you... with Cowan and Jones right behind them."

"So, anyone know who they are?" I said. "The drug pushers," I mean.

"The DEA boys informed Cowan, but only a shorthand account," Mick said. "The big guy is called 'T-Bone' on account of that ugly scar on his forehead. They're not saying about the little shifty one, except that he has a long record and even served time in Canada, and they seldom jail anybody up there. Cowan and I want 'em gone. So do the tribal officials. Stump and his scumbag friends apparently feed the dope pipeline to the Reservation. Cowan believes they bring the stuff across the Alberta border, easy to do in that remote part of the world."

"Not too much longer now," Dan said, "and they'll make a mistake. "I can feel it."

Within a spell of silence, three guys needed relief from the scourge of low-life crime. The Mick hailed his assistant, "Peggy, a pitcher of High Line Thunder over here, please."

Mick did the pouring. He raised his glass and we three clinked and guzzled. Mick exhaled vigorously and nodded at me, "So Jack, you write crime fiction. Do you see this story ending well?"

"I'm the wrong one to ask, Mick," I said. My wife says I do decent pulp fiction, life not so much. Anyway, for my part, I'm relieved. We've got you guys, Cowan, the state cops, and DEA on the case. I'm takin' tomorrow off."

Dan was taken aback, "And Sheriff Cowan is informed of this? You must know he's worried for your safety. He'll want to know your whereabouts."

"Yeah, I agree," Mick said. "Maybe just start with Dan and me. 'A day off.' Meaning what?"

"Bo and I are going hunting."... That's all I admitted to. I couldn't stomach overblown promises about super detecting with DNA technology, which I know almost nothing about. Worse, I couldn't rest my detecting reputation on a longshot called "the shit print." True, Bo and

I were headed to the Sweetgrass to hunt. But, like a politician, I'd omitted the important part, exercising a lie of omission. Bo and I would hunt, yes—hunt for clues to a homicide.

You better turn in early, ego said to id; *you may need to star in this show.* With a badge comes responsibility. I said goodnight to Mick and Dan and headed to my bunker in the Glacier Motel.

Bo and my Winchester 12 came in to spend the night. I went to bed with Cowan's amalgamated lawmen's report. Oops, I mean the "No-Name" report.

No-Name turned out to be a snoozer. In fact, that's what I was doing—snoozing—when around midnight the report fell out of my hands. A short time later, Bo growled a warning. Car headlights flashed through the curtain. I heard the driver's engine idling, maybe a deputy, maybe a thug. I reached down next to Bo and put my hand on Winchester's stock. She held two in the magazine, one in the barrel—three inch magnums, 5-chill. Should the guy bust through the door, I'd probably take out his knees... minimum, all depends. Chilling seconds passed. I'd never pointed a loaded gun at anybody; but I know the sort of bloody mayhem a shotgun accomplishes at a range of 10 or 12 feet.

Sneaking to the window, I scootched the curtain aside. My backup, Bo, sustained a continuous rumbling growl. I saw a man shadow sitting behind the wheel of a dark sedan, so I grabbed Winchester and took a seat in a hardback chair facing the door. Fortunately, a minute later the midnight mystery car pulled out. I rewarded Bo with a premium dog chew and myself with two fingers of Johnny Walker.

7 A.M. – Pumper Café.
Short night, short sleep, but the morning Pumper felt okay. No longer do gangsters carry tommy guns and murder their enemies in barbershops and cafes.

I took a little booth for privacy, feeling sluggish... a lot of bleary in me. I waited for my third cup of crow-black coffee before beginning another speed-read of the "No-Name report." It hadn't improved overnight. Written in official-eze, No-Name identified no suspects, specific leads, or strategies, though it was rich in details of what hadn't been discovered.

While waiting for The Pumper's famous "Gusher special"—a month's supply of cholesterol embedded in biscuits, sausage, and gravy—I stepped outside and called Joanie. She was filling in for a colleague, teaching a graduate level class in histology. "I have ten minutes," she said. "I have them taking a quiz."

Joanie listened to my brief synopsis of our new plan followed by silence, meaning, *Jack, why don't you stay on track for more than one day?*

The Pumper cook could re-heat my "Gusher." I climbed into Big Red to finish something more important, putting Joanie at ease.

My most professional presentation garnered maybe a C-minus. She said, "You may pull it off, Jack, but keep someone with you."

"No worries, Joanie. We're working as a team."

"We?"

"Yes, Bo and I."

"Wonderful—you and an innocent hunting dog practicing on-the-job training for law enforcement." I aimed to protest, but she cut me off: "Hold on, Sherlock. You force me to break my rule of classroom punctuality. I'll be back on in three minutes. Don't hang up."

I nudged the volume on my radio to better hear Pancho Sanchez. He thundered toward his finale as Joanie returned to her telephone.

Her bright voice had improved, "I have my students toiling away, Jack. Are you prepared to toil away?"

"Absolutely. Bo and I in the incredible Sweetgrass country. Wish you were here to enjoy it. But meantime, you have nothing to worry about."

"Well, maybe that's my problem—the nothingness. You forget. You've shared the substance of your mission. So, you cannot obfuscate danger into nothingness."

"Listen to you, Joanie my love. You've obviously been talking with Kerner, a master complicator. He can't be here, so he channels his drama through you. Just remember, I'm cagey and smart. I have a dog and a gun and I'm going into the Sweet Grass Hills where I'll see the bad guys coming from miles away. Can you see Kaniksu grizzlies coming from miles away?... I didn't think so."

"Jack, you know Grizzly ferocity is highly exaggerated."

"I'll grant you that; but let's talk about you. Being a modern woman, you refuse to subscribe to the story line borne by old novels, wherein all the hard stuff, save childbirth, is shouldered by the macho man. And you're jealous because you can't be here to prove the premise wrong."

"Nice try, Jackson; but changing the subject won't work. So why can't you go with your full team?"

"Because they have real jobs. Bo and I are on a bird hunting vacation."

Joanie didn't answer, which—knowing her—was *the* answer. She opposed my solo Sweetgrass excursion. I waited. Finally she said, "Promise you'll call me?"

"You'll have a full report in triplicate," I teased.

"You're impossible, Jack. Why do I love you?"

"The mystery of the century," I said. "Even better than the puzzle I'm working on."

I signed off with a pair of audible kisses. She answered with three of her own and a promise: "Rusty, you need a tune-up."

Chapter Fourteen

STINGERS

On the morn of September 27, rejuvenated—belly full and cheerful-ly optimistic—I pulled out of the Pumper's parking lot and headed north toward Sunburst. Clear skies, 26 degrees. I marveled at the snow topped Sweet Grass Hills poking from the distant prairies. I was bound for the Larigan ranch home to meet Chet Forster, and from there journey into the high country to pursue a couple of hunches. Or, was I on vacation from reality?

On bird alert, Bo danced repeatedly from my side across to the pas-senger window, interrupted by intermittent stare downs: "Boss, when will you stop to hunt?"

As before, the narrow blacktop east of Sunburst was pleasantly empty. Ahead, the highlands rose majestically and peaceably, an incon-gruous setting for a homicide.

Our first stop came at the end of 20 slow miles. On a knoll above a dry coulee sat a two story log ranch home presiding over a log barn and a maze of corrals. The Larigans' highlands grazing operation, without modern trappings, had apparently changed little from "Old West" tra-ditions.

Just as I stepped on the porch, Chet opened the door, "Howdy. Jack Lindquist, I'll bet." He extended a leathered hand, blue eyes a-flashing, "Chet McCrary. I been expecting ya'. Sheriff Cowan said you'd be com-in' out."

I chuckled, making light of it, "The sheriff likes to keep tabs on me."

"Well, come on in why don't-cha? I got fresh coffee."

Chet was 60ish, wide shouldered, narrow hips, like a bulldogger.

And energetic, with parts that needed movement, he shifted from one foot to the other. Without his Stetson, his face was classical ranger rider's two toned—white forehead above a weathered face—a "deer jerky face," my gramp would say.

I trooped behind him through a darkened, old timey living room with bulky stuffed furniture and a grandfather clock, on into a well-lighted kitchen with 1960's appliances. Chet pulled out a kitchen table chair for me, "Pay no mind to the mess. My missus only comes for long weekends now since hirin' on with the county clerk."

We sat at a round, red-checkered oilcloth table, dunking sugared doughnuts in thick-creamed coffee. Chet 's black and white heeler dog lay on his belly between his chair and mine. Naturally, I smiled at the heeler, since I naturally admire cow dogs. Chet was pleased. "He answers to 'Fred.' He's crazy for lady dogs like the yellow one sittin' in yer rig."

"Could make for interesting pups—hunter-heelers."

Chet set his coffee cup, "I seen ya' last time ya' came out. "You was comin' off Yucca Ridge. I was ridin' the same fence-line that had yer interest up there. I stayed back in the ponderosas 'till you turned tail down the ridge. Then I knew you was the fella' Sheriff Cowan said was comin' out. 'Cept I was sorry to be too late to ketch up an' say howdy."

I laughed, "Chet, if you're hinting at an apology, forget it. Since I set foot in Toole County, practically everybody's been a step ahead of me. Folks know my whereabouts before I do."

Chet refilled our mugs. "I'm thinkin' you want my take on Charlie's supposed axe-dint."

Chet began his accounting, sparse and bare-boned. He'd taken charge of the Sweetgrass Ranch in August of '08 two months after Charlie's death. Chet's knowledge of facts and particulars came to him second hand... except for one thing. He said, "The one thing I know fer sure is the 'Canadian Trail.' Know what I'm talkin' bout?"

"Vaguely."

"Come on, we'll talk about it on the way."

Chet ambled out his back door with his heeler and me in tow. We gathered next to a saddled gelding. Chet's leather thong chin-cinch secured his black domed horseman's hat against the Sweetgrass's feisty winds.

A nice touch. He rested his backside against his buckskin's front quarters and thumbed over his shoulder, east—in the general direction of the cone buttes of the Sweet Grass Hills, "Did they tell you about the marijuana farm up there? BLM rehabbed the ground, you know. Too bad the law couldn't jail the scumbag caretaker. He might have spilled the beans on his bosses."

"He might yet," I said. "I presume you're talking about Jonathan Slimann."

"Yup. Don't matter what people learn about 'em. The Slimanns skitter free."

"So far," I said.

Chet confirmed my Slimann assumption and added more. Busted marijuana farms, like the one on the mountain northwest of Syringa and the one in the Sweet Grass seldom lead to convictions. They're operated by small time druggies who are poor farmers, but quick evacuators, leaving public land officials to clean up their messes. Except, in this case, the mountain marijuana garden was but one tentacle of a family's nefarious dealings.

Chet nodded and swung smoothly into his saddle. "Gotta check on some fences. A couple weeks back I found another break north of the stock pond. Cut wire, four wheeler tracks—the makin's of that scissorbill Slimann. Like I tol' the sheriff, it's only 15 miles to Canada from there. You might wanna' check it out." As his anxious horse danced, Chet added a parting comment, "I see ya' got a gun an' a gun dog. You might want to kill a few prairie chickens up there. You got my permission."

I saluted him, "You're a gentleman, Chet."

Like a modern Tom Mix, Chet whirled his horse and they loped away, with Fred running alongside.

Bo and I found grouse "up there" only half-way to the crest of Yucca Ridge. She pinned a covey in buffalo berry by wisely circling to keep them from blasting out the back side. The birds were forced to lift out vertically, and I dumped three for three. Perfect, one for lunch and a pair for Chet.

I spread a tarp under a giant juniper and lit the hibachi. Coffee went on first, then—while sipping it—I slow-roasted a sharptail slathered with cherry chipotle. While waiting, I scanned Sheriff Cowan's packet of papers, *noting* little noteworthy (Kerner would laugh cynically), until the word "Canada" practically jumped from the first of four pages, about an emerging investigation regarding Canada and drugs. Heroin, cocaine, and high potency marijuana imported into Vancouver, from there east to, as yet, unknown destinations. Chet's supposition about Stump and a "Canadian Trail" was becoming credible.

From the end of the road we hiked through an inch of snow up the trail of eroded ATV tracks. Just before noon, I sighted the knurled dead snag by the fence corner, the crime scene—possibility of an accident no longer tenable.

A soft breeze wafted through the easterly ponderosas, carrying a drift of falling frost, like a million sun sparkled diamonds, a rare ethereal scene. Briefly, I thought, *leave this be. Justice is out of our hands, and we can't bring Charlie back.*

Putting cowardly thoughts aside, I shifted gears. If Charlie was murdered, the evil-doer must pay. I would do what I could, pursuing a longshot: the shit print theory...

The first part was easy, locating the circular snow covered mounds. I broke off a stick of dead juniper for a poker. Sure enough, with a little practice I learned to quickly lever and flip the dried pods.

Walking from the flat rock where I first viewed the place of Charlie's demise—a distance of about 25 paces—I flipped a dozen cow pies, some soft and fragile, of recent vintage. Others, firm and atrophied, could have been dropped a year ago, soon after Charlie's gunshot death.

Onward I searched, finding a perfect deer hoof imprint on the underside of a cow pod, but no signs of tire prints. Doubt settled in about Pearl's pearl of wisdom and my longshot hope. Nevertheless, I expanded my vision of the crime scene, walking a wider circle. Bo seemed to be catching on, snuffling and nosing in the snow. But our inspections revealed only ordinary grass and pebble imprints.

"Bo, it's time for self-counseling." She stopped with me, and came to plop her fanny on my boots. Speaking loudly for emphasis, I said: *"Remember, Lindquist, nothing you do in crime investigation is silly. A hunch is worthy. You gotta believe.* Bo stretched her neck, brown eyes staring me down. I patted her head, "Here we are, Bo, talking to the Sweet Grass Hills."

In the fence corner where Charlie had fallen, I stood contemplating, searching for ideas. "North," Chet had said—a possible trail from the north could have been used to bring packaged dope those last few miles from the Alberta border. "Bring your sniffer, Bo," I said. "We're not done."

We started west along the fence line, hence turning north where the fence curled around a rock outcrop. Checked a dozen cow pies in a short distance, one with a curious imprint along its very edge. It could have been made by the cow crapping on a stick. I carefully hand-whisked the snow, finding no stick, but possibly the very edge of a tire print—encouraging; but we needed a full, clear print to match the suspect's ATV print.

Almost frantically, I hurried to flip more snow covered cow pies. Bo had the fever too, thinking we had a game going. I lost count, but had no rational reason for counting anyway. I'm guessing it was about cow turd number 30 where we hit pay-dirt.

When I flipped the dried dung pod, Bo jumped after it, alert, as if she knew, and *yes*—plain as can be—a perfect tire print covered the entire underside of the specimen. "Yahoo," I hollered, and my cheer echoed from the steep incline of West Butte. I snapped a close-up with my mini camera, wrapped the treasure in burlap, and stowed it in my backpack.

Since Chet's advice, "north," had paid off, we hiked a mile further north where the ridge gentled to a plateau. A low dam blocked a swale, creating a half-acre pond of mostly ice-coated water. A half dozen mallards lifted from a nook of open water, apparently kept warm by a spring. Maybe I could spot trout? I had no other reason to proceed except my compelling success playing Pearl's hunch. Go with the gut, I decided.

Springwater trickled from a pile of rock rubble, apparently waste rock left from pond excavation. Bo climbed into the rubble, tail wagging, snuffling. It was too cold for rattlers, so I let her go. Oddly, she began digging in the rock. "Okay Bo," I said. "Hunches are working today. Let's see what you've found." I helped roll away the bigger rocks while she scratched and snuffled. Abruptly, she plowed her nose in and emerged with a dirt encrusted red strap. "Drop, Bo," I said, and she delivered her prize to my hand—dirty and worn, but definitely a red fabric dog collar. My inspection confirmed suspicion. The collar's dog tag was inscribed: "Ginger," and "C. Larigan" followed by a phone number. Though wearing fall wool, I shivered.

Stunned and saddened, I sat on a rock, arm around Bo. But she wasn't finished. She went back to sniffing and scratching. Out came loose blond hair. I pulled Bo back and looked closer, finding hide and bones. Ginger had been buried... and murdered like her master.

Now I regretted coming to a crime scene without a lawman witness. I folded Ginger's dog collar into my bandana and knelt for a last look into her grave. Bo, sat with her hip against my leg, looking at me as if to say, "What now boss?"

Again, persistent Bo poked her nose into the rocks, snuffling. She had something more. I lifted her chin and there lay an inch of brown papered cigarillo, mostly disintegrated, but recognizable. "Organic," as Joanie would say. I pinched it in a piece of toilet paper and stowed it in my backpack with the dog collar and cow pod. Bingo! Stump was on record, claiming he hadn't set foot on Yucca Ridge since his confrontation with Charlie Larigan two years ago. I'd be willing to place money on forensic verification of Stump's ATV tire print.

In an easy lope, Bo and I took off down Yucca Ridge. I'd seen a reflection of sunlight from glass on the slope of West Butte. I remembered my ridiculous assertion: "Joanie, I'll have a shotgun for defense, and from my high vantage on Yucca Ridge the bad guys can't sneak on me." That was gross exaggeration. I'd be an easy target for a high powered rifle with telescopic sights. Quickly, Bo and I dropped into a coulee and below line of sight from the heights of West Butte.

I paused to survey the terrain before descending the draw. Dammit! Another vehicle was parked below in the swale next to Big Red. I grabbed my mini-binoculars from a backpack pocket. Aha! A quick focus confirmed a comforting scene—Sheriff Cowan perching on his pickup tailgate looking at me through his own binoculars. We hurried down the hill to join him.

Before I came within speaking distance, Cowan climbed into his truck and started away, driving in a crawl. He beckoned me to follow. Appropriately, he never left granny gear over those 5 or 6 miles to the

Larigan homestead. A thinking man: the harder the puzzle, the slower his speed.

We found Chet's buckskin still saddled and hitched by the front yard gate. Chet sat on his porch in a rocker. He didn't wait for a porch conference, but strolled out to meet us with Fred at his heel. Cowan stepped out to greet them. So did I.

Nobody announces a toe-digging driveway conference. It surfaces out of tradition, spurred on by convenience: high-level business in a gravely driveway, all accompanied by clucking chickens, bawling mother cows, and Chet's horse sweat cologne flavoring the air.

Sheriff Cowan began, "Chet, you have a serious problem with your neighbor. He crossed swords with Charlie Larigan, as you know. I'm convinced he's increasingly unstable and dangerous. You'll want to avoid him. If it was me I'd keep a weapon handy."

"Stump, you mean. I seldom see him, Sheriff. He must be mostly bunking in town, 'cuz I rarely see his rig at the Slimann Ranch. Don't know why he comes out. Sly sold off their herd two years ago."

"Well Stump was there today." Cowan nodded and pointed to the south fork of Nine Mile Road. "He came past your gate early this morning, drove over to the old Slimann place and unloaded his ATV, went out the back gate and up the trail toward West Butte."

Chet dug gravel with a worn boot toe, "Suppose he went across the border for another drug shipment?"

Cowan eyed Chet quizzically, "How do you know about that?"

"Common knowledge, Sheriff. Ask anybody out in this corner of the county. The marijuana farm was only a sideline. I hear their marijuana crop had some sort of blight when the Feds raided it."

"Interesting," Cowan said. "Anything else newsworthy out here?"

Chet dug more toe gravel. He said, "If you call rumors news, there's a bumper crop. But no, I get everything third or fourth hand. Most of it goes in one ear and out the other." Chet looked at me and grinned. "I did hang onto a piece of news about Jack here."

"Care to share it?" Cowan said.

"Sure. Yesterday I stopped by the Silver Dollar in Sunburst. They were yacking about Jack bein' a Federal lawman. I knew better, but kept my nose out of it."

The sheriff grinned, "Perfect, Chet. You're a good man. You proved that our strategy is working. We need extra eyes and ears out here, unofficially, of course. I don't mean to be pushy, Chet; but you could help me with a logistical problem."

Chet gestured toward the snow-capped cones of the Sweetgrass, "You mean watching who comes and goes up there?"

"Mainly. I have a deputy covering the back side. On the Yucca Ridge side, though—if you could check on my trail cam, I'd appreciate it. We need to know who's using the trails."

"Not a problem sheriff. I cover the high country once a week, more if necessary. Lemme put Copper up. Then we'll sit down in my kitchen. I'll brew a pot a coffee." He looked at his watch. "Scratch that. We'll have a beer."

The sheriff, being "Sheriff" refused a beer. Chet refused to drink alone. So did I. We qualified as a pair. He confirmed my assumptions—country smart, and ready to help. He and the sheriff poured over a map on his kitchen table while I eavesdropped. The map was marked with blue ink trails and notes on its borders. Cowan pointed out landmarks, beginning with the joining of two trails a mile south of the Alberta border. "My trail cam is here at the forks, hidden in the crotch of a juniper."

"Small world, Sheriff," Chet said. "I've been there many times... good place to shade up for lunch."

"Somehow, I'm not surprised." Cowan stood and pushed his chair back, "We'll get outa' your hair, Chet; but one more thing: You should expect visits and interviews from DEA and Montana Special Investigations gathering information on the Canadian drug connection.

"Not a problem, Sheriff; but I've gotta be honest. "So you send Stump up on a drug conviction. Great; but how does that square up with Charlie?"

"It can't," Cowan said. He lowered his eyes on me. "That part is up to Jack here. And I promise, you'll know every particular when the deed is done." What? I'd never heard Sheriff Cowan embellish. Why now? And what deed? Beat the truth out of Stump Slimann?

As we stepped off his porch, Cowan added a warning: "Chet, leave your lights on and your doors locked. Crazy Stump will be in a rage knowing you let Jack come through your property again. Jack and I are headed to his place now, keepin' tabs on him.'"

"Keep the beer cold," I said.

I pulled out behind the sheriff as he'd requested. Three miles south on Nine Mile Road he pulled over next to an oversized mail box lettered "B. Slimann." A narrow lane to the east led to the Slimann's paint-peeled two story ranch home tucked into a grove of cottonwoods. A broken limb lay unattended on the damaged porch roof.

Stump's truck and ATV were parked at the side of the house. He'd left his driver's side truck door open.

Cowan stepped out of his truck with his laptop, came around to Bo's side and got in. "Nice girl," he said, stroking her head top. "Jack, we need to visit some."

"I was about to suggest the same," I said. "First, why are we sitting in plain sight of our suspect?"

"Pressure, Jack. I'd like him to blow his cork, show his guilt before his old man shows up. My source says Sly will finish his case in North Dakota in a few days. He'll return and cover Stump in his version of lawyered custody. "

"So what is this 'deed' I'm about to do?"

"He fears you Jack. Believes you're a high level cop, just as we planned. He got drunk and blabbered all over The Mick's saloon, blames you for the arrest of his pusher bosses."

"T-Bone, you mean?—and his weasely side-kick?"

"Yup. The Hill County sheriff is holding them in Havre. They both broke parole. The Feds are coming for them."

"Will they come for Stump?"

"Nah. He's low-level. They'll leave him for us locals. Suits me fine. I want him for a bigger rap—capital murder. So do you."

A curtain parted in a front window. "He's watching us, Sheriff," I said. "What kind of weapons does he own?"

"No long guns, if that's your worry. My unofficial deputy performed an unofficial inspection when he escorted him home with a DUI. Something else you should know. I'm told my, uh, assistant's Ford truck carries a coded GPS tracker and a signal emitter. His ATV is wired too." Cowan winked, "How that happened is a mystery to me. Not important." He opened his laptop. "If my battery has juice, I'll show you where old Stumpy went today."

I watched over Cowan's shoulder as he narrated, energized as if he'd found gold: "Jones is 77, but can still cover the back country a-horse-back. He tailed Stump today... to the top of West Butte and back."

"Jones? Would that be Juniper Jones by any chance?"

Cowan turned to glare at me. "And how would you know? He's supposed to be working undercover."

"The day we first met, your office deputy, E J, gave him away. Juniper Jones, the name goes in the ear and registers." Cowan's sour-puss look was sufficient to indict both E J Burns and me. "I wouldn't blame her, Sheriff," I said. "I flustered her, tricked her into talking. I'm good at that."

Cowan softened, "Okay, okay, let's keep Junie Jones undercover. He's important; and he'd work for free if I let him. He's developed a unique style of backcountry surveillance aboard the world's best electronically equipped horse."

"And he sends info to your laptop, right?"

Cowan laughed, "I had Junie on my satellite phone when you were messing around on Yucca Ridge. His saddle horn emitter boosted the signal."

Sheriff Cowan adjusted his laptop to favor me. He narrated the show while I watched, fascinated by Juniper Jones' marriage of technology and horsemanship. Tiny bright icons scurried upon a backlit terrain augmented by topographical features, including green contour lines and subscripted landmarks. Cowan waved across the screen: "This view includes the players in the Sweet Grass Hills today, all three of you. If you stopped to pee, I guarantee Junie Jones recorded the event."

"Updated from 1984, huh? Damn, talk about 'Big Brother.'"

The sheriff blasted on: "We'll zoom in now, on the segment where Stump watched you and this pup of yours digging like badgers. Junie observed everything through his 30 power telescope. His long lens video recorded you recovering something. So now you can tell me what in hell you discovered. In fact, you can show me what you stowed in your backpack. Here, watch this"—

A small font digital clock in the corner of the screen ticked off seconds while two lighted icons—a crude canine and a slow motioned man went about their business. Meanwhile, Stump's icon—an irregular black blob—sat motionless on the second contour below the summit of

West Butte. The fourth icon was a stick-man rider and horse profiled at the summit. "Which is Mario and which is Pac-Man," I said.

"You're 20 years behind, Jack," Cowan laughed. "Without Junie Jones up there, I might have worried for you. On second thought, I am worried for you."

"Any particular reason?"

"You tell me. Junie's movie shows you and your sidekick poking around a knob on the shore of Larigan's stock pond. Look here, you can see yourself in action."

"I saw the curtain move again, Sheriff. Stump is edgy."

"You're right, Jack. Let's head back to town and let Junie cover Stump's movement. Junie's up the hill, watching from an aspen grove. Cowan checked his watch, "You and I, Jack... we'll meet at my office where you can show me what sort of treasure you stowed in your backpack. Let's say 6:30."

Next stop: the Toole County Sheriff's Office for a "debriefing." The sheriff forgot to mention that Deputy Burns would sit in. She brought a video recorder and joined us in Cowan's office. "E J, shut the door please," he said.

Cowan plopped in his fake leather office chair and tilted back, hands clasped behind his head. Speaking as if boss to underling, he said, "Jack, you're in over your amateur head. That's my fault. I think it's best to grab what evidence you have and sideline you for your own safety. So, I've asked E J to film this session. You good with that?"

"I have nothing to hide, Sheriff."

"Great, then you won't mind telling us everything you know. You're foray up on Yucca Ridge may someday be instrumental as prosecutorial evidence. "Just a hunch, that's all."

"Nothing would please me more, Sheriff; but what happened to my role as a mysterious lawman from out of town?—the guy who will scare Slimann shitless... brainless too. Your plan for a squeeze play."

Looking like a doe who'd lost her fawn, E J stared open-mouthed at Cowan, "Sheriff... ?"

"Never mind, E J. Just roll your camera." She frowned, irritated. As I began retrieving items from my backpack, E J punched a button on her tripod-mounted camera. She documented two mushed cigarillos unrolled from toilet paper, the dried cow pod in burlap, and Ginger's collar. Leaking a little pride, I placed the evidence carefully upon Cowan's desk. I should have known better. The pride part, I mean.

I'm afraid I lost my Sherbinski cool, unloading on the sheriff, rambling on for 10 minutes—visualizing, picturing the setting, reconstructing the double murder—dog and master. I rose from the table and paced, gesturing like a courtroom prosecutor. Why the drama? Pent up frustration, I suppose.

I stood, a man of—shall we say—delicate build, looking down on a 220 pound, muscled sheriff with testosterone oozing from every pore. He looked up with a wry grin. I inadvertently stiffened, wanting to stand taller, "What are you waiting for, Sheriff? Why not arrest him right now. We've got the goods on him. We have a tire print which we can match with his ATV, proving he was at the scene. So will his cigarillo's DNA matching the ciga-butt he tossed by the Plainsman. We have Ginger's collar. Her body can be exhumed. Clearly, Stump hid evidence, the incriminating kind."

Cowan never changed expression. He stood, backing away from the camera's radius, signaling E J to shut down her recording camera. "Great work, Jack," he said. "But it's all vulnerable evidence. Bennett Slimann will cut it to shreds. Like it or not, he's notoriously successful defending crooks, especially his own kin. Then there's the problem with chain of custody. You're an amateur. You gathered potential evidence using amateur methods. Problems—all kinds of them. The DNA labs are overloaded and subject to scheduling priorities unlikely to include Toole County, Montana."

I was stunned, to put it mildly. Angry too. "So, it was all a waste of time?"

Cowan smiled, "Lighten up, Jack. We're changing course, that's all. You've done your part. Miss Burns, here, will finish her recording... tomorrow, when you're well-rested. Give her your best recollections, photos and notes." He waved over my exhibits, including the burlaped shit print that was becoming odiferous in his heated office. He said, "I'm asking you to sign a statement consigning these items to me."

"Then what, Sheriff? Just walk away? I have an investment here, you know."

"Your investment will prove out, Jack. I have a feeling... . E J, take a break, please."

Buck got up and closed the door behind her. As a born-again civilian, my calling him "Buck" sounded appropriate. Apparently "Lindquist" was back in style as well. "Lindquist," he said, "you've been terrific."

I sank into a chair. He paced behind his desk, energized. "This is the toughest case I've ever chased, and you have possibly pried it open. All depends on Stump's frame of mind, how resilient he is without Daddy by his side. No matter how it turns out, I'll be forever grateful. So will the Larigans."

"Thank you, Buck; but I'm going to miss crossing the finish line."

"Maybe not. If you stick around another day or two, you may see it happen. Now, I respect your judgement, Jack; so, I'm asking your opinion, off the record, of course."

I snickered, could have been a cynical snicker if I didn't honestly like the sheriff—surprisingly so, since he'd "hired" me and "fired" me twice already. I agreed to hear him out, but couldn't resist pesky pessimism. "Justice is already a year late, Buck. Anything less than a full confession means a marathon trial in another unprejudiced county. And his lawyer daddy is clever, you say. He'll hire a master defense lawyer, and together they'll reconfigure Stump as a sympathetic figure."

Buck's jaw dropped. He nodded in agreement, "I couldn't have said it better myself. However, it ain't gonna happen that way. Now you are familiar with the players, and you've dabbled in law enforcement with your crime fiction. If you think I'm headed down the wrong road, then speak up."

"I'm listening."

"I see a confession in the making, Jack. Stump is becoming more and more unbalanced, possibly using dope as well as Jack Daniels. He'll make mistakes. I can exaggerate his inattentive driving as reckless or catch him with another DUI. The Shelby Blues will help if I ask nice. We'll talk about his drug running, harboring convicted felons, and maybe discover a concealed weapon. I can get a bold printed arrest warrant including a laundry list of charges. Once in custody, he'll be subject to pressure, all Mirandized, of course."

"And you think he'll convict himself?"

"Not immediately; but he isn't the brightest bulb. He won't ask for a local attorney, because he'll want his mollycoddling lawyer dad who's out of town. Just between the two of us, my sheriff friend in North Dakota is—shall we say—*complicating* Bennett Slimann's life. While Bennett is tied up, I'll smother Stump with your stuff: the shit print, forthcoming DNA evidence, and the buried dog. He'll come apart. That's when I'll *suggest* that a confession gets him no worse than 20 years with parole for good behavior."

"Huh? Good behavior?" I chuckled. "You think good behavior is possible?"

"Nope."

"I don't either."

"That's the point." Sheriff Cowan rubbed his hands together. "He'll never set foot in the Sweetgrass or Shelby again."

We stood, facing off. With exaggeration, I could claim to be Cowan's equal. "I like your strategy, Sheriff, and I like your confidence. As a bonus, his conviction—by association—will also besmirch his shyster father... the final disgrace."

I stood and shook his hand, "Best of luck, Buck."

As I turned to leave, he said "Meantime, where will you be?"

"I haven't the faintest, Sheriff"—and I honestly didn't. "Why do you need to know?"

"Part of my job, Jack. You're in my jurisdiction, and you're vulnerable. And if I wasn't so damn prickly, we'd probably be considered friends."

"Or if you were a civilian."

"Soon as I turn "civie," I'll let you know. Sheriff Cowan laughed his "Buck" laugh, before again turning serious. "Anyway, for now I have Junie Jones tailing Stump. Still... watch your back."

CHAPTER FIFTEEN

DOWNTOWN SHOWDOWN

September 28. I strolled past Emma Jean Burns, tipping Lucky's brim. Free of the Toole County Sheriff's Department... and terminated, I should have felt liberated, but didn't. Bo knows me. With her sixth sense, she feels my temperament. I climbed in behind Big Red's wheel. Bo squirmied against my hip, sat, and licked me behind my right ear.

"You're right, Bo. I *am* worried. Buck has only two or three days to work on Stump Slimann before hotshot Bennett returns. And we're helpless, out of the picture now."

I cranked up Big Red, hung a right on Mineral Street and east on Central, headed for downtown and the Plainsman. Four blocks down Central my cell chirped. While stopped at a pedestrian cross, I picked up, "Jack, at your service."

"Sheriff Cowan," he said—no amenities. As if out of breath, "heads up, Jack. Junie Jones lost our pigeon."

"Louder, Buck," I said. "A freight train's rumbling past." Cowan's voice resounded stronger: "Stump outfoxed Junie. He's on the loose and 'squirrelier' than ever. He buzzed in and out of our parking lot, probably looking for you. E J spotted him."

"How could he lose Junie with Houston Command at his fingertips?"

"I'll explain later. Stump is nervous and desperate. He changed vehicles, took his dad's collector's model Mercedes out of storage. Junie has no electronic tag on it. You better watch for Stump. He's nuts and he's stoned, Junie says."

"No prob. I've got a dog and a gun."

"Yah, great. So, where are you headed?"

"I'm on Central, headed for the Plainsman to quaff a couple cold ones. I was fired, remember? So the Mercedes, what does it look like?"

"Black roadster, 300SL Gullwing, diesel. Look for black diesel smoke."

"Perfect, Sheriff. You're a great cop."

"Meaning what?"

"Meaning that, as we speak, I see a black Mercedes in my rear view mirror... close, riding my bumper. Gotta go."

Stump waved frantically, motioning me to pull over. I snapped a decision, figuring he'd be slow to react; so I tromped on the gas, jerked the wheel left, and careened into a narrow lane between a grain elevator and a warehouse. By circling the backside, I'd return to Central Avenue with a big lead. If Stump was still on my tail, I could jump out and fast draw Winchester from the rear window rack. Of course, all this calculating happened in three adrenaline-boosted seconds.

In my rear view, I saw Stump's diesel puff smoke as he gunned his engine coming off Central. I wheeled left at the warehouse corner. Damn the luck! A parked grain truck blocked the lane, and here came Stump roaring in behind. He skidded to a stop just short of my rear bumper. Big Red was trapped between the truck in front and Stump's relic Mercedes behind. The warehouse hid us from view; slim chance for a rescue mission from Cowan.

Assuming the fight meant weaponry, I leaped out, scrambling for Winchester in the back window rack. Too late. With only a single door to negotiate, Stump beat me to the punch. As I reached for the rear door handle, he already stood by his front left fender pointing a long barreled .44 at my nose, a single action revolver, meaning I'd have a second to rush him if he missed. He cocked the hammer, and my heart raced wildly. I considered my odds. Stump was unsteady on his feet. His gun hand trembled. I figured he had a 50:50 chance of hitting me on the first shot. He whined, "Hands offa' that door handle, or yer a dead man"—a pathetic sopranoed pleading, unbecoming for a gunman.

"You can have my truck," I said; "but I'll take my dog with me, if you don't mind." Growling steadily, Bo pressed her nose against my driver's side window.

Stump waved his gun barrel, "See this, asshole? Step back, Sumbitch. You know what I came to get, an' I ain't got time to fuck around."

I spread my hands quizzically, playing dumb. *Stall for time*, says the spook writers' cliché. A siren wailed in the distance, hopefully Sheriff Cowan to the rescue. Stump's pale, watery gray eyes flickered beneath the bill of his catawampus Seattle Mariners' cap. He was darkly unshaven, dirty as a 5-day drunk, jittering like a tyke about to pee his pants. Clearly, dope had him in its grip, possibly the same shot of courage that helped him murder Charlie. I said, "You should know my truck has one dead cylinder."

"Quit stallin' shitbrain. I know exactly who you are and what yer gonna hand over... got 'xactly five seconds ta gimme that backpack before I blow a hole in ya'."

Oblivious to the scene behind him, the grain truck driver pulled forward, giving me room to make a move. In a compliant tone I said, "Sure, sure. It's on the passenger side—nothin' in it; but let me get it for you." I stared past his huge .44 death muzzle into ferret eyes, judging them as confused. I pled eagerness, "If that's all you want, hell, there's only a hundred bucks and change in my backpack; let me grab it for you." Without hesitation, I started around the nose of my truck. He stumbled after me.

Stump jolted, "Nope, nope, nope. Freeze right there. Sumbitch. You got a gun in there dontcha?"

Hands up, like an arrested crook, I said, "Uh, no. I have a .38, but not in there."

How to stall him off? A siren sung again, closer this time. Stump waved his .44, blabbering, spittle running down his chin. "Move it," he said. "Up against the truck, shithead. Sumbitch. I oughta plug ya' right now." He jabbed his gun barrel in the small of my back as he passed behind, sidestepping to reach for the door latch. His gun muzzle waved alternately at sky and across my face as he opened the door, reaching, reaching... and Bo leaped, chomping down on his wrist, shaking her head, as if killing a rat. He screamed, blood spurted, and his finger tightened on the trigger.

The .44's discharge was explosive, a metallic collision—bullet and fender. I charged and karate chopped his gun hand, breaking his thumb with a sickening sound, as if snapping a dead stick. The gun dropped, he staggered and fell hard on his back with a "whump." Bo landed with four paws on his front, snapping, wolf-like, inches from his face, ready to kill. "Leave it, Bo," I said—my command akin to "drop the rat."

I picked up his .44 and stood over him aiming at his bulbous, whiskey nose. With measured deliberation, I said, "We'll need to tourniquet that wrist, Bubba, or you're gonna bleed out." Stump was sitting up now alongside Bo, who panted joyfully as if she'd just brought a cock pheasant to hand. Stump, dazed and groggy, held his fang-punctured wrist over his chest and squeezed with his left hand—ineffectually, at best. Blood soaked the middle of his shirt and pooled in the folds of his fat belly. His eyes narrowed. He snarled, "Bastard, you'll pay for this."

"Like Charlie Larigan, you mean? Now, when you're ready to talk sense, I'll stop the bleeding for you, otherwise..."

Finally. Sheriff Cowan's tires squealed coming off Central. His siren's wail ended, and seconds later he stepped out of his squad truck hustling to us, slapping his thigh with a billy-club. In formal, official-ease voice, he said, "I'll take over here, Mr. Lindquist. This man is facing a number of charges."

"If he lives, Sheriff," I said. "He's running short of blood."

Stump's eyes glazed over. His arms flopped, and he fell back, unconscious. I said, "Sheriff, he's opted to use his right to remain silent."

Drugs, shock, loss of blood—he could have died. Fortunately, the EMTs arrived and went to work. Death would have been too quick and easy, and convenient for daddy Sly.

The *Havre Daily* headline could have read: "Jonathan Slimann, son of noted attorney, Bennett J. Slimann, dies in confrontation with Idaho man and his vicious dog." And Bennett would have escaped responsibility for grooming Stump, criminal son number two to compliment criminal son number one, who had just been indicted in North Dakota for felony fraud. Now, in Dempseytown, Montana, Stump was left like a bone for the hounds of justice.

CHAPTER SIXTEEN

VAGARIES OF JUSTICE

After a night in the hospital with Juniper Jones standing guard outside his room, Jonathan B. Slimann was awarded a suite in the county jail. E J called me with the news, said the sheriff wanted me to know that Stump was "squawking like a magpie." She laughed pleasantly, an obvious good omen.

On the advice of the city attorney, after Bo's morning run I took Bo to a veterinary clinic where the vet on call drew a vial of blood, a precaution to verify that her "attack" on Stump wasn't precipitated by rabies. When I returned to the Glacier, the clerk knocked on my door with a message: Sheriff Cowan wanted to see me. I was more than ready.

I pulled into my privileged parking lot at the sheriff's office. 10 A.M. The office was a-buzz. Nevertheless, E J discreetly took possession of my copy of the Cowan Report and guided me through the bustle of waiting newsmen and local officials to Cowan's office. With the sound of my voice, he was on his feet, pointing out his window toward the county jail, "Glad you showed, Jack. I think you should see the jailed killer. Do you good."

I followed Cowan out the side door to the stone jailhouse. The young deputy at his desk eyed me carefully as we filed past, headed for a quartet of jail cells. We stopped in front of the first cell, where Stump sat on his bunk. He didn't rise. "Anything you want to say, Slimann?" Cowan said.

"Go to hell," he mumbled into the front of his orange jumpsuit.

There. Done—my privileged glare at our captive through iron bars. Not unsurprisingly, the event provided little fulfillment, like looking at a broken-legged skunk in a trap. With a sideways glance at Stump, Cowan said, "I'd like you to stop by my office, Lindquist ... tomorrow; the hullabaloo will run its course by then." 'Lindquist,' he'd said, unnatural, but part of the façade of official-ese.

Cowan walked me toward Big Red, pausing in front of his office, and his stash of dog cookies. He had other things on his mind, "My report, I suppose you have it in your truck."

"Nope, E J has it in her desk." I paused at my truck door where Cowan, Bo's easy mark, ignored her whining. He grabbed my door latch, a gesture of dismissal.

With uncharacteristic terseness, he said, "Our little contract, Jack... you and I will terminate it tomorrow. E J will block out the time. Meanwhile, I'm asking you to keep a low profile around town. Invisible would be perfect. Know what I mean?"

"Understood Sheriff," I said. His forehead wrinkles were noticeably deeper. At the moment, I was thinking: *he's a dedicated sheriff. With the job comes incessant worry.*

"One more suggestion," he said, as I hopped into my driver's cockpit. I lowered my window, and Bo poked her nose over my shoulder, her black eyes shining on her potential benefactor.

"Besides invisibility?

Which brought a welcomed chuckle. "Yes, I'm adding an addendum: Keep your room at the Glacier for a couple more days. Take Bo hunting, read some books; but don't vacate just yet. Just a precaution, that's all.

"I don't get it. Precaution against what?"

"Bennett. He's a wily sucker. He's over his head in legal trouble in North Dakota. But he has tentacles. He could hire a stand-in to file for a hearing on Stump's confession, in which case you'd be subpoenaed."

"You're sure there will be one?

"The confession? Already happened. He blabbed to the guy in the next cell. The official confession will come down this afternoon in front of a public defender."

"I don't get it. You don't need me as an observer, or witness, or something?"

"Nope. Later, we'll talk. You need to fade into the background now, like Junie Jones."

Bo followed our discussion with bright eyes and twitching nose. Buck laughed, He said, "Give me a minute. I'll be right back." He only needed seconds, returning with *two* bowser cookies—premium, smelling of bacon. She would have kissed him, had he leaned over. He banged on Big Red's roof, "Be a good sport. Take her hunting." A reporter had advanced from the rear. The sheriff broke past him, headed for his office.

Daylight, September 30th, in a cattail swamp by the Marias River.

The swamp was a place of ducky dreams: a hidey place with warm springwater, wind protection, and grain fields in every direction. A place of hunter dreams too, with permission granted by my new farmer friend. "Sure," McClain said. "Just bring me a couple of mallards afore you leave."

The swamp reeked of musky duck. I parted cattails, wading ankle deep water with Bo at heel. Ahead, we heard low mutterings of happy gabbing mallards.

Suddenly, we ran out of cattails at open water, where a dozen mallards stretched necks before blowing skyward in a storm of quacking and spraying water.

Bo glared at me as I stood with Winchester harmlessly at my side, while the fat mallards circled back to see if I was real.

I read Bo's mind: *have you lost your mind boss? I haven't retrieved a bird all week.*

"There's no sport in a jump-shoot, Bo. We'll hunker down here and wait for the next bunch to glide in."

Ten minutes later, Bo's wish was granted when I dropped the first pair of greenheads. She sniff-snuffled, splashing amongst reeds in a whirlwind double retrieve. Within in the hour, she retrieved three more singles in succession. We were done: a pair for McClain and three for the Glacier's night clerk, who had somehow learned to like me.

Over the next three hours, Bo and I remained invisible to all but jackrabbits and antelope. I found a rutted track suitable for three miles an hour. My map called it "unimproved road," a gross exaggeration—though perfectly suited for a guy who wanted to avoid humans. I engaged Big Red's four wheeled power train and climbed up Squaw Butte and down the far side, headed for Mission Lake. I turned off a mile short of the lake.

Back at the Glacier, I took a thinking man's shower without success. I would show up at Cowan's office with a clean slate, in other words, an empty head.

With my attitude, Big Red seemed to have a mind of her own. I found myself tooling down Main, skirting the edge of "Downtown," where curious pedestrians gawked at me: the Idaho guy in the red truck doing *"funny business."* I mostly looked straight ahead.

Before my ass found the chair, Cowan started in. Understandable. He'd waited more than a year to lift leaden shackles from his shoulders. "It's over, Jack. We got 'im. I'm ninety percent sure." The sheriff blew air through his lips. "He signed a confession, Jack." Cowan bounced a fist on his desk. The big announcement. Huge. He'd delivered it without smiling.

I reached across his desk to shake his hand, thinking: *in the short time I've known Sheriff Cowan, he's taken on a grayness, as if tainted by dirty air. A fresh breeze was in order.* I said, "He signed without encouragement from rubber hoses?"

Cowan's chuckle was insufficient, but a start. "He gave up, Jack. In my amateur's judgement, I'd say two and a half days without booze or drugs dropped him into hopeless depression. I suppose his defense could claim his innocence by reason of insanity."

In the mode of counselor and prosecuting attorney, I blustered, "Naw, trying to prove insanity a year after the homicidal day would be the epitome' of insanity. Besides, you've been copacetically lawful in handling the case."

"That is something we need to discuss," he said in his best worry voice. Though fidgety, Cowan was primed to unload when interrupted by a knock at his door. Without waiting for a response, E J opened the door, looking past me to the sheriff. Obviously, her curiosity trumped protocol.

"Anything you need, Sheriff?"

His glance was hard, "Lindquist and I are in conference, EJ. We don't want to be disturbed."

"Sorry," she said, quickly closing the door behind her.

Cowan grinned, "She does my worrying for me. Now, where were we? Oh, you were saying about copacetic law. Yes. Maybe we should tie up some non-copacetic loose ends."

"We? How would *I* know about such things?"

"Dunno." Cowan paused, tapping his desk with his pen. "A lawman's badge, for instance?"

With a world class blank face, I said, "What badge?"

He nodded, grinning, "Perfect. Couldn't have said it better myself."

Half in jest, I said, "Just another valuable tip you've taught me about the intricacies of law enforcement, Sheriff."

" 'Buck' will be fine, Jack, now that you are about to become one hundred percent civilian, rather than a pretend cop."

"But I haven't resigned."

'Buck' didn't take the bait. "I'm resigning you. Resigning myself too, for all practical purposes. We'll leave the Sweetgrass killer in the hands of the justice system."

"So you're satisfied his confession will hold up?"

"I'll bet on it, Jack. Fortunately, a public defender stood as a witness to Stump's delivery of fanciful mitigating circumstances. He's hopeless, learned nothing of law from his dad and brother. He says the dog attacked him, as if that would excuse killing Charlie in cold blood with the victim's gun."

"First degree homicide?"

Behind Buck's window, tires squealed, and a deputy departed the lot, siren wailing. Buck ignored it all. He said, "We'll take first or second degree and add Stump's weaponized attack on you. Sparky Smith, my electrician friend, witnessed his assault from the top leg of the Farmer's Union elevator."

I spread my hands, as if catching manna from heaven, "Incredible, Buck. It's about time we drew a lucky card."

Buck stood, the sort of man whose inner twitches fire after 20 minutes of containment. I stood out of respect, thinking our meeting was over. Instead, he turned to stare out the window, studying the incredible view of a parking lot. While analyzing pebbles and blowing plastic bags, he mused, "Lucky card, eh? Don't get big-headed on me Jack; but I gotta' say, you were the lucky card that filled my inside straight—when was it?—I lost track. Anyway, now I want a perfect finish."

"Don't know what's left to worry about."

In lieu of an answer, he looked at his watch. Four o'clock. He turned for the door with his hand guiding my shoulder. I said, "Anything I can do to help?"

He whirled to a stop outside his door. "Yes, there is." He jerked his thumb over his shoulder in the direction of *Downtown*. "Go see The Mick. It's the "dead hour" at the Plainsman, good time to talk."

We shook hands, said our goodbyes—me with a puzzling face. I trooped past E J with a puzzling face of her own.

I took Bo to the weeds, then drove to the Plainsman. Entered the side-street door and paused just inside, where my unadjusted eyes saw The Mick as a dark blob behind his bar. No patrons sat before him.

"Jack, good to see you," he said. I leaned against the bar, letting my eyes adjust. I made out his business-like smile and proud tender's posture. He turned and tossed his bar towel to a cute blonde in a very short skirt, "You're on, Leah." He came around the bar and led me to a far, darkened corner table."

We settled in. "Need a beer?" he said.

"Naw, too early," I lied. "But it's apparently important to visit with you."

"So you saw Cowan."

"Just left. We had a 'fruitful visit,' in his words. He 'resigned me,' more or less a firing, and—for me—a relief. Then I discover there's more. You're the spokesman. So, what the hell's going on?"

"Jack, Jack... be cool. No worries, mate. I'll make it simple and quick. Sure you won't take a beer?"

"You?"

He nodded, "A tall one. Tuesday nights, nothing much happens. Leah can run this place in her sleep."

Leah seemed alert to Mick's thirst. She brought 20 ounce micros, "Browning Brown."

After one slow draw on my "Brown," I said, "Business, Mick—it will be simple and quick, you said."

He plonked his mug on the polished pine table. "Okay, Jack. I believe you know all this, but just to be certain—"

"Just to be certain, Cowan wants assurance that I won't blow his case. So he appoints you as unofficial emissary."

Mick grinned, "No comment on that, but just for the helluvit, listen." I nodded in agreement. He began in an uncommonly serious tone.

Mick's short form was designed for simplicity: one, two, and done. "Keep a low profile. Avoid news reporters. Reporters from the *Havre Daily News* and the *Great Falls Tribune* are in town. If they corner you, stiff 'em."

"I'm good at stiffing. Anything else."

"Yes; and it could be important"... he half-turned in his chair, eyes sweeping the dimly lit room. Nothing had changed. Nobody sat within earshot, not even close. Still, he tipped toward me like a Tom Clancy conspirator, "There's a bit of unfinished business."

"What? A certain officer of the law led me to believe the suspect has confessed... more than once."

"I heard the same rumor, but the suspect tipped his hand... apparently. Yapping about entrapment and impersonation of a law officer. We citizens wouldn't want to be seen with a lawman's badge, for example."

I smiled at its last sighting, known only to me... a slightly cupped golden disk catching glint of the afternoon sun as it sails across the blue pool of the Marias. It didn't skip like a flat stone. Too heavy. But it seemed to pause for an instant, dimming... then gone, gone deep forever.

"So, the badge? The Mick said.

"Badge? Now, why would I have one of those?"

"Why, indeed," Mick declared. We drained our beers just in time for Leah's arrival with a second pair.

Mick and I ordered burgers to complement our brews. We talked football, collegiate and high school—all about star athletes, over-achievers, and thrilling finishes. Yet, our stories seemed labored and ill-timed. Mick's heart wasn't in it, nor was mine. Justice was parting the storm clouds over the Sweetwater, its job nearly complete.

"Mick, I've enjoyed this." I said, pushing back my chair. "Great conversation and great beer; but for some reason, I'm running short of go juice."

"Me too," Mick said. "Strange. All I've done is stand around all day."

Back in my Glacier refuge, I punched Joanie's number. She knew my circuitry better than anyone and would happily commiserate. Not so fast. Her recorded message reminded me of her grizzly bear conference in Missoula, one of those torturous affairs mixing scientists, environmentalists, and politicians holding keys to vaults with public funding. All day long, a succession of experts pose conflict and imagined solutions, gather for drinks and dinner, and repeat the day's agenda, only now in common, everyman language. At this very moment, Joanie would be sipping wine, smiling, an earnest and expert pacifier. Though Kerner had no such talent, he often struck a useful chord. I punched his number.

I chuckled, waiting for him to pick up. Why am I doing this? I know he'll cite the book again. He picked up on ring number eight, and—yes—after listening to my listless status report on the Sweetgrass Case, he cited "THE BOOK."—*Studies on Normal and Pathological Psychosomatic Energy Partitioning*, by Leonetta J. Hanson, PhD. Kerner surely hadn't forgotten our previous animated discussions on the ebb and flow of human emotions; yet he delivered a fresh synopsis, laboring through a 10 minute monologue: Hanson's theories, citations, her studies, case histories, and summarization. I laughed, and immediately felt better. Why do we need PhDs to define commonsense. A person pours heart and soul into bringing about Justice, all the while haunted by the thought of failure. His emotional fuel tank pegs at zero just as Justice triumphs, and he wonders why he has nothing left. Well, in my case my tank was running on fumes. Sheriff Cowan had reassigned me to obscurity.

Oct. 1, Obscurity. Obscurity went well, in my opinion. Like the way I handled a trio of businessmen in the Pumper Café.' They talked over one another, shooting questions, hungry for details: "You can tell us," the insurance man said. "Are you a private detective or do you work for Sheriff Cowan?" I changed the subject to fishing and hunting... well, I tried anyway. The hardware store manager spoke as if head of a committee, "We could use a lawman of your caliber here full time." Discomforting, all of this, and strangers stopping me on the street to shake my hand, fertilizing reports of heroism.

I suppose stroke of luck heroism is like dreaming of becoming a millionaire. You think *how wonderful*, then meet a millionaire and discover he is no more content than the barber next door. On second thought, contentment is the wrong word. Better, satisfaction, a more realistic assessment that must be savored immediately. Like fresh homemade ice cream, today's satisfaction won't taste quite as good after a month in the freezer. Furthermore, satisfaction shrinks with time, leaving space that needs refilling. Toole County Montana, however, makes way for satisfaction.

That's why we gathered in a Plainsman's private meeting room on the first of October—The Mick, Dan the coach, Chet McCrary, Police Chief Willert Wight, and mayor Sweeney—a retired marine. A waitress came in with a young assistant toting a giant tray of snacks that qualified as a full meal. She took our drink orders.

We partied for two hours without receiving a bill. Duncan Pierce, owner of the Plainsman, picked up the tab. He came in to kibitz and listen to a succession of speeches interrupted by laughing, high times. And—once again—we stood to toast Charlie Larigan.

A spate of satisfaction was due the Dempseytowners. They wanted their town back. The Mick, sitting beside me, explained it well: "For more than 100 years, the good, honest, and industrious ruled this part of Montana. The other kind tried for traction and failed—drifters, grifters, and leeches."

"Except the Slimanns got a toehold," I said.

"I'll concede that, but they're finished," Mick said. "Cowan gave you the rundown. Stump is headed for the slammer, the serious one with tall stone walls and men in towers with machine guns."

A knock came at the door, and Emma Jean Burns stuck her head in. She spotted me, and beckoned. I went to the door for a whispered conversation. "Sheriff Cowan wants to see you," she said.

I waved at my gathering of worried faces, "Be back in ten minutes."

E J led me out the side door into the darkening side street, where I joined Buck Cowan on a butt-flattening steel bench abutting the Plainsman. E J adjourned to the passenger side of the sheriff's squad truck, which was parked next to Big Red.

The sheriff didn't need to explain his clandestine behavior. He was a canny one, like my sheriff friend in Kooskia, who's been re-elected four times in Clearwater County, Idaho. Both are savvy about the inescapable realities of politics and law. Play close to the vest; Bennett Slimann could still leverage his residual importance in Toole County, Montana.

Cowan reached into the inside pocket of his official brown sheriff's jacket, pulling out a pair of fat cigars. Offered me one, correctly assuming I would smoke. "Cuban prime," he said, "probably black market, almost enough to get a sheriff canned."

I harbored queasy feelings in this shadowed place adjacent to the Slimanns' defunct agency. Sherbinski-ism at work, I saw a puff of smoke float from the shadows across the street, alerting me to a dark figure with a distinctive swoop of hat brim—Junie Jones. "You have him spotted, huh?" Cowan said. "I'll keep Junie on the job until the Feds tell me Toole County is clean."

"You're a helluva cop, Sheriff—big city policing on little town crime. "I suppose we're celebrating."

"We are. And remember, you can call me 'Buck'." He whooshed a cloud of smoke, "This is as close as I get to being off duty. My people expect 24/7 from me, you know. I've a notion to take off this uniform and go back inside with you."

"So, no more worries about Slimann slithering free?"

"Not enough to count. I just heard from my friend in North Dakota. Two more landowners came in with evidence implicating Stump's daddy and his brother." Buck reached over and banged my thigh with his fist. "If I was you, I'd head down the road; pay your grizzly bear woman a conjugal visit."

"Wait? How do you know... ?"

"Smoke signals, Jack. They come from the west, out of Idaho. But, seriously, if I knew how, I'd find a way to repay you."

"Easy, Buck. You promised an interview. Remember?"

"Interview?"

"You, a War Baby; you could pony up insight for my demographic study."

"Yes, and you are, what?—supposedly a social scientist? An egghead?" His face was a pool of disbelief. A smart man, Buck Cowan; he allowed a sly grin, "If you say so, Jack, if you say so."

"And you will submit to my interview?"

We stood from the bench, facing off. He swayed from foot to foot, tossed his half-smoked Cuban into the sand bucket, nodding affirmation, "Let's shake on it Jack, but with one condition: You'll come back for Stump's sentencing hearing. We'll do your interview then."

Buck grasped my hand with his shaker and whopped my right shoulder with his open left hand. I said, "I'll be back, Buck. Meantime, maybe you can gather evidence supporting offspring abuse and arrest Stump's old man."

Grinning broadly, Cowan tipped his hat. In three long strides he reached the door of his sheriff's truck, gimpy leg be damned. His truck was parked directly in front of Big Red and Bo.

Buck started away, but stopped, lowering his window. He poked his head out, hollering, "Jack, you've got time now. Take Bo bird huntin'. She's done her man-hunting." I waved goodbye and turned for the door of the Plainsman, where Mick held the door.

"We need you in here, Jack," Mick said. "Bring Bo. We're doing pictures."

Chapter Seventeen

GRAND AND GLORIOUS

6 AM, October 2nd. Free once more and feeling marvelous, full of piss and vinegar, as my grandpa would say. I pointed Big Red south on I-15, headed for Great Falls and the greater tribe of Larigan.

Kerner, the relentless arranger, kept me on the phone last night for a half hour. It would have been an hour had I not cut him off in favor of Joanie.

Kerner informed me that during my High-Line and Sweetgrass escapades, he'd been routinely communicating with the Larigans and their friends. Yesterday, Kerner left the college at noon and traveled to the L Bar L where he met Angus, Jimmy, and Walker. Said they'd just come out of high country range, gathering cows. "They had a mess up there, Link. The big gray renegade wolf come through. They spent two extra days gatherin', gettin' all the calves mothered up."

I laughed to myself. Kerner's quest for Western has him speaking their language. On he went, putting himself in the middle, one of the "boys" at the Larigan fire pits, where "20 neighbors magically showed up, "gatherin' in to hear about the apprehension of Charlie's killer. They don't even need cell phones, Link, and they come out of the hills."

"You never heard of smoke signals?"

Kerner's voice portrayed an uncharacteristic level of emotion. "You need to know, Jack, Angus will hold you to your promise to return for a bird hunt. I'm included. He's planning a mountain hunt for blue and ruffed grouse, horseback hunting with Bo ranging out front, pointing birds."

Well, I had no choice. I appointed Kerner to deliver my commitment.

Locked on cruise control, ears tuned to satellite radio, I slowed on the Marias Bridge, savoring a look at the historic river. "At last, Bo, we're getting our mojo back."

We helped "fix" an injustice, imperfectly at best, but our part concluded. We gained a coterie of new Montana friends. How could a lucky man ask for more? But, in fact, there was more. Last night, Joanie announced her plan to book a Missouri River fishing trip for the two of us, my birthday present a month early. She agreed to meet me following the Larigan gathering. "You can come with a red bow tied around your middle," I said.

How could life be better?—as if life's rhythm had returned. "Psychic restoration," Kerner would say. Speaking of... he called again. I pulled onto a side road to answer my cell phone's "call of the pheasant." Bo danced and panted, confused by the artificial bird's crowing.

"I'm listening, Bob," I said, "but I'm very busy at the moment," a remark to hold him at bay. I was enjoying "Viva De Funk" by The Crusaders, whom I could not dismiss in mid-funk. I stalled long enough to know Kerner's professorial brain was roiling. "What's up Doc?" I said.

"Jack, we need to talk." His tone was a dead give-away.

"No, *you* need to talk. The question is why?"

I'd been his silent counselor before. Ask a question and he delivers *War and Peace*, in this case *"War" On the High-Line*. Stump's jailing didn't end the "War" for Kerner, nor did he approve of my disengagement. With the help of his professional contacts in North Dakota, Kerner was preparing to dig into the Slimanns' shystering enterprises.

Kerner geared his long distance voice for urgency, "Jack, listen now. We have a 30 page dossier, and it grows daily."

"Who's we?"

"I and Vasaraba, my professor friend from the University of North Dakota. Recall that we talked of him before. He's brilliant, Jack, and believes..."

"No, not on the phone, Bob. Let's go man to man, say about six o'clock this afternoon in the King of Hearts." I didn't wait for his answer, "Weak signal," I said, signing off.

With windows lowered, I drove down I-15 giving carefree a loose rein. Bo too. On her passenger side, she stretched her neck out the window, peering into the wind, her busy nose sorting a myriad of scents.

Her lips blubbered with the rush of air. All she lacked was Snoopy's Flying Ace scarf. "Bo," I said, "You sniff 'em, we'll hunt 'em."

The Interstate descended gently onto a sloping plateau of grain fields... pleasing, apropos. I chose the slow lane and cruised 50 tranquil miles at 50 miles per.

The highway curved down from Cedar Hill, where a silvery bend of the Sun River appeared in the distance. I bumped my radio volume for George Duke, hammering on his keyboard with "Stones of Orion," somberly important, high drama. I said, "Aha, Bo, how about *Bloody Purple* as a movie? Duke and his "Stones" will open with his soundtrack. I'll write you into the screenplay, Bo. You can be the hero dog and save an innocent person like you saved me."

King of Hearts, Montana. I found Kerner tucked into a King of Hearts booth with a view of the parking lot. He jumped up to hug me, as usual, but added a brisk shoulder thump. "Max said to keep you around. He'll be along later." Kerner had pre-ordered, I know, because a twinkly waitress immediately appeared with a pair of 16 ounce drafts, a craft brew called "CAPTAIN CLARK."

Sounds impossible, but Kerner was even more animated than usual. I let him talk without interruption. Seems that Hanna had returned home in a perky mood, having won a "menopausal skirmish." She was 'clear headed, and bubbling with newly discovered romanticism.' Kerner "compromised," he said, by renting an irrigated pasture for her horses. I toyed with a cynical comment about afternoon soaps, but quickly dismissed the thought. Time to wind down. I requested a hiatus from high level parlay. Not a chance.

Kerner's turmoil would not wait. As I listened, I thought, *Hanna can't change him; I can't, nor should I. He's a driven contrarian, insatiably curious and stubborn.*

That's why his long distance snooping in North Dakota took him deep into a fraud case implicating Marcus Slimann and—very soon, Kerner said, Marcus's father, Bennett. Dr. Roman Vasaraba, Kerner's professor friend, had done most of the legwork. Dakota court records, conversations with a hyperactive newspaper reporter and a rookie deputy—all begged for further investigation. The biggest bombshell?—a former Slimann client was missing. He was a badlands rancher and named as a witness in the Slimann fraud case. Even more intriguing from a Juneau Sherbinski point of view, was Kerner's imaginative theory based on a piece of obscure North Dakota history. Nothing is out of bounds for either Sherbie or Kerner—in this case, a most bizarre and hideous method to destroy human evidence. ...

In North Dakota, speculations had bounced about for more than a century, all about bodies incinerated in "burning coal mines," in actuality, veins of lignite coal ignited by prairie fires years earlier. I cut Kerner's description short, since I was better informed than he.

I was 10, my brother 12, when Uncle Pete took us to see the freakish fires. Uncle Pete rode bulls and broncs into his mid-forties, the sort of guy who'd go looking for danger.

We tied our horses to juniper snags a quarter mile from a jagged, smoking cleft in a dead grass meadow. Uncle Pete warned us, "No running, follow my path exactly, single file."

Uncle Pete stopped us about 50 yards short of the smoking cleft venting from the inferno below. From deep in the earth came a ghostly moan of variable pitch, like an angry monster. I wanted to turn back, but wouldn't admit cowardice; so I stood close to my older brother, listening to Uncle Pete's rules, explaining how he'd lead out, creeping the last dozen yards to the crevasse. Crawling, he said, reduced our risk of falling through the thin, undermined shell of earth.

On all fours, Uncle Pete crept forward and peeked over the edge, a quick look before backing out, cat style. My brother crawled forward next with Uncle Pete grasping his ankles as a precaution. He did the same for me, warning: "Go slow and steady, and only far enough to get a quick look." His admonition was unnecessary. Fiery heat seared my eyes and cheeks, forcing me back, but not before I'd gazed into the roaring "Furnace of Hades," a deep hollowed cavern cradling a continuous bed of burning coals interspersed with pillars of shooting flame. My three second look has stayed with me forever.

I provided Kerner an abbreviated version of my boyhood visit to Hades, but added Dakotan lore, tales so exceptional they begged to be told. I'd heard stories repeated over the years: Horses, cattle, and deer were victims of the "burning coal mine." Perhaps humans too, like the bachelor cowboy in the 50's who disappeared.

Kerner was fascinated by my boyhood recollections. He said, "So we could have a no body homicide?"

"Or, a nobody homicide, Bob. You're getting way out there with your farfetched hunch involving the Slimanns. So what will you do with unsupported theory?"

"No, what will *you* do with it? Vasaraba and I have random but un-connected facts. Only an investigator's ground work will connect them. We'll explore other tangents. Meantime, I have the entire file on a flash drive for you. You're the *"man,"* in the vernacular of your pulp fiction. You proved yourself in the Sweetwater Case."

I laughed, "Bob, you are straying from orderly, scholastic certi-tude—wild theories, Professor. That's *my* bailiwick."

"That's why you should go."

"Go?"

"Go to North Dakota. Expand the investigation."

"You know I can't."

"I don't know that, Link—quite the opposite, in fact."

Deep in conversation, I hadn't noticed Molly and Sunny enter the King's saloon. Kerner alerted me with a wink and head twitch, right out of Sherbinski's opening sequence in *Blood on Her Stilettoes*. I could accuse Kerner of pseudo-plagiarism.

Like advancing shadows, Molly and Sunny walked in from the rear. They stood behind, waiting, and I accepted their accommodation: to stay on the sidelines, let Kerner and I resolve our dispute, which—in-credibly—became a beautiful settlement. I hadn't a sniff it was on its way.

I said, "Let me remind you, Professor, why I cannot fly off to North Dakota. You are the one, and you encourage Joanie as well, to insist that I demonstrate initiative—'scholastic maturity,' you called it, 'ex-pand horizons,' you said. War Babies, remember? In three weeks I hav-en't interviewed a single subject, nor have I entertained an intellectual notion."

Molly and Sunny were unequivocally drawn to our discussion. Without a word they pulled out chairs and sat. I didn't mind eavesdrop-pers, having grown accustomed to my strange role as a semi-public project. Kerner didn't mind because he's a master of fixation. He said,

"Jack, please allow me to release you from your dilemma. I want to...
I will consent to... would you agree to my taking on the—how shall I
say?...

"Spit it out, my friend."

"I'll accept your decision should you disagree with the very idea..."

"Which is?"

I found myself tilting forward, like Bo as I begin dropping hamburger bits into her dish. Deeply serious, Professor Robert Hamilton
Kerner, Esquire, licked his lips. He said, "Jackson, I'm requesting that
you relinquish your intellectual property, *The War Babies*, including all
supporting documents that I previously gifted to you.

I jumped to my feet, surprised, ecstatic, the "weight of the world
lifted," in this case not a cliché. I said life could not be better. It just
got better. "You have a deal, Professor," Kerner rose, and we shook
hands. Without conscious thought, I wrestled him to a manly hug.
"Thank you, you old curmudgeon. Joanie and I have a date to fool some
trout before Bo and I head out to Dakota. If we fail to crack the case,
Sherbinski waits in reserve. I'm thinking *Blood and Ashes* is a catchy title
And now, Truly North—at last she and Sherbie will become more than
private eye partners."

I could have come clean right there, but decided against it. I had assembled prose in my head—a confrontation in the North Dakota badlands. Before sleep foundered me that night in the Drop Inn, I polished
my meadow scene...

*He's a stooped ectomorph with a cold, bony face, a wheeler-dealer lawyer
wearing a straw hat, checkered sports coat, and shined beetle-black
wingtip shoes. He opens his thick black leather briefcase on the hood of
his silver Lexus, removing a paper and pen. He looks over his shoulder
at a mounted cowboy. The cowboy nudges his coal black stud horse forward to bump against the Lexus' fender. The lawyer steps aside, fearful;
but his sinister bull rattlesnake's smile betrays him. He takes the pen
and extends it toward Lucas, the mounted cowboy, as if offering a gift.
No reaction from Lucas, only from his grinning horse, who stretches his
neck over the hood of the Lexus. His nose hovers over the paper and a
string of horse drool falls, forming a translucent pool covering the paper's dotted line, the place where Lucas is asked to sign, the place that*

is accompanied by a notary's illegal, pre-dated stamp. Luke says, "My horse, here, is readin' the fine print. Me, I need time to think on yer offer. Maybe need a couple a yars." With that, his blue heeler, Willy, lifts his leg and pees a ringing stream on the Lexus' wire wheel, and Luke deftly spins his horse, hollering "hee-yah." The horse whinnies, Willy yips, and they race away in a cloud of dust, last seen wheeling around the flank of a clay butte.

I was anxious to wheel away myself... from our King of Hearts gathering. Max appeared on my left, Sunny on my right, I assumed for handshake and hug—an adios moment. It was not to be.

"Jack, if you'll help me move these tables together," Max said; but before I could question why, came a ruckus from behind in the King's glassed entry. They whirled in like wind-racing mustangs. The lead mustang, Angus, burst through the double doors followed by Jimmy Young Man and Grace, Summer, Walker McCloud, Curly the wrangler, and Lobby Soup Pearl. They jostled toward me in a pack, all wearing smiles, grand and glorious. What followed wouldn't be considered a resolution. It was a *wake* for Charlie Larigan, a boisterous celebration lasting until closing time. According to plan, our foothills bird hunt would begin in just 8 hours.

As we milled around the table for festive good nights, Angus pulled me aside. Through his look-alike John Wayne grin, he said, "Jack, in the morning I'm putting you on my best hunter's mount."

Angus's "best mount" turned out to be Doubtful, a 10 year old riding mule. Angus explained as he watched me saddle: "Don't worry 'bout her name. She was a slow starter... 'doubtful.' We about gave up on her." Angus patted her neck, and Doubtful smiled, of which mules are so inclined. Angus turned to me with his own wry smile, "Man or beast—we can all improve ourselves."

Angus rode side-by-side with me. There were 8 of us born, bred, or schooled westerners—and I now include Kerner—plus Walker, the Tennessean, the only hunter with southern style bird hunting experience. He advised, "Take yer time arybody; hol' back an' let our dog work. We cain't go slow enuff."

Angus, Jimmy, Grace, Summer, Walker, Max, Pearl, Kerner, and Jack Lindquist. We began on the rounded crest of a brushy ridge, riding abreast with scabbarded shotguns. Bo roamed hard and fast out front, blasting through buckbrush and huckleberry, sometimes disappearing, and after consternation, discovered patiently holding a covey of Huns or a solitary ruffed grouse. Someone would holler, "She's over here, bring up the shooters," and the assigned pair dismounted and moved in for the flushing. We managed to down a few birds; but all-in-all we were equivalent to a rookie baseball team on the first day of practice.

The biggest question: could Bo last all day quartering ridgetops in front of 9 mounted hunters?

By mid-afternoon Bo was still going strong when the ridge steepened against a rocky outcrop. A spring trickled from its base, water suitable for man and beast and a welcoming place for a break. Bo waded in, lapping water, nose by nose with Doubtful, who noisily sucked in water. With a cold, full belly, Bo stretched out, resting in the shallow pool.

We had 8 birds in the bag and had bagged twice as many laughs at our equestrian hunting ineptitude. Walker strolled out to a rocky point and came back with a directive. Authoritatively, like a Civil War captain, he announced, "We'll take the finger ridge goin' down to the low country." He reflexively turned to Angus.

"Good plan, Walker; now how will ya' train these honyocks ta' shoot?"

"What I seen so far... cain't be done."

Walker had a valid point. Typically, our flushed ruffed grouse rocketed through lodgepole and aspen on zigging, zagging trajectories. I'd drawn laughs with my 0 for 3, but gained slight redemption nailing 2 out of 3 Huns on the low ridge. Now the assigned shooters, Summer and Kerner, rode point on the ridge crest, astride Duke and a gelding named "Smoke."

Kerner was likely poised to disappoint, maybe embarrass himself. Though he'd studied and practiced wing shooting, I'd never seen him score more than 40 percent in open, treeless habitat. Here, in steep and timbered terrain, he'd be fortunate to touch a feather.

100 yards ahead the tip of Bo's tail vibrated above buckbrush. She had birds pinned. Summer and Kerner dismounted, and riders moved in to tend their mounts. The shooters crept forward, shells chambered,

ready. They were barely in range when the Huns blew out at a low angle, chirping and whirring—an unnerving moment to all but well-seasoned hunters. And Kerner was anything but seasoned. Then how to explain what happened?

Two birds broke out of the flock, zooming right, on Kerner's side. He swung on the lead bird, his gun barrel tracking a fast, continuous path. "Boom"—perfect, puff of feathers, rack of pump shotgun. "Boom," number two down, and Bo is off for a double retrieve when a third late flusher escapes through a tangle of aspen; but no—the greatest surprise of all—Kerner swings a big lead on a long shot, touches off, and number three tumbles, colliding with the trunk of a ponderosa. And a cheer erupts from a bunch of "seasoned" hunters, honoring an "unseasoned" one. Excepting Angus and me, our crew trotted their mounts forward to gather near Kerner and Bo, a very happy pair.

Angus leaned forward, elbow on his saddle horn, cradling his chin with a thumb. Doubtful and I were close by, the only ones in earshot. Angus says, "If I wasn't here to see it, I wouldn't a' believed the story. I was happy enough already that ol' Smoke didn't dump the professor."

"Well, Mr. Larigan, Kerner has been surprising me for most of 20 years," I said.

Angus nodded, wearing a big smile: "Let 'em know; I'm goin' down." He looked westward... "A squall comin' in. I'll have a little fire goin' at the road."

An hour later we arrived at the horse trailers to Angus's welcome and his magnificent embered campfire with its giant coffee pot. Our circle of warming bodies grew as one-by-one riders unsaddled and gathered. We clustered around the fire, warming hands on an assortment of old, wounded coffee cups from Angus's "grub box." He topped our coffees with "whiskers" of whiskey.

"Walker, you think we can get good at this fancy bird huntin'?" Jimmy said.

"Hope not. Twouldn't be so much fun."

Came a pause, and quiet took over, as if we were all on the same train of thought. Jimmy confirmed the obvious: "Charlie would have loved this. He'd head up the laughter committee."

Angus raised his mug for a toast: "Charlie woulda' had us huntin' before 10 in the mornin' too. Next time, Jack, you and Bo will come back to a bang-up horseback hunt, two or three days at least." He paused, nodding at Kerner: "Dr. Kerner, you too, you're welcome any time."

"Yeah," Walker said. "Max an' me figure: shootin' like that, he's sort of a ringer." Walker stepped toward Kerner and clinked his coffee cup with his own. "The good doctor, here, is kinda' store-bought. Max, will ya' do the honors?"

Max promptly stepped in next to Kerner, took his immaculate white Stetson by its brim and punched its innards, erasing its perfect, virginal creases. We all cheered as Kerner rocked back on his heels, beaming, topped by his domed Hoss Cartwright hat. We toasted the new Kerner, laughing, spirits soaring.

We snuffed our fire with promises all 'round that next season we'd organize horse hunts.

Angus and his tribe couldn't have done more to ensure a happy ending. Yet, something was woefully missing. I found it two days later on the Missouri River near Gates of the Mountains.

Bo and I met Joanie at a Hauser Lake marina where she had rented a 16 foot aluminum fishing boat with an old fashioned 15 horse outboard steered by a hand held tiller. Perfect—and no deposit required for rock dings.

Joanie and I kissed long and promising right there at the public dock. Then we made our way to the marina picnic grounds where Bo chased a tennis ball and the three of us celebrated family re-unification by rolling in green grass. Lunch featured Joanie's smoked loin of white-tail and my surprise of Montana Mills whole grain honey-bread paired with Walker McCloud's "Tennessee Stout:" home brew in hefty brown bottles.

Noon is a ridiculous starting time for serious fishermen. Unserious, we gathered gear and piled into our boat. Bo played navigator, standing over the bow, testing the wind. I motored us out to big water where Joanie and I fished with deep water fly lines, appropriate for slow fishing, leaving ample space for talking.

I've never succeeded hooking Joanie on fishing, a matter of dueling priorities. I wanted to fish and talk only when necessary. She wanted to necessarily talk while holding a fly rod. She probed for details about my Montana adventure of which I could not deliver. Despite good intentions, I'm socially inept on the water while contemplating what lies beneath the surface.

I killed the motor and let our boat drift before a westerly breeze of about 10 knots, perfect for a drift troll and perfect for sightseeing on a cool, blue sky day. Soon we'd intercept Moon gulch. I was anxious to show history buff, Joanie, where Meriwether Lewis discovered the Gates of the Mountains.

Dead ahead, a pair of mergansers alternately dove and swam excitedly, fish hunting, probably picking off minnows underneath, minnows trying to escape predacious trout.

Without explaining why, I replaced our Muddlers with weighted Clouser Minnows. Joanie watched with disinterest. She said, "You actually grew close to the Montana people in a short amount of time."

"I did, and not necessarily smoothly."

"I don't understand."

"Well, my new friend, Buck Cowan, for example. He had to learn to trust me. He studied me, and he spent considerable time doing so. His countenance can shrivel cactus. I'd like you to meet him."

"I look forward to it. Do you want me to meet "Lobby Soup" Pearl as well? And should I be a tiny bit jealous?"

"I hope so, and don't forget 'Sunbeam Sunny'."

"Who else?"

"There's an entire bibliography of beautiful ladies. But, to balance the equation, you should meet the studly men characters. I say 'characters' because I'm in the process of using Angus, Jimmy Young Man, and Walker McCloud as models for fictional characters." As she studied my face, a violent strike nearly took her rod, leaving her with a limp line and no Clouser.

Her lunker could have been a twin to my thick muscled five pounder, which I eventually netted. Sure, Joanie was pleased for my trophy catch, but not enthralled either. She quickly returned to semi-serious talk. "So what of War Babies?"

"You first," I said. "Your DNA advice proved invaluable in the Sweetgrass. Now I want to hear how it played out with grizzly bears."

She laughed, "Sure Jack. You'll love this. It reads like a novel.... We've been looking for a gnarly old boar griz. He didn't play by the rules of civilization. Authorities suspected him of breaking into cabins, and—this much was verified—he waltzed into campgrounds, scaring off tourists. The B.C. Parks and Recreation officials trapped him in '06 and outfitted him with a locator collar."

"Like a felon with an ankle device."

"That's unfair, Jack. He was disrespected for acting bear-like. When he escaped the collar I was secretly happy for him, pulling for a good pine nut season so he'd stay in the high country and away from people. Fortunately, the white barks grew a bumper crop of nuts. Unfortunately, our grizzly had acquired a taste for mutton on the hoof and campground bacon."

"Speculation? Or did they find evidence?

"No, *they* didn't. *I did*—at the scene of the crime, as your man Sherbinski would say. In May I was called to a campground east of Kalispell. Found his DNA in scat. Remember?—we talked about it. Then came my August lab report on evidence from the Yaak River Valley, where he killed a ewe and a Pyrenees guard dog. This week I received a call from a Canadian researcher. Based on his excellent trail camera photo, our big boar currently hangs out 200 miles north in three Sisters Park. He's a dedicated drifter. I've named him Jack." Bo turned from her place on the bow, listening, her brown eyes smiling.

"Joanie," I said, "Look at her; you've confused her with this second Jack."

"And you've turned your good friend, Bob Kerner inside out."

"What do you mean?"

Joanie reached in her fishing duffel and retrieved a sheaf of papers. "I pulled Kerner's report from my computer. He included separate remarks, insisting you study his report."

I laughed, "Insisting—his favorite pastime."

"Well, you need him. He needs you; he can't stay on track any better than you." Joanie laid the papers on my fishing duffel. "His abstract, here, proves the point. He held it back, didn't want to distract you in the midst of your Sweetgrass investigation."

"Except he did, on a daily basis." I held my rod with my knees while I read Kerner's cover title:

Imposition of Generational Paradigms on The Rural American West.

GRAND AND GLORIOUS

Societal Consequences as Measured by Demographic Indices Modeled Upon the Cultural Class, Western Rustic. Dr. Robert H. Kerner

"Yeah," I said. "They thought Freud was nuts too." I arranged a seat cushion next to mine. Bo jumped onto it. "Nope. Not for you Bo." I nudged her down and patted the cushion for Joanie. "For you, Joanie, love of my life." She squirmied in hip to hip. I said, "Do you still want me to return to the battlegrounds of academia?"

"You kidding? And ruin the man I love?" She planted a warm one on my mouth to seal the deal.

Bo pushed her butt between my knees and sat on my feet. *Ya', boss. You ain't leavin' us.* I snapped my fingers, and Bo hopped onto her blanket covering the boat prow.

I had largely given up fishin', unable to concentrate. I said, "Joanie, while I have you inescapably enthralled, I have a favor to ask."

"Yes, in a long line of favor-asking, what is it?"

"Simple. You can do it. The bear people love you. Please ask them to leave Sir Jack alone. If he kills another sheep, you richly compensated scientists pay for the stinking sheep. And above all, do not... ever... put another damn tracking collar on Jack."

"Here's what I think about that, Rusty," she laughed. She tugged my rod from my hands and stood it next to hers. Our boat rocked gently in the waves, and we fell together onto my mackinaw. I remembered the sign at the dock listing Authorized Activities. Ours wasn't listed.

> *"This above all: to thine ownself be true,*
> *And it must follow, as the night the day,*
> *Thou canst be false to any man."*
> *-Shakespeare*

> *"Be yourself. Who else is better qualified?"*
> *-Frank J. Giblin, II*

On October 8th Joanie left Bo and me in Syringa and returned to her U of I laboratory. The next day I received an incredible letter—

"Dear Jack: Around the 9th or 10th of October, I want you to visit Hunter Duggan at his Muleshoe Ranch. It's a mile west of Kamiah. He's between pack trips; he'll be ready for you. So will SHE. Ha-ha. A

small reward for all you did for us. Angus."

Angus didn't need to tell me about the famous grizzled old "skinner," Hunter Duggan, and his impeccable reputation. In Clearwater country, anyone who matters knows of Hunter.

At mid-morning of October 10th I drove over two inches of squeaky new snow into Hunter's little ranch in Dogwood Canyon. Old Sol slanted down over the ridge, just now reaching Hunter's corrals and his prize mules.

"SHE" was tethered on the outside of a round corral, warming her thickening October coat. Hunter stood with one arm draped over her neck. He turned to greet me and shake my hand, "You must be Jack." With a smile as wide as his face Hunter said, "I named her 'Belle.' She's four, had three years trainin'. Solid. Rarin' to go. She'll pack or ride, guaranteed. Don't know what you did for this Angus fella, but he paid top dollar for the best young mule in my outfit."

Hunter backed away so Belle and I could become acquainted. She stood quietly at attention, her radar ears erect, pointed forward. She stretched her neck to reach her black nose to the back of my hand, blowing a soft approval. I untied her and squared up with her face from a mule length distance. It was love at first sight.

P.S. - Jonathan Stumpy Slimann got 25 years to life. I got a world class mule and a happy wife.

GRAND AND GLORIOUS

GRATITUDE

To: my parents, Bill and Ruth Erickson
grandparents: Frank and Ida Erickson,
Grandparents, Rollie and May Millhouse

Joy of life was forever reflected in their faces.

To Carolyn, my determined editor, I'm thankful for her eagle eyes and
keen perception... she works for campfire trout and fine red wine

To Steve and Scott, story advisors

And to
Shena Bingham, a delightfully talented illustrator

J. David Erickson is a retired fisheries biologist living in Buhl, Idaho with his wife and editor, Carolyn. He was born and raised in North Dakota, degreed at Montana State University, and spent a career fish farming in Idaho. His first two books, *The Muddy River Boys* and *Beyond Muddy River* are true stories of boyhood and coming of age. *Jack and The War Babies*, Erickson's first work of fiction, is a tale of a free spirit who's wanderlust leads to a life-changing experience.